A *Duke* TO *Die For*

Praise for Amelia Grey's Novels

Never a Bride

"Readers will be quickly drawn in by the lively pace, the appealing protagonists, and the sexual chemistry that almost visibly shimmers between them in this charming, light-hearted, and well-done Regency."
—*Library Journal*

"Witty dialogue and clever schemes... Both of Grey's vivid characters will charm readers."
—*Booklist*

"Will keep you up all night... praying for a wedding. Fresh and original and destined to be a keeper. Charming and delightful... a must-read."
—Joan Johnston

"A delightful Regency romp. You'll have lots of fun with this one."
—Kat Martin

A Dash of Scandal

"Absolutely charming... a wonderful, feel-good, captivating read."
—Heather Graham

"Fans of Regency romance will relish this amusing tale... delightfully cheerful."
—*Midwest Book Review*

THE ROGUES' DYNASTY

A *Duke* TO

Die For

AMELIA GREY

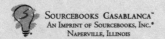

SOURCEBOOKS CASABLANCA™
An Imprint of Sourcebooks, Inc.®
NAPERVILLE, ILLINOIS

Published by Sourcebooks Casablanca, an imprint of Sourcebooks, Inc.
P.O. Box 4410, Naperville, Illinois 60567–4410
(630) 961–3900
FAX: (630) 961–2168
www.sourcebooks.com

Library of Congress Cataloging-in-Publication Data

Grey, Amelia.
A duke to die for / Amelia Grey.
p. cm.—(Rogue's dynasty ; #1)
I. Title.
PS3607.R4988D85 2009
813.'6—dc22

2008038770

Printed and bound in the United States of America.
QW 10 9 8 7 6 5 4 3 2 1

One

My Dearest Grandson Lucien,

You would do well in life to heed Lord Chesterfield's wise words: "Never put off till tomorrow what you can do today."

Your loving Grandmother,
Lady Elder

LUCIEN TRENT BLAKEWELL, THE FIFTH DUKE OF Blakewell, strode through the front door of his town house, taking off his riding gloves.

"Your Grace, I'm glad you're home."

"Not now, Ashby," Blake said, tossing his gloves, hat, and cloak into the butler's hands without breaking his stride. "I don't have time." He'd stayed too long at the shooting match, and now he was running late.

One of his cousins was racing a new horse in Hyde Park at four o'clock, and the other had a high-stakes card game starting at six. Blake didn't plan on missing either event. But in order to make both, he had to finish reviewing at least one account book for his solicitor. The poor fellow had been begging for them for over a month.

From the corridor, Blake walked into his book room. Piled high on his desk was the stack of ledgers, numerous miscellaneous correspondence, and invitations he'd left unopened for weeks.

He shrugged out of his coat, loosened his neckcloth, and sat down at his desk with an impatient sigh. There were times when being a duke was downright hellish.

Grudgingly, he opened the top book, determined to make a dent in the work he had to do.

"I'm sorry to disturb you, Your Grace," Ashby said from the doorway.

Blake didn't bother to glance up from the ledger he was thumbing through, trying to find where he'd left off the last time he looked at it… which was too many days ago to remember. He still hadn't become completely used to hearing himself called 'Your Grace,' even though his father had been dead almost two years.

It was a time-consuming task, keeping up-to-date with all his holdings and property, not to mention the details of the various businesses in which his father had invested over the years. His solicitor constantly sent documents for him to sign or account books to check. And, last year when his grandmother had passed on, her estate had added more responsibilities to his already full desk of unattended paperwork.

His new role in life had certainly curtailed his once daily and quite enjoyable activities of riding, fencing, and late afternoon games of billiards and cards at White's or one of the other gentlemen's clubs he belonged to. He was not accustomed to being on anyone's schedule but his own.

The butler cleared his throat.

"Yes, Ashby, what is it?" Blake finally said when it was apparent the man wasn't going to leave him alone until he had his say.

"There's a young lady here to see you, sir."

That got Blake's attention. He glanced up at the tall, thin, and immaculately dressed butler, who wore his long graying hair held neatly away from his sharp face in a queue.

"A young lady, you say?"

"Yes, Your Grace."

"Who is she?"

"Miss Henrietta Tweed."

"Tweed," Blake said aloud as he thought about the name for a moment. He couldn't place it. "Who is with her?"

"Just her maid."

"No other chaperone?"

"None that I saw."

That was odd.

It was unusual for a young lady, or any gentleman, to call on him without making prior arrangements—and altogether inappropriate for a lady to do so without a suitable chaperone. Blake shrugged. On another afternoon he might have been intrigued by this strange request to see him, but not today. He didn't have time to entertain anyone.

"Just take her card and send her away."

Blake picked up his quill, dipped it in the ink jar he'd just opened, and returned his attention to the numbers in front of him.

"I tried that, Your Grace. She says she doesn't have a card."

The quill stilled in his hand. That was most curious, too. A woman without an appropriate chaperone and without a proper calling card. For half a second he wondered if one of the ladies he'd met earlier in the day at Hyde Park had followed him home. And there were other possibilities. It was rare, but he knew that sometimes a lady of the evening would be bold enough to seek out a titled man in hopes of bettering her station in life by earning a few coins or becoming his latest mistress.

Blake's interest was piqued once again, though he had to admit almost anything could take his mind off accounts and ledgers.

He glanced back up at the butler. "What does she look like?" he asked, thinking that would help him determine if she warranted interrupting his work.

Ashby's chin lifted and his eyebrows rose slightly. "Like a young lady."

Sometimes Blake wished he hadn't kept his father's annoying butler. The old man could be downright impudent at times. But Ashby kept the household and the sizable staff running in near-perfect order. The butler's work was testimony to the care with which his father had trained the man. That, and that alone, was what kept the aging servant at his job.

"Did she say why she wanted to see me?"

"Not exactly, Your Grace."

In exasperation, Blake laid down the quill he had just picked up. "Ashby, what the hell did she say?"

Unflustered, the butler replied, "She said you were expecting her."

"Was I?" Blake asked. Since Blake had turned off his father's secretary a few months earlier, the butler had tried to help him keep up with his social calendar, but so far neither one of them was doing a good job.

"Not that I'm aware of, Your Grace. She also said that her trunks were on the front steps."

Blake made a noise in his throat that sounded like a mixture of a grunt and a laugh. He must have been in too big a hurry to notice her luggage when he came through the front door.

"What the devil?" Blake said. "I'm expecting no one, especially a young woman with baggage and no proper chaperone. She obviously has the wrong house." He rose from his chair. "Did you question her about who she is looking for?"

"Yes, Your Grace. She said the Duke of Blakewell was expecting her."

"That's not bloody likely when I have no recollection of knowing anyone by the name of Tweed."

"She also suggested that I should speak to you at once so that you could clear up what she called my obvious confusion."

That sounded rather impertinent coming from someone who was apparently befuddled herself. No doubt the quickest way to handle this situation was for him to take a moment or two to speak with her.

Blake looked down at his paper-cluttered desk. His eyes centered on the open book in front of him, and he swore softly to himself. Reviewing the latest entries would have to wait again.

"Show her to the front parlor and say I'll be in to see her."

"Right away, Your Grace." Ashby turned stiffly and walked out.

Blake marked his place in the ledger with a dry quill. He hastily retied his neckcloth and reached for his coat. No doubt the woman had him mixed up with someone else. The sooner he dealt with the waif and sent her on her way, the faster he could get back to checking the balances in the accounts book so he wouldn't miss the race or the card game. For the most part he got along quite well with his cousins, but they would be unforgiving if they felt he'd slighted them.

When Blake approached the doorway to the drawing room, he saw a short, rotund lady with her back to him warming herself in front of the low-burning fireplace. It took only a glance at the fabric of her cloak and bonnet to know that she was not a lady of means.

What was Ashby thinking to allow her entrance into the house?

"Miss Tweed," he said, striding into the room, determined to set her straight and then have a word with his errant butler.

The chit turned to face him and he immediately realized she had on a maid's frock. At the same time, from the corner of his eye, he saw a rather tall, slender, young lady rise from a side chair in the far corner and come toward him. When he looked at her, Blake felt his stomach do a slow roll. She moved with exquisite grace and an inner confidence lacking in most of the young ladies in Society.

Big, almond-shaped eyes—bluer than a midsummer sky and fringed with long black lashes—pierced him with a wary look of impatience. Her lips were full, beautifully sculpted, and the shade of spring's first rose. The color of her skin was a sheer, pale ivory, and her complexion was flawless.

She was the loveliest creature he'd ever seen.

She wore an expensively tailored black cape that parted down the front as she walked, showing a blush-colored traveling dress. Her wide-brimmed bonnet with tightly woven trim matched her cape and gloves. He couldn't help but wonder what color of hair was hidden beneath her headpiece.

For some reason he found it exceedingly seductive the way the satin ribbon of her bonnet had been tied into a perfect bow under her chin. He had a sudden urge to reach up, pull on the end of the black ribbon, and untie it... despite the fact that every inch of her said "lady."

"Yes, I'm Henrietta Tweed." She inclined her head a little as if pondering whether to say more. "I'm waiting for the Duke of Blakewell."

Blake bowed and then said, "At your service, Miss Tweed. I am he."

Her eyes narrowed slightly. That was the only outward sign that she was confused for a moment. Quickly, she regained her air of confidence. She lowered her lashes as she curtsied in front of him.

"I apologize, Your Grace; I didn't recognize you."

A prickle of desire rushed through him and settled low in his groin as he watched her dutifully acknowledge his title. He found everything about her tremendously seductive.

"No harm done," he said.

Blake's gaze swept over her face once again. She appeared to be a self-assured, capable young lady who wasn't the least bit intimidated by his title. He also noticed she wasn't indifferent to his appearance as her gaze slowly swept down to his riding boots and then innocently crawled back up to his face. Her close observation of him sent a rush of heat like he hadn't felt in years searing through his loins.

Ashby cleared his throat. "Should I have Cook prepare tea, Your Grace?"

Despite all the work he had to do, not to mention contending with a cheeky butler, Blake found himself agreeing. Quite frankly, how could he say no to this intriguing lady?

"Yes, Ashby, and take the young lady's wrap. Have tea served in here after you show Miss Tweed's maid to the kitchen for refreshments."

"Yes, Your Grace."

Blake watched as his unexpected guest took off her gloves and then untied the bow beneath her chin. Her hands were lovely and without jewels. He'd never realized just how stimulating it could be to watch a lady take off her bonnet until he found himself experiencing another twinge of desire as the soft, fluttering ribbons slid along her shoulders.

She had lush, golden blonde hair arranged neatly on top of her head, and Blake had no doubt that it would be gorgeous hanging down her back. She handed her bonnet, cape, and gloves to her maid and softly told the woman she would be fine alone and to follow the butler to the kitchen.

Blake waited to speak until the maid and Ashby

left the room. "I'm afraid I don't know of you, Miss Tweed. Who is your father?"

With ease and more self-confidence than anyone her age should have, she walked closer to him, keeping her gaze pinned on his. He liked the way her carriage was straight but not stiff. He liked the way she looked directly at him and didn't try to impress him with batting lashes, false smiles, or the unnatural soft voice some ladies used when talking to him.

Blake also liked the way she looked in her simple, high-waisted traveling dress. It was long-sleeved and quite modest for the current fashion. The fabric was of a fine quality, though not the best available. The neckline was high and trimmed in dainty pink lace that made her look absolutely fetching.

He was more curious than ever to know who she was.

"My father was Sir William Tweed. Considering your age, you probably never met him. I must assume your father knew him."

"And what makes you say that?"

"Because the Duke of Blakewell is the last name on my father's list."

What in the hell was she talking about? He became more intrigued with each word she spoke.

"What list is that, Miss Tweed?"

She clasped her lovely hands together in front of her, and once again she looked straight into his eyes. "If you don't know what I'm talking about, Your Grace, we have a problem."

"At last we agree on something. Those are the truest words you have spoken thus far."

A wrinkle of concern settled between her eyes, but it in no way detracted from her beauty.

"You were supposed to receive a letter and some rather important documents from a solicitor named Mr. Conrad Milton that would announce my arrival and explain everything about me."

Blake immediately thought of his desk. Not only was the blasted thing covered in account books that hadn't been reviewed, along with papers and documents that hadn't been signed, it was littered with all kinds of correspondence that hadn't been opened.

For the first time since becoming a duke, Blake wished he had taken his responsibilities as the Duke of Blakewell a little more seriously.

"I've been behind on mail recently. Just tell me why you are here."

"All right." She unclasped her hands and calmly let her arms fall comfortably to her sides. "I am your ward and your house is supposed to be my new home."

Blake couldn't have been more shocked if she'd thrown cold water in his face.

"What? No. This is ridiculous." A strained chuckle caught briefly on his breath. "I can assure you that you are not my ward, Miss Tweed."

She took a deep breath but otherwise remained composed.

"If only that were true, Your Grace, but I'm afraid it isn't. I don't know what happened to the letter or the documents you were to receive, but rest assured there are papers that prove the Duke of Blakewell is next in line to be my legal guardian and the sole trustee of my inheritance."

"Guardian? How old are you?"

"Nineteen."

"But you carry yourself like…"

"Someone older?"

She was not only beautiful, she was perceptive, too. Why was he finding everything about her appealing? She was obviously laying out some elaborate scheme and expecting him to swallow it, yet still he found her fascinating.

"Yes," he said.

"I assure you I've had to grow up quickly."

For a moment Blake thought he saw a hint of wistfulness in her bright blue eyes, but it was so fleeting he wasn't positive. And nothing else in her manner had caused him to think she was in the least unsure of herself, which was remarkable concerning her situation, if the tale she told was true.

"Regardless of your age, I can't be your guardian. Don't you know who I am?"

A knowing smile gently lifted the corners of her attractive lips. Blake's lower body responded once again.

"Your reputation stretches much farther than all of London, Your Grace. In the scandal sheets, you are referred to as the Devilish Duke."

Far from being insulted that she brought up that nickname Society had placed on him some years ago, he threw up his hands and said, "My point exactly. Who in their right mind would expect me to be the protector of a young lady's reputation? I'm the kind of man fathers safeguard their daughters against. There has been a mistake."

She didn't appear perturbed in the least. "I agree.

I can only assume your father was the Duke of Blakewell who agreed to be my guardian, should anything happen to Lord Palmer."

"Who is Lord Palmer? I thought you said your father was Sir William Tweed."

Another smile played at the corners of her lips, irritating the hell out of him even though he found it extremely provocative. There was nothing humorous in this debacle if, by some cruel twist of fate, she had truly been left to his care.

"Lord Palmer was my guardian for the past year and a half. Before him there was Lord Brembly, and before him, Viscount Westhavener."

Blake stared in disbelief. "How many guardians have you had?"

Very sensibly she said, "Far too many, I assure you, Your Grace."

"I'm trying hard not to be frustrated, Miss Tweed, but I'm not making much progress because I'm not seeing a connection between you and me, or my father."

She remained so calm it was maddening. It annoyed the hell out of him and challenged him at the same time. This lady was very confident of her place in life, though he couldn't imagine why, considering the convoluted story coming out of her.

She lifted her slightly arched brows. "I'm afraid the explanation is rather lengthy."

Blake glanced up at the clock on the mantel. It was past three o'clock already, and he hadn't even started on the accounting ledger. No doubt he wouldn't make it to see Morgan's horse compete at Rotten Row—and he wouldn't make Race's card game either if he didn't get Miss Tweed settled right away. The work for his solicitor would just have to wait until tomorrow.

"As soon as I find or receive the correspondence you've mentioned, I'll have my solicitor look it over and straighten this out. In the meantime, tell me where you need to go tonight, and I'll see that you get there."

Her shoulders stiffened, though just barely. "I have nowhere to go, Your Grace, but here."

Those simple but unflinching words took the starch out of him. Either she had come up with the grandest scheme imaginable to get in his good graces, or she was serious.

Blake turned away from her for a moment and silently cursed under his breath. What the bloody hell was he going to do with her?

He turned back to face her and said, "Perhaps you have a relative or a friend who will take you in."

"None that I know of."

"You have no relatives at all?"

His question brought a long moment of silence from her. There was an uncertain quality to her eyes as they searched his face.

"Surely if there were anyone, my father would have put their names on the list before that of a stranger."

That she had no one was hard for him to believe. Sometimes Blake felt as if he were in some way related to half the people in London, and because of his grandmother's four marriages, he probably was.

"I've had a very long day, Your Grace. May I sit down?" she asked.

He couldn't very well say no. "Yes, of course."

If he'd been thinking clearly, he would have asked her to take a seat earlier, but nothing had gone as it should have from the moment he walked through his front door. Ashby had even had to prompt him to do the proper thing and offer tea.

She sat on the dark-green brocade settee with surprising assuredness for a nineteen-year-old with no place to stay. Blake was in no mood to sit still, but he took a side chair opposite her anyway.

Mrs. Ellsworth, his housekeeper, brought in a tray with tea and placed it on the table that stood between him and his guest. Blake waited impatiently while tea was poured, though he declined a cup.

He watched Miss Tweed sip her tea from the dainty china and noticed her hands again. He liked the feminine look of them. Her fingers appeared smooth and nimble, nails neatly trimmed. He had the sudden thought of those hands feather soft on his chest, trailing seductively over his body.

Blake mentally shook himself and said, "It looks as if I'm going to need that lengthy explanation after all, Miss Tweed. Where exactly did you say you come from?"

"Originally?" That wistful look came into her eyes, but again only for a moment. She took a deep breath, and he had the feeling she was calling on some inner strength to sustain her.

Blake realized that she wasn't one to feel sorry for herself, and he liked that about her. He rarely noticed so many things about any young lady. Over years of attending the Season, he'd come to think that there was little difference among them, but Miss Tweed could have him rethinking that.

"I was born in Dover, but I haven't lived there for quite some time. My parents were killed in a carriage accident when I was seven. I went to live with my only relative, my father's half brother, Lord Phillip Bennett, and his lady. Unfortunately, Lord Phillip met with an untimely death at sea a couple of years later. Viscount and Viscountess Westhavener were next on the list. They were wonderful to me. They hired a governess who taught me to read, write, and add numbers as well as all the things a young lady is supposed to learn to adequately manage a large household. I was with them for four-and-a-half years."

"Then what happened?"

"Viscount Westhavener was struck by lightning late one afternoon as he walked in his garden. The viscountess asked that I be allowed to stay with her, but unfortunately it couldn't be allowed. My guardianship had already been decided by my father's long and able list.

"I had to go live with Lord Brembly and his lady in Dorset. When he died by falling off the roof, I was uprooted once again and sent to Mr. Henry Pippin's home in Essex. He was thrown from his horse and killed shortly after I arrived, so I was moved yet again to Lord Palmer's home. Regrettably, he succumbed to consumption only a few weeks ago."

"Bloody hell, that's way too many guardians to have had in twelve years!"

"Yes, it's been most unfortunate. And now I find myself at the door of the last man on the list."

"Mine. The Duke of Blakewell."

"Yes."

Damnation. If all she said was true, and it was too bizarre not to be, what was he going to do about her? He was having a devil of a time just keeping up with his duties as a duke. And now he was being pressured by some political hogs to take his father's place in Parliament. But all that aside, there was no way he could take on the responsibility of a young lady. He didn't have a thought in hell about what to do with her.

"Miss Tweed, if my father and mother were here, I'm sure they would be honoured to abide by your father's wishes and take care of you. But as you can understand, I can't be your guardian."

He wasn't sure what he expected from her, but it wasn't the spark of triumph that flashed in her bright eyes. She looked pleased, as if he'd said exactly what she wanted to hear.

"I understand perfectly, Your Grace, if you feel you can't be my guardian. I'm going to be twenty at the end of summer, and I truly don't need anyone to look after me. I'm more than qualified to take care of myself. All you need to do is draw up a document and sign it, giving me power to be mistress over my inheritance."

Blake gazed at her lovely face. He could see in the expression on her face and in her blue eyes that she believed what she was saying. She thought she could handle her affairs and take care of herself as proficiently as a man. He almost laughed. He, of all people, knew how difficult it was to keep up with account books.

She had the countenance of an innocent, not the

guise of a woman of the world. Looking at her then, he knew a guardian was exactly what she needed, because he was thinking how kissable her lips looked, how soft her skin appeared, how he would love to feel her shapely body pressed solidly against his.

He cleared his throat and tamped down his wayward thoughts. She was not trying to be seductive in any manner, yet he found her immensely so.

"I'm still not totally convinced I'm in charge of you, but I'm certainly not about to sign anything at this point."

She placed her empty cup on the tray. "Once you are convinced that what I say is true, I hope you will reconsider allowing me to be mistress of my inheritance. Besides, it's in your own best interest. I don't want to see anything happen to you."

That was an odd statement. "What are you talking about?"

"The inevitable, Your Grace. All five of my previous guardians have died. There is a curse on the list of names my father made all those years ago. If you take on the responsibility of being my guardian, I'm afraid you will die, too."

A quick smile parted his lips, and then he laughed with ease. She was so refreshingly direct that he was absolutely taken with her.

"You must be trying to amuse me, Miss Tweed. Congratulations. It's working. But I'm afraid your mind is playing tricks with you. There is no such thing as a curse."

She gave him an indulgent smile but said, "I beg to differ. Everyone who has ever been responsible for me and my considerable inheritance has died an untimely death."

Blake had no intention of dying any time soon.

He gave her a roguish smile and said, "Bad luck, Miss Tweed. It's all just bad luck."

She sat back in the settee and folded her hands in her lap. "Then perhaps you need to think long and hard about that, Your Grace, because all that bad luck just landed at your door."

Two

My Dear Grandson Lucien,

I recently remembered more words of wisdom from my long-departed friend, Lord Chesterfield: "Whatever is worth doing at all is worth doing well; and nothing can be well done without attention."

Your loving Grandmother,
Lady Elder

"Perhaps, Miss Tweed, it was Lord Chesterfield who said something along the lines of 'If not for bad luck, I'd have no luck at all.' I think I can weather any purported curse you believe lurks around you or your previous guardians."

The Duke of Blakewell was laughing at her. Henrietta's heartbeat faltered and then quickened again. Why was he not taking her plight and his obvious danger seriously?

Defiance kicked in, and suddenly Henrietta's shoulders lifted as if she'd suddenly been set free of some imaginary chains. The Duke of Blakewell might be the first duke she'd ever met and surely the most handsome man she'd ever laid eyes on, but he was also the most infuriating.

Just because her heart had tripped at the sight of him when he first strode by the drawing-room doorway, carelessly tossing his gloves, hat, and cloak into the hands of his butler as he went, was no reason for her to allow him to use her for his own private amusement.

"You jest, Your Grace. I've read the published letters Lord Chesterfield wrote to his son, and I'm quite certain that quote was not anything he wrote. I think it's far more likely something you just made up to amuse yourself."

A playful smile lifted the corners of his mouth. "Humor has its benefits, Miss Tweed."

"You might find hilarity in the deaths of my previous guardians, but I do not."

His smile slowly faded at her reprimand, but his eyes in no way appeared contrite. "Of course, death is no laughing matter. I didn't mean to imply it is. I found humor only in your suggestion of a curse."

"Why does that amuse you so? I don't consider a curse a laughing matter, either."

Once again a smile, easy and genuine, curved his lips. "I don't believe in hocus-pocus rituals, Miss Tweed and, quite frankly, until you mentioned a curse, you seemed so… sensible."

Henrietta drew in her breath and held it as she studied him for a moment, trying to decide if he'd just bestowed a compliment or a criticism on her.

Not that it mattered. It was hard not to believe in curses when she had seen them come true. Henrietta had never forgotten the words of the old woman with whom she'd stayed until she could be taken to her first guardian after her parents died.

Mrs. Goolsby had been a frightful person who didn't try to hide her fear of Henrietta and the curse she said followed Henrietta. Over the years, Henrietta had tried to forget the sharp-faced woman and her talk of curses, ghosts, and death, but it was difficult when, just as Mrs. Goolsby had predicted, every one of her guardians had died—except the one sitting before her now.

Because of what she'd read about the duke in the scandal sheets, she hadn't expected him to be as old as her previous guardians, but she certainly hadn't anticipated that he would look like the paintings she'd seen of Adonis: tall, proud, commanding, and powerful-looking with his wide, strong shoulders, flat stomach, and lean, narrow hips.

The duke was faultless in appearance, dressed in fawn-colored breeches and shiny black riding boots. His broad chest was covered by a white shirt, a red quilted waistcoat adorned with brass buttons, and a black riding coat made from expensive, lightweight wool. The bow of his neckcloth was uneven and looked as if it had been hastily tied. But far from making him appear disheveled, the informal bow made him look like the devilish rogue the gossipmongers claimed he was.

His unfashionably long, light brown hair was stylishly brushed away from his face. It hung thick and straight to just below his earlobes. Clean-shaven, his chiseled cheekbones and well-defined jawline accentuated a slightly square chin. His full, masculine-shaped lips and narrow, high-bridged nose matched his aristocratic demeanor, not to mention making him handsome enough to set her heart to fluttering.

But most intriguing of all were his eyes. They were an unusual shade of grayish brown that was similar in color to that of weathered wood. And for a moment, when she first stared into his captivating eyes, she had the feeling she could look into them forever and never grow tired.

"I am sensible, Your Grace," she finally said, taking issue with his unstated assumption that believing in curses made her foolish. "My good common sense is what prompted me to warn you about the danger to your well-being."

"Just as my good common sense tells me there is no such danger from something that cannot be seen, felt, or heard," he countered.

"How can you doubt there is a curse when you are the only man on my father's list of guardians who is still living? Even your father—my intended guardian—is no longer living."

He casually folded his arms across his chest, looking very relaxed and uncomplicated. "Perhaps that has something to do with age, Miss Tweed. No doubt all the others were my father's peers and not mine."

"Perhaps, indeed, but none of the men in question died of old age. Unless, of course, that's how your father died."

He paused before he spoke. "No, he was leaving his club one night, and he slipped on some ice and fell, hitting his head on a stone planter. He never woke up."

She lowered her lashes out of respect and then said, "I'm sorry to hear that. I'm sure it was dreadful for you, but as you can see, all my guardians were killed by accident, except one who died of illness."

"How strange," he said in a fake serious tone while a twitch of a smile worked the corners of his lips. "Accidents and illnesses are the very two things that cause most people to die."

Henrietta bristled inside but tried to remain calm. The last thing she needed to do was annoy the duke, but he seemed to be twisting everything she said.

"You are mocking me, Your Grace."

His smile widened just enough to make him even more devilishly handsome. "Yes, but only because you make it so very easy for me to do."

"Me? You can't lay the blame for your ill manners on me."

"True. I wouldn't, so to put your mind at ease, let me just say that I'll consider myself forewarned about this curse you believe in so that you may live with a clear conscience, should anything happen to me."

Now he was the one sounding sensible! And even though that infuriated her, she couldn't help but feel a slight catch in her breath as she looked at him. The man was far too appealing to her senses, especially when he was teasing her.

"Thank you for that small consolation," she said with true appreciation in her voice for his concession.

He glanced at the clock on the mantel. "We still have the problem of what to do with you."

Henrietta lifted her chin. "I did suggest a possible solution that you may want to revisit."

The duke's gaze dropped to her lips and lingered there so long that her cheeks heated. She felt a slow stirring of something she didn't understand low in her abdomen. It was unsettling that sometimes when he looked at her, she felt these strange sensations: a tightening in her breasts, an unusual warmth low in her stomach, and a shortness of breath.

"You're referring to your proposal that I sign your inheritance over to you and be rid of you?"

"Yes," she answered, trying not to sound too eager or too hopeful. "If you did that, I would never have to cross your mind again and—" She deliberately hesitated. "You would be free of me and from the curse that has plagued my guardians."

"The supposed curse is the least of my worries, Miss Tweed. And, since I don't even know for sure that I am your guardian, as I said before, signing anything is completely out of the question and need not be mentioned again. Besides all that, I don't think you realize everything that is involved in taking care of an inheritance. Young ladies simply are not capable of understanding the difficulty of all that's involved."

What nerve! She knew most men felt that way about women, but to say it to her face was an outrage.

Henrietta leaned forward in what she hoped was a nonthreatening way and quietly said, "Realizing I am a guest in your home, I'm reluctant to challenge you, but I must take issue with you on that point, Your Grace. I am well versed in numbers and many different types of business transactions. Lord Brembly allowed me to help him with his account books, which were considerable. He and his ladyship had complete trust in my calculations and reasoning abilities."

"I am not Lord Brembly, Miss Tweed."

She would never argue that point, considering the fact that Lord Brembly had been at least thirty years older than His Grace and was short, pudgy, and bald.

The one thing she wanted now, more than anything else in the world, was not to have to worry that this man would have the same fate as all her other guardians because of her. She wanted to be free of the curse. She wanted a home she could call her very own. She wanted to be in one place forever so she could feel like she belonged. She wanted to make friends that she would never have to leave. She wanted to live an ordinary life without fear of being uprooted once again and sent to a different town to live with new people.

If she had control of her inheritance, she would purchase a small house in a suitable district. She would hire a housekeeper and, with her maid, she would be adequately chaperoned wherever she went. And she would never have to worry about anyone dying because of her again. She would never be forced to move again. She could spend her days with her needlework, writing poetry and reading, or engaged in any number of other activities that brought her contentment.

Henrietta had been a burden, a ward of others, for twelve years now. Perhaps it had been futile to have hoped the duke might be more forward-thinking than most of his counterparts and ancestors about a woman's comprehension and ability to care for herself without the aid of a male guardian. Or maybe he, like most men, just didn't want to give up any control.

Whatever the reason, she felt the need to remind the duke of a certain fact.

"Your Grace, we have had queens who have more than adequately managed entire countries for many years at a time. Surely, I can control several hundred thousand pounds in an account and not spend myself into the poorhouse or debtors' prison."

For a moment she thought she saw a spark of admiration for her in the depth of his eyes, but just as suddenly his lips slid into the maddening smile that made her heartbeat falter and her breath quicken.

Taking a cue from her, he leaned in close and softly said, "Why take the chance?"

Henrietta gasped at his outdated thinking. Her cheeks heated at his cold response to her plight. "Does your arrogance know no bounds?"

"Probably not, Miss Tweed. No one has put boundaries on me for quite a while."

"Then perhaps therein is your problem, Your Grace." She was going beyond the pale in speaking so audaciously to someone as important as a duke, but something about this man made her throw caution to the wind.

He chuckled, seeming not the least affronted by her boldness. "Perhaps, though I'm impressed with your courage to try to persuade me. Even if what you suggest could be a viable possibility for the future, we still have no solution for the present."

The duke glanced again at the large, ornate clock on the mantel. Henrietta had become so caught up in her quarrel with him that she had forgotten she was keeping him from an important engagement. She should have realized that he had appointments when she first arrived and wanted to see him. Obviously, his position in Society kept him very busy, and she was being inconsiderate.

"Since you were not expecting me, as I thought you would be, I don't want to inconvenience you further. My maid and I will be quite comfortable in an inn, if you will be so kind as to suggest where we might find safe and adequate lodging and a carriage to take us there. This is my first time in London, and I'm not at all familiar with the city."

A wrinkle of concern formed between his brows. "Surely, you know I can't allow that, Miss Tweed. For the immediate time, I suppose my housekeeper can be considered your chaperone. I will tell her to prepare a room for you and see that your trunks are sent up."

Though he was quick of wit, he'd clearly been caught off guard by her arrival and had no idea what to do with her. But, for now at least, he wasn't going to throw her out into the streets.

She couldn't imagine what had happened to Mr. Milton's correspondence, but its absence had certainly put her in an awkward position. His Grace had mentioned that he was behind on his mail, and his butler had to remind him to offer refreshment. It wasn't too difficult to assume that the Duke of Blakewell didn't have a lot of order to his life. And order was the one thing that had always brought calm into Henrietta's topsy-turvy life.

Her unusual childhood of being shifted from one new home to another had taught her to be strong, adaptable, and capable. She had learned a long time ago to accept whatever fate dealt her and make the best of her current surroundings. That's exactly what she would do now.

"I should think that we need to post a letter to Mr. Milton at once to see if he has any idea what could have happened to the documents you were to receive concerning my guardianship and ask him to do whatever is necessary to put your mind at ease."

His eyes narrowed. "First, Miss Tweed, I don't need you to make suggestions for me as to what to do. Secondly, it's rather late in the day for that. And thirdly, there is the possibility I have the papers from Mr. Milton somewhere on my desk. As I mentioned before, I'm behind on my correspondence."

The thought that he might have the means to clear up this misunderstanding quickly brought Henrietta to her feet. "Then shouldn't we go look for them at once so you'll know I speak the truth about who I am and my circumstances?"

The duke rose, too, as his gaze darted over to the clock on the mantel once again. "I don't doubt you speak the truth. Quite frankly, your story is too preposterous to have been made up. And we will get this situation straightened out as to what to do about you. Eventually. But right now, I haven't the time to look into this as I'm already late for a pressing appointment."

Another thing the past twelve years had taught Henrietta was to know when to back away from a conversation and save her argument for another day. She had done all she could for the time being.

"Of course. I'm sorry to have kept you from your engagement, and I do appreciate your hospitality in allowing me to stay here. I'll try not to be of any further trouble to you."

Ignoring her apology, he said, "Mrs. Ellsworth will

show you upstairs and see to your supper and anything else you might require."

At the mention of food, Henrietta's stomach rumbled softly. Dining would be most welcome as she'd been traveling since before daybreak with only cheese and bread to eat along the way.

"Thank you, Your Grace."

The duke acknowledged her gratitude with a simple nod, went to the doorway, and called for Mrs. Ellsworth. The short, stodgy housekeeper with kind, dark brown eyes and silver-streaked hair walked hesitantly into the drawing room. Ashby, the tall and thin butler with a dour expression, materialized too. The two servants listened dutifully as the duke gave instructions concerning Henrietta's welfare.

He then turned to Henrietta and said, "Ashby and Mrs. Ellsworth will take over from here. Until later, Miss Tweed."

Henrietta stood in the drawing room, watching her new guardian grab his cloak, hat, and gloves from his butler's hands and disappear out the door. How could the most handsome man she had ever met also be the most infuriating one she had ever met? He was autocratic and high-handed, too!

Mrs. Ellsworth and Ashby remained in the doorway of the drawing room, speaking softly to each other and occasionally looking in her direction. Henrietta couldn't hear what they said, but she was certain they were discussing exactly what they should do with her.

It didn't take a scholar to know they had no idea what to do beyond their employer's pointed words of "See she has a room and food."

This wasn't the first time she'd found herself in a situation where the staff was perplexed by her arrival. It had happened to her far too many times. They didn't know what to do. But Henrietta did. It was time to take control of the situation and put order back into her life.

She took a deep breath, lifted her shoulders and chin, and started towards the duo with a kind smile on her face. "Mrs. Ellsworth, why don't I go upstairs with you, and together we can decide which room is best for me. And perhaps we can find a small space on the servants' floor for my maid. I assure you, we'll do our best not to disrupt your efficiently run household any more than absolutely necessary."

Little less than half an hour later, Henrietta's packed trunks lay open on the floor of her elegantly furnished bedroom. The décor was soothing in a pale shade of green that reminded her of spring's first blades of grass. Her maid shook out the folds of a green velvet dress while Henrietta splashed cool water from the basin on her face.

When Henrietta was twelve, Peggy, who was more than twice Henrietta's age, had been hired to be her maid, and they had been together ever since. The short Irish woman had no trouble taking orders from the younger Henrietta. Peggy's round figure was always hidden beneath a simple, dark grey dress and white, starched apron. Her thick red hair was always neatly covered with a white mopcap trimmed with delicate lace.

"I don't think you have ever been given a room this splendid, Miss Henri," Peggy said. "Look, there are two wardrobes in here. You don't have enough clothes to fill one of them, much less two. What are you going to do?"

"I'll leave one of them empty, of course," Henrietta said in a good-natured tone as she patted her cheeks dry with a small towel.

No doubt the kind of women who usually stayed in this spacious room brought several dresses for morning and afternoon as well as gowns for the evening and bonnets, gloves, and shawls to match them all. They would attend parties held in the best homes and go to balls that lasted all night. They would probably be at all the operas and take long walks along the secret paths of Vauxhall Gardens.

For a moment, Henrietta closed her eyes and imagined herself at a fancy ball where hundreds of candles brightened the room with golden light. Men were twirling beautifully dressed women across the dance floor. She heard music and laughter. She felt the excitement of the moment. She imagined herself drinking champagne from a crystal glass and smiling at a handsome gentleman.

Suddenly her eyes popped open. The gentleman standing in front of her at this imaginary ball was the stimulating Duke of Blakewell.

Henrietta shook her head in exasperation. She wasn't usually given to such fanciful notions. She had read about the lavish soirées of High Society London and had often wished that some day she could attend one of the extravagant events. Or perhaps one evening she could go to Vauxhall Gardens and watch the fireworks display. She believed it would be as lovely as drinking champagne, which was something else she'd like to do some day—when she was no longer controlled by the whims of a guardian.

In the small country towns where she had always lived, there had been a few dances to attend from time to time, but Henrietta had had no need for a wardrobe full of fancy dresses and lavishly trimmed ball gowns that were ghastly expensive and would seldom be worn.

"You know what I mean, Miss Henri," Peggy said, interrupting Henrietta's thoughts. "This is a mighty fancy house, and His Grace looked like a dandified gentleman for sure. Pardon my big mouth for saying what wasn't asked, but I don't think he's going to want us around all the time like your other guardians. He didn't seem at all happy to see you."

From the looking glass, Henrietta watched her maid worry over a wrinkle that ran down the front of the green dress. She was trying hard to press it out of the thick fabric with her hand.

"He wasn't happy, Peggy, but the Duke of Blakewell is an honorable man, and he will see to it that we are well cared for."

Peggy shook her head. "I hope you are right, Miss Henri, because we don't have any other place to go."

"Chin up, Peggy," Henrietta said with more cheerfulness than she was feeling. "He will not neglect his duty to us. Have no worry on that point, as I am sure of it."

Henrietta looked at her reflection in the mirror. She would do all the worrying for both of them, but she didn't want her maid to know that. Peggy could be excitable, and Henrietta was hesitant enough herself without having to constantly reassure her maid that they indeed had a home with the duke.

Later that evening, Henrietta headed back down the stairs, feeling much more relaxed than when she had gone up them a few hours ago. She had washed off the day's journey and changed into a simple, pale-green dress with a round neckline. The long sleeves and high waistline were trimmed in a matching satin ribbon, and one simple flounce adorned the hem.

Cook had had a scullery maid send up a bowl of piping hot lamb stew, a thick slice of bread, and a delicious serving of cooked plums, which Henrietta had eaten with relish.

It was much too early to think about retiring, so Henrietta had left Peggy to finish unpacking her trunks. After sitting in the lumpy carriage for most of the day, she felt the need to stretch her legs for a bit. A tour of the duke's house would give her that opportunity.

Night had fallen quickly in London, but a lamp had been left burning on a side table, giving off a golden, welcoming glow. As she stood in the vestibule, she realized the house was surprisingly quiet for the number of servants in attendance. She could only assume that Mrs. Ellsworth, Ashby, and the other servants were allowed to retire to their own rooms or attend private matters after their chores were done for the day and the duke was out of the house for the evening.

Henrietta picked up the lamp, walked over to the drawing-room doorway, and looked inside. This time she saw things she hadn't noticed before when she was in the room with the duke: a large floral painting hung over the fireplace; a tall, brass candelabra stood in one corner, and a pianoforte occupied a place against a far wall. The room was well appointed and seemed in perfect keeping with what she expected of a bachelor's home.

She turned away from the doorway and started down the dark corridor, stopping to glance inside the dining room, which held a lovely rosewood table with fancy carved chairs sitting around it. A large fruit compote had been arranged on top of a corner table.

The honeyed glow of light reflected off the highly polished furniture, showing there wasn't a speck of dust anywhere. Opposite that room was a doorway that led to the kitchen, which she didn't bother to enter, but she could smell a welcoming scent of fresh baked bread wafting from inside. Farther down she found another smaller room that looked far more cozy and inviting than the perfectly decorated room where she'd met the duke.

Each area seemed well proportioned and elegantly decorated with fine furniture and expensive artwork. Gold tassels hung from classical swags framing the windows, and luxurious carpets covered the floors.

The duke had a large, comfortable home. It was just the kind she would like to have as her very own, but Henrietta had learned long ago not to get too contented in any one house.

Opposite the rear parlor was another room. Before she even approached the entrance, something told her this was the duke's exclusive domain.

She hesitated. Should she infiltrate it?

Maybe just a quick peek inside to satisfy her burgeoning curiosity about the man who now had control over her life.

Without further thought, she stepped over the threshold into the book room and instantly caught the mellow fragrance of beeswax, the acrid smell of burned wood, and the masculine scent of leather. She couldn't resist turning up the lamp so she could get a better look at the contents of the room.

One side of the room held floor-to-ceiling book-shelves, completely filled. She ran her hand over first one and then another of the thick, handsome, leather-bound volumes of science, history, and poetry. Suddenly she stopped and smiled. The duke even had copies of her favourite books: thin, cheaply bound, horrid novels. It was the largest collection she'd ever seen. She couldn't help but wonder if the duke had read them all.

A perusal of the spines told her she had read some of them, but not all. Her hand rested on the title *The Forbidden Path*. That one sounded like a delicious read. She slowly traced her hand across every book, seeing many titles she hadn't read.

Having all these wonderful books at her fingertips would be heaven—if she were allowed to stay in the duke's home. After talking to him, that didn't seem a likely possibility, and that thought caused the same deep longing inside her to have a home of her own.

Surely he wouldn't mind her borrowing a book to read from one of his well-stocked shelves.

She turned away from that feeling, and the books, to

scan the rest of the room. On one wall was a fireplace
with a stately mantel that held ornate candlesticks.
Soothing warmth emanated from the banked ashes. In
front of a set of windows stood the duke's desk. She
felt a little naughty and a little guilty perusing everything without his knowledge or permission, but that
didn't keep Henrietta from walking over to the desk
and giving it a closer look.

Two upholstered wingback chairs had been placed in
front of a richly dark mahogany desk, and an important-
looking leather chair sat on the opposite side. A tall
stack of ledger books and several jumbled stacks of
envelopes littered the top of the desk, along with
many loose sheets of vellum, foolscap, and parchment.
There was no place on top of the desk where you
could see the fine wood.

How could anyone live with such disarray?

No wonder the duke hadn't known she would be
arriving today! From the looks of all the unopened
mail, she would guess it had been weeks, not mere
days, since His Grace had tended to his correspondence. A reasonably competent secretary would have
this hodgepodge of papers straightened, sorted, and
properly filed or answered in no time at all.

Obviously the duke didn't have a well-organized
secretary, or could it be that he didn't have one at all?
No, he was a duke. He probably had more than one
secretary taking care of him.

Henrietta remembered him telling her that a lady
wasn't capable of managing an inheritance. What
nerve he had to say that when his desk looked like a
winter storm had hit it!

Henrietta had no idea how someone as important as a duke could be so neglectful. If this were her desk and she didn't go crazy from the disorderly look of the stacks of mail, she'd surely die of curiosity from wondering who had written her and what they had to say.

As she stared at the untidy heap of papers, her first impulse was to dash behind the desk to clean up and rearrange everything. She'd start by making the stacks of envelopes neat and tidy. Once that was done, she'd open each letter and scan its contents, determine its significance, and make three orderly stacks: one for things that needed immediate attention, one for things that could be handled at a later date, and one pile for informational letters that needed no reply.

The duke definitely needed a system that sorted his correspondence and a competent secretary to implement it for him.

But no, she couldn't touch anything on his desk—as much as she wanted to. It would be the height of presumption, not to mention downright disrespectful of his kindness to her. Besides, how his desk looked was no concern of hers.

Reluctantly, she turned away from the untidy desk and focused her attention on the bookshelves again. She found *The Forbidden Path*, plucked it from the shelf, and tucked it under her arm, determined to leave and go to her room, and read until she fell asleep.

However, she made the mistake of looking at the desk once again and, despite every fiber of her being telling her no, she walked back over to it and stood near enough to touch it.

But she couldn't touch one thing on the desk.

Not one.

However Blakewell maintained his affairs was none of her concern. Maybe he worked very well with such clutter around him.

Yet… perhaps she would just put the lid on the jar of ink so it wouldn't dry out, or worse, be spilled on an important document. Yes, leaving an open jar of ink around valuable papers was very dangerous.

"The duke would want me to cap it," she said to herself as she carefully pushed some papers aside and placed the lamp and book she'd been holding on the edge of the desk.

She reached over a stack of letters, picked up the lid, and carefully secured it on the ink container.

"There," she said. "That one small thing makes the desk look a little better and safer."

And maybe she could just straighten the stacks of letters and put them in some kind of order for him. Surely the duke wouldn't care if she just made them a little neater.

And perhaps she should look through the mail stacks just to see if there was indeed a letter from Mr. Milton. She wouldn't open it, of course. That would be inexcusable, but if it was there, His Grace would be happy she'd found it for him and put it on the top of a very neat stack.

Wouldn't he?

Three

My Dearest Lucien,

You may want to recall these wise words from Lord Chesterfield and study on them as you go about your daily duties: "Every man does not pretend to be a poet, a mathematician, or a statesman and considered as such; but every man pretends to common sense."

Your loving Grandmother,
Lady Elder

BLAKE PULLED ON THE REINS AND SLOWED HIS GELDING to a trot as a group of men standing at the far end of Rotten Row came into view. Dark gray and purple clouds of dusk hung low in the wide blue sky. The fresh, rich smell of early spring foliage and a breezy chill stirred the late afternoon air. Perfect weather for a horse race, but thanks to Miss Tweed, Blake seemed to have missed the entire competition.

His cousin Morgan was easy to spot, not only because he was taller than most of the men standing around him, but because he was the one accepting handshakes and claps on the back, a sure sign that his thoroughbred had won again. Blake wasn't surprised. Morgan had an eye for good horseflesh, and he seldom bought a loser.

The chestnut-colored stallion stood behind Morgan, stomping and pawing at the earth as if he was ready to run again. The high-strung animal wasn't accepting his congratulatory pats as graciously as his owner.

Off to the side Blake saw his other cousin, Race. He was talking to the loser and no doubt trying to make the poor fellow and his cronies feel a little better about how much money they had lost.

Blake was friendly enough with his two cousins, but an unspoken rivalry had always simmered just below the surface of their relationships.

To the ton, the three grandsons of Lady Elder always appeared united, taking up for each other if need arose. But when they were alone, it wasn't unusual for one to try to best the others, be it at shooting, racing, or fencing, though they never admitted to the competition unless it was to gain the favor of a young miss.

They all had their strengths and their weaknesses. The one thing none of them wanted to do first was marry. This unstated vow among them had grown out of frustration with their grandmother's continuous machinations while she was alive.

Everyone in the ton knew that, before her death, their grandmother had tried many times, by fair means and foul, to force her grandsons to marry. After all, she had been happily wed four times. Each time she took a husband, she elevated her station in life until finally, late in life, she became the Earl of Elder's countess.

But not even vast fortunes had tempted Blake or his two cousins to propose matrimony to any of the young ladies who fancied them.

Decades earlier, Lady Elder had successfully married off each of her three daughters to titled gentlemen, making her the most famous woman of her time. In turn, each daughter had given her a grandson, all in the same year. The firstborn grandson was Lucas Randolph Morgandale, who became the ninth Earl of Morgandale. The second was Alexander Mitchell Raceworth, who became fourth Marquis of Raceworth.

Blake was the youngest grandson by nine months, and Race and Morgan had never let him forget it, even after his father died and he became a duke, outranking them both.

All three cousins were tall, handsome, and available. They were continually sought after by young misses, aging widows, and beautiful heiresses, but all three men happily remained bachelors in the beginning of their thirtieth years.

Blake stopped his mount not far from the excited men and jumped down from the saddle. The group had thinned to only a few as he walked his gelding toward Morgan. Now that he was closer, Blake saw that one of the men still in the park was Clayton Rockcliffe, the ninth Duke of Rockcliffe, along with his tag-along brother Lord Waldo. Blake had never considered Rockcliffe a good friend and, after a high-stakes card game a few weeks earlier in which Blake was sure the man had cheated to win, he didn't like the fellow.

It was ridiculous the way Lord Waldo followed his brother everywhere—and that Rockcliffe tolerated it. Blake couldn't imagine having such a constant shadow.

He had always detested the advice his grandmother sent him each month from her dear, departed friend Lord Chesterfield, but the man had hit on a few truths in his long and utterly useless letters to his son. One of them was that if a man would cheat at a game of cards, he'd cheat at everything else in his life.

Until Blake had become a duke two years earlier, Rockcliffe was the most eligible man in England since, at the time, he was the only unmarried duke. Because of his much younger age and good looks, Blake had taken the title of most-sought-after bachelor away from Rockcliffe and, in subtle ways, Rockcliffe had let him know he didn't like having a rival.

Blake nodded to one of the men he passed, shook hands with another, and completely ignored Rockcliffe and Lord Waldo as he made his way over to Morgan and Race.

"If you were going to be so late as to miss the contest, Lucien, why show up at all?" Morgan asked as the last well-wisher walked away.

Blake frowned at his cousin and threw his horse's reins over the saddle horn. Morgan knew Blake hated to be called by his first name, the name only his grandmother had used. He knew Morgan wasn't happy that he had been delayed, and calling him "Lucien" was his attempt to get back at him. Morgan, the eldest of the three cousins, was a stickler for convention, and he wanted to make his annoyance clear that Blake hadn't been there to see his horse's latest win.

Ignoring Morgan's pointed remark, Blake walked over and patted the warm, firm neck of the thoroughbred. The animal snorted and shook his head at the attention.

Blake never intended to be late for anything, but far too many times he seemed to arrive past the appointed hour. He wasn't sure why, but time wasn't something that he usually paid much attention to.

In hopes of making light of his tardiness, Blake said, "Was it Lord Chesterfield who said 'Better late than never?'"

Morgan grunted as the wind whipped a strand of long dark hair across his face. "If he did, he was wrong about that, and he was wrong about all the other bloody things he wrote in those damn letters."

"Don't get so riled, Morgan," Race said, jumping into the conversation. "And you know very well our grandmother said that herself about being late. Who the bloody hell knows where she heard it or whether she just made it up? But we all know she attributed every blasted thing she ever wrote to us or said to us as coming from her good friend Lord Chesterfield."

Blake grinned at Race even though he didn't need his intervention where Morgan was concerned. If there was any controversy, Race wasn't one to be left out.

"Actually I believe the phrase was first noted in Chaucer's *Canterbury Tales*," Blake offered, "but then do any of us really give a damn who first said the words?"

"Hell no, we don't care," Race said with a grin, "but our grandmother sure did."

At that, Morgan grinned, too. "You're both right; no one cares."

"Is Gibby already gone?" Blake asked, not seeing the old man. Sir Randolph Gibson considered himself a grandfatherly figure to the three cousins, though he had no blood connection to them.

"Like you, he was a no-show," Morgan said. "But he had manners enough to send over a note saying that he couldn't be here."

"That's rare for him to miss a race," Race said, a wrinkle forming between his brows.

"Most unusual. In his note, he mentioned he was meeting with someone who wanted him to invest in a fleet of hot-air balloons."

"A fleet? You can't be serious," Race said.

"Gibby can't be serious," Blake added.

"There's only one way to find out." Morgan turned to Blake. "And I believe it's your turn to see what the old man is up to now."

Of late, Sir Randolph Gibson's mind seemed to be failing him when it came to good common sense and sound business decisions. This hot-air balloon idea sounded very much like two other outlandish ventures in which he had recently invested and that had ended with major financial repercussions to his income. The three cousins felt duty bound to watch out for him, not only because their grandmother had asked them to, but because Gibby had been such a constant companion to her during the last few years of her life.

"I'll make a point of visiting him tomorrow to try to find out who's after his fortune this time—and what I can do about it."

"Let us know what you find out," Race said.

"Or if you need any help," Morgan added.

Blake nodded and then took off his hat and ran a gloved hand through his hair. "Sorry I missed the race, Morgan. I was unexpectedly tied up with something urgent this afternoon."

"No doubt your mistress had you tied to her bed," Race said with a laugh.

A picture of the very proper Miss Tweed flashed in Blake's mind. No, he couldn't see her ever being uninhibited enough to go for that kind of sport.

"Don't answer that," Morgan said. "We really don't want to hear about your escapades with your latest mistress."

"Speak for yourself, Morgan," Race said with a mocking sparkle in his dark eyes. "I might be interested in hearing a few particulars. Not too many, Cousin, mind you, but a few details could be, shall we say, intriguing if not instructive for us."

"Back to the reason I'm here," Blake said, ignoring Race's ribald comment. "Congratulations on the win, Morgan, though I never had any doubts what the outcome would be."

Blake pulled a clump of sugar out of his pocket and held it up to Morgan with a questioning expression on his face. Morgan nodded his consent, and Blake gave the sweet to the stallion.

"And what about your winnings?" Morgan asked as his horse snorted and pulled at his bit, looking for more of the treat in Blake's outstretched hand. "Or did you bet against me this time?"

"You know better than to even suggest that," Race said, taking up for Blake again.

"Sorry, ole chap. I didn't get my bets placed on this one. I had planned to do it today before coming over here, but with all that I had to do, the time just got away from me."

"At least you can make it up to Morgan by being his partner in the card game tonight," Race said. "Rockcliffe and Lord Waldo are coming. I know you've wanted to have a go at Rockcliffe for weeks now."

Months.

"Yes, how much was it you lost to him the last time you played him?" Morgan asked Blake as he handed the reins of his horse over to his groom, leaving the three of them alone.

"More than I care to remember," he answered his oldest cousin as he looked behind him and saw Rockcliffe and Lord Waldo riding away, their impressive horses kicking up dust from the road.

"Or more than you'll ever forget," Race said with a grin.

"I guess it could be said that way," Blake answered, turning to Race. "Sorry, but something has come up, and I can't make your card game tonight."

"Why the hell not? Are you going back to see Constance?"

"Or, perhaps you've finally found another mistress?" Morgan questioned.

"As a matter of fact, I am going to see Constance, but not for the reason either of you are implying."

Both his cousins' expressions indicated they didn't believe him.

"I get the feeling there's something you're not telling us," Morgan said.

"No. There's something I've been trying to tell you ever since I got here, but the two of you seem more interested in idle chatter."

"Then out with it," Morgan said.

Blake wasn't sure where he needed to start or just how much he wanted to tell his cousins, so he simply said, "A young lady showed up at my house this afternoon and promptly told me I was her guardian."

"What?" Morgan asked.

"Are you sure?" Race echoed.

"Of course I'm sure. I haven't seen documentation to back her claim, but she seems very credible to me."

Morgan grunted. "There's a scoundrel born every day who thinks he can pull the wool over a nobleman's eyes, Blake. No doubt some man is out to make fast blunt and has put her up to something sinister."

Blake hadn't gotten that feeling at all. Miss Tweed appeared legitimate in every way.

"Did she have any kind of proof to back up such a claim?" Race asked.

"None with her," Blake answered.

"Not surprising," Morgan said. "Besides, there is no way this could be true. You're not old enough or wise enough to be the guardian of anyone."

"That's right. You can't even take care of yourself," Race added with a laugh. "There's no way you could be responsible for anyone else. No one in their right mind would even ask you to be a guardian for their dog. I hope you showed her and her chaperone the door."

Blake hesitated. "Not exactly."

Race and Morgan looked at each other and in unison asked, "Why?"

"First, she doesn't have a chaperone with her—other than her maid. Secondly, there is the slightest possibility that she knows what she's talking about."

"Don't tell me you got too deep in your ale one night and agreed to be someone's guardian," Morgan said.

"Of course not," Blake said, starting to feel somewhat exasperated by the whole turn of events.

"Did you lose a bet in a hand of cards?" Race asked cautiously.

"Or possibly win the honor of being her guardian in a high-stakes game?"

"It's nothing like that. She said a solicitor should have notified me of this. The problem is that I haven't been through my mail in weeks."

"Good lord, tell me it's not true," Morgan added to Race's breathy swear.

"It's very much true."

"Why haven't you yet hired a secretary to keep up with your correspondence?" Race asked.

"Obviously, he hasn't had time," Morgan said, in a slightly mocking tone. "You never should have turned off your father's secretary until you had a damned good replacement for him."

Blake knew Morgan spoke the truth, but he would never admit that to his cousin. When Blake's father died, he made arrangements to keep on his father's secretary, butler, housekeeper, and a host of other servants employed at the town house in Mayfair. Over the course of time, he'd accepted Mrs. Ellsworth and he'd somehow, so far, managed to tolerate the dour-faced Ashby. But Blake couldn't abide his father's demanding and condescending secretary. Now he'd been without one for far too long.

Blake had every intention of replacing the man, but days had turned into weeks and weeks into months without him interviewing anyone for the post. And even though his mail was left unattended for weeks at time, that had never been a problem or bothered Blake until now.

"So did you find these documents she spoke of?" Race asked.

"Not yet."

Blake really had little doubt that the letter was there. Miss Tweed didn't strike him as the kind of young lady who'd say something so outrageous if it wasn't true. Besides, who in their right mind could make up such an extraordinary story about the previous five guardians dying? It was so excessive it had to be true.

"Why the hell not?"

"Yes, damnation, Blake, what are you doing standing here with us?" Morgan asked.

"Pardon me, if I wanted to inform you two that there was a young lady at my house before anyone else heard about this situation and told you."

"Oh, yes, you're right about that," Race said. "We would be upset if we heard this news from the gossips."

"What is her name?"

"Henrietta Tweed. Her father was Sir William Tweed. Apparently he was an old friend of my father's."

Blake took the time to tell them Miss Tweed's wild

tale about the deaths of the previous guardians and her belief that there was a curse.

"Damnation, she's had an extraordinary life if what she says is true," Morgan said when Blake finished. "It's no wonder she believes there's a curse."

"Yes, but the question is, what are you going to do about her?" Race said.

"For now, I'm going to Constance's house and ask her if she'll be Miss Tweed's chaperone until I can figure out what needs to be done with her."

"I don't believe it. You're going to ask your lover to be this girl's chaperone?"

"Former lover," Blake said in an exasperated voice. He hadn't been romantic with Constance for quite some time now. They had had a torrid affair that flared quickly, but just as abruptly died away.

"Constance is out of her mourning now and well-respected in Society. She will be the perfect person to chaperone Miss Tweed."

"She's respected only because no one knows she became your lover just a few weeks after her husband died."

Constance sounded like a doxy when Morgan put it that way, and nothing could be further from the truth. Constance's husband had been in a coma for months until his body simply withered away. She was lonesome and needy for affection of any kind at first. It didn't take either of them long to realize they weren't suited for each other as lovers, and they had settled into a comfortable friendship.

"No one but the two of you knows about my liaison with Constance, and it had better stay that way."

"You know you have our trust," Morgan said.

"If nothing else," Race added.

"Constance will know what to do with Miss Tweed, I'm sure."

Suddenly Race laughed. "I would give anything to see Constance's face when you tell her you want her to take care of a young miss."

A satisfied grin flashed across Morgan's face, which then dissolved into laughter. "I'd rather like to see that myself."

When Blake didn't join their merriment, it soon died away with the clearing of throats.

"You have to admit it's quite ludicrous," Race said. "What is the girl's age, thirteen or maybe fourteen?"

"I wish," Blake admitted aloud. "She is not a child or a young miss."

His two cousins looked at him with curious expressions.

"She's a nineteen-year-old young lady with enough confidence to put the two of you in your places."

"At nineteen?"

"A beauty you say?" Race's eyes lighted.

"Don't get any ideas, either one of you. She clearly has been raised as a lady of quality, and I won't have either of you thinking to change that."

"Where is she now?"

"I left her in Mrs. Ellsworth's care. I have little doubt that Miss Tweed has finished her dinner by now and will be sound asleep when I return."

The wind kicked up, and Blake realized the sky had turned dark. He settled his hat back on his head.

"Sorry, Race, the card game and winning my blunt

from Rockcliffe will have to wait until Miss Tweed has been taken care of."

Twenty minutes later, Blake was sitting in Constance's parlor waiting for her to see him, but he was thinking about Miss Tweed. Instead of wondering what he was going to do with her as he should have been, he was remembering her sparkling blue eyes, her full and shapely lips, and how he couldn't help but admire the courage she had needed to walk into his house and declare to a total stranger that he was her guardian.

When he had first seen her coming toward him, heady warmth had spun through his veins, igniting a sharp, purely masculine response of sudden desire in his lower body. What he felt was in no way what a guardian should feel for his ward.

He had wanted her as a man wants a woman.

"Blake," Constance said as she walked into the room, "what a rogue you are to stop by to see me without an invitation or notification of your desire for a visit."

Constance wore a beautiful smile and a low-cut black velvet gown. Her long, vibrant red hair had been shaped into tight curls on the top of her head. Her wide green eyes were filled with delight as she walked toward him with the confidence of a woman who knew where she stood with a gentleman.

Blake knew that several men had already made known their intentions to offer for her hand, but she was set to decline them all. And he had a feeling she would continue to do so. That wasn't because she was pining for her dead husband—or any other man. Rather, Constance was enjoying the life of a wealthy widow and all the freedoms it afforded her.

Blake rose, took both her hands in his, and gently squeezed them as he kissed one of her cheeks just below the eye and the other near the corner of her mouth. Blake would always love her fresh womanly smell, even if he no longer wanted her in his bed.

"My grandmother tried to teach me proper behavior. I hope you'll forgive my bad manners."

Constance looked up into his eyes and said, "I'll forgive you anything—once."

He chuckled. "Then I'm a lucky man. I try never to make the same mistake twice—especially with a woman. You look lovely, Constance."

"Thank you, Your Grace. And you are as handsome as ever. I don't have to ask how you are doing. I can look at you and see you are doing very well."

He shrugged off her compliment and said, "I have no complaints. How are you?"

"I, too, am well. Sit down and tell me why you stopped by. I'll pour you a drink."

Blake remained standing. He watched her walk over to the side table behind the floral-printed settee and lift the top off a decanter. They had been lovers less than a dozen times. Even at that, their affair lasted longer than it should have. The exciting rush of anticipation had only been between them the first time. They both knew it and accepted it with no misgivings. Constance was intelligent, loyal, and caring, and he would do anything for her, but she wasn't the lover for him.

"I hear only silence," she said as she splashed wine into the glasses.

"That's because I was just thinking that I would have liked for you to have been my sister, should I have been fortunate enough to have one."

Constance turned and smiled at him. "I think that's the nicest thing anyone has ever said to me."

"I mean it."

"I don't doubt that you do, and it makes me feel rather special."

He sighed to himself. "I hope you still feel that way after I tell you about a favor I need to ask of you."

Constance walked back over to him and handed him the drink. He waited for her to take a seat on the settee, and then he joined her.

"You know you have only to ask what you will and, if it's within my capabilities, I will do it for you."

She held out her glass for a toast.

"You may want to hear what I have to say before you agree to do it."

"I trust you," she said.

The way she looked at him, the way she said those three little words, told Blake he had made the right decision in coming to her for help.

Blake touched his glass to hers and said, "And I trust you, Constance. That's the only reason I would ask this of you."

She laughed softly. "You're making this sound terribly important. You have my curiosity brimming. Now tell me, what do you need from me?"

"I've been trying to decide if I should start at the beginning and tell you the entire story, or if I should just tell you what I want of you."

Constance took a sip from her glass. "You decide, of course, but the night is young, and I just poured our wine. I have plenty of time for a long story, if you do."

Blake took a deep breath. Time and his duties were two things to which he had to start paying more attention.

"Unfortunately, and as lovely as it would be, I don't have all evening to sit with you. The short of it is that I need you to be a chaperone to a young lady for me."

Her eyes narrowed, and the smile slowly faded from her lips. She lowered her glass. "A chaperone? Me? You look serious."

"As I can be."

"I'm not in need of any kind of employment, as you well know."

"Of course not. This would be temporary, a few weeks at most. It's complicated."

"Perhaps you should tell me the whole story."

Blake took a deep breath. He still didn't understand the whole story himself.

"Apparently many years ago a friend of my father's listed him, as the Duke of Blakewell, in his will to be the guardian for his daughter. There was nothing wrong with that as long as my father was the duke. Regrettably, as you know, my father is no longer with us, and the duty of seeing to her welfare has apparently fallen to me as the current duke."

Constance relaxed and set her glass on the rosewood table in front of them. The smile returned to her face.

"That's simple enough to take care of. You can hire a suitable governess for her and send them both off to one of your country estates. Give them permission to ride horses every day, and they will never bother you again. All little girls love horses."

Blake chuckled ruefully and relaxed against the back of the settee. "If only it were that uncomplicated, but I'm afraid that won't do."

"Why not?"

"She's not a little girl. She's nineteen."

And she's lovely, poised, and very desirable.

"Good heavens," Constance said. "Nineteen. That does present a problem. Doesn't she have a doddering old aunt, a long-lost uncle, or even a disreputable cousin she can turn to for help?"

"Apparently not."

"Such a pity. It must be dreadful to be so alone in the world."

Blake had felt the same way when he'd heard she had no living relatives. Not only did he have his two cousins, he had a host of close and distant relatives from his grandmother's many marriages. And then, of course, he had Gibby. Now that Blake thought about it, he had no idea how it would feel to be totally alone in the world with only strangers and servants to turn to for help.

"From what I gather, her father's will listed several names as guardians, with the Duke of Blakewell being the last one."

Constance frowned. "So she's been through all the others, and suddenly she's your responsibility. That doesn't bode well for you, Blake. She must be hellish to deal with."

Not wanting to go any further into the sketchy details about Miss Tweed's bizarre story, Blake simply said, "No, it's not anything at all like that. It has nothing to do with her behavior. Unfortunately, all her other guardians have gone to meet their Maker."

"And she lost her parents, too? What a shame. So tell me, what is she like? Is she well-mannered and of quality?"

"Without a doubt," he answered.

"Intelligent?"

"Extremely."

"Is she beautiful?"

"Absolutely."

Constance pursed her lips for a moment before they spread into a smile. She said, "Well, Blake, there's no problem at all that I can see."

"I'm glad you don't see any, my dear friend, because problems are all that I see."

"I have the perfect solution. You should have no trouble getting rid of her quickly with what I have in mind."

Blake eyed her warily as he took a sip of his wine. "And what exactly is it that you propose I do?"

"It's very easy, my friend." She smiled. "Find a man to marry her."

Four

Dearest Lucien, my youngest grandson,

Lord Chesterfield once wrote to his son: "Speak the language of the company you are in; speak it purely, and unlarded with any other. Never seem wiser, nor more learned, than the people you are with. Wear your learning like your watch, in a private pocket."

Your loving Grandmother,
Lady Elder

"MISS TWEED?"

Startled, Henrietta looked up from the envelope she was staring at and froze. The Duke of Blakewell stood in the doorway, tall, broad-shouldered, and scowling. At her. His stance was rigid. His dark, serious eyes seemed to pierce straight through to her soul. There was a commanding presence about him that suddenly felt primal. He looked at her with a single-minded intensity that, for a brief moment, made her want to slink into a corner and curl up so small that no one could see her.

And no wonder! She was sitting in his chair, at his desk, sorting through his mail.

Oh dear! She was in a basketful of trouble.

Tamping down her fear and embarrassment at being caught sorting his correspondence, she rose slowly and, as calmly as she could under the condemning circumstances, she smiled pleasantly and said, "Good evening, Your Grace."

Blakewell appeared momentarily thrown by her polite greeting. His severe expression didn't change, but his shoulders relaxed a little as he stepped farther into the room. He was undoubtedly a formidable man to deal with. She had to remain strong and in control.

"I suppose you are wondering what I'm doing in here," she said with all the aplomb she could muster, given how fast her heart was beating.

"No, I'm not wondering at all. I know *exactly* what you're doing."

Her breath grew uncomfortably shallow. "You do?"

The furrow in his broad brow deepened. His eyes narrowed. "Yes. It's quite clear to me that you are snooping into my private letters."

Henrietta gasped. Scorching heat flared in her cheeks. His words were a blatant insult to her character, and she needed a moment to find her voice.

"Snooping? Me?" Her hand flew to her chest in indignation. "Never, Your Grace. That's an outrageous accusation to make."

"Is it?" He pointed to the unopened letter on the desk in front of her. "I don't think so."

She had never been more mortified in her life. "This is not what it looks like."

"Really?"

His voice sounded doubtful. And no wonder, considering her predicament.

"Yes."

"Then perhaps you should explain to me why I'm not seeing what I'm seeing."

Regaining her composure, she said, "I'd be happy to do that, Your Grace."

Henrietta walked from behind the desk and stood beside it. Clasping her hands together tightly in front of her, she continued, "Even after the long and tedious coach ride today and the rather trying conversation with you earlier this evening, I was restless and not ready for sleep so I came in here hoping to find a book to read." She reached over, picked up the copy of *The Forbidden Path*, and held it up for him to see, confident the evidence would prove her innocence.

But he didn't deviate from his allegation as he said, "If a book was all you wanted, why were you sitting behind my desk rather than standing over by the bookshelves?"

Her hope that she could get out of this precarious situation with her dignity intact was fading fast. But she wasn't going to give up. Yet. If she were to hold her own with this formidable man, she had to stand firm and not waver an inch.

"There is a perfectly innocent explanation."

"I'd be rather interested in hearing that, Miss Tweed, because right now you are looking quite guilty of snooping into my private papers." The duke's expression remained firm as he folded his arms across his chest in a casual manner.

She took a long steadying breath. "While I was looking over your titles, I noticed quite by chance that the lid had been accidentally left off the ink container on your desk. Knowing that could cause a major mishap, I walked over and put the lid back on for you. I was sure you wouldn't want the ink to dry out or, perhaps worse, for it to be knocked over and spilled on some terribly important document."

He glanced down at his orderly desk, surveying it quickly but thoroughly. His eyes narrowed, and skepticism showed in their brownish-gray depths as he looked back up at her.

"Are you certain that is all you did, Miss Tweed?"

A blind person could tell that his desk looked nothing like it had when he left the house. She had carefully arranged loose papers and letters that had been opened but carelessly tossed aside into small, orderly piles. The massive jumble of unopened mail had been straightened into four manageable stacks. Even the quill had been taken out of his ledger book and positioned in its stand, with a clean sheet of vellum left in its place to mark the duke's page.

But what was most telling was the fact that the beauty of the polished mahogany could now be seen. Its richness gleamed invitingly in the soft lamplight. By the dates she'd seen on some of his correspondence, the duke hadn't seen the top of his magnificent desk for a long time.

Her handiwork could not be hidden or denied, but she wasn't above being evasive or vague.

She cleared her throat and took a step away from the desk. "I may have moved a few sheets of paper and straightened your mail."

"You *may* have?" he asked in a mocking tone as his gaze continued to pierce hers.

She knew that had been an incredible thing to say, but she really had no choice. She couldn't tell a duke how inconceivable it was to her that he left his desk in such disarray. And that she considered it downright inexcusable to go so long without reading and answering his correspondence.

"Yes, but not to worry, Your Grace. I assure you, I didn't remove or discard anything from your desk, nor did I read anything that was already open. I am not a snoop. I simply made tidy what was there." She motioned in the direction of the neat stacks of paper.

Henrietta held her breath and tried to remain composed as she stood staring at him, watching his expression fade from annoyance to uncertainty to something far different. Not only did his demeanor change, but the stormy gleam in his brooding eyes slowly melted into a soft and dreamy look. His lips relaxed into a faint, heart-stopping smile that made her legs feel weak. It was as if everything in the room changed and she saw nothing except Blakewell.

He walked closer to her.

Too close.

Her heartbeat was already racing in her chest, and her breaths were coming in short little gasps. She had never felt quite like this before. It should have disconcerted her, but these new unexplained feelings intrigued her.

"And why did you do that, Miss Tweed?" he asked, taking another step toward her.

"What?" she asked, finding it difficult even to

remember what they had been talking about while he advanced on her. The only thing she could concentrate on was her awareness of the nearness of the handsome duke.

"Why did you sort and tidy my private papers?"

She realized his voice had changed, too. It was smooth, low, and more seductive than any voice she'd ever heard. It caused her skin to prickle with tingles and her stomach to tighten.

Henrietta had been much more comfortable with the scowling, demanding duke who first stood in the doorway. She didn't know quite what to say or how to handle this seductive man who was making her aware of things she shouldn't be feeling for someone who was supposed to be her guardian.

His Grace had her discombobulated, which was a foreign feeling for her. She was usually very together and not easily unsettled. She was a sensible person, despite what he thought about her believing in a curse. What was it about this man that made him so different from her other guardians? She had to get control of herself. Henrietta knew for certain that when anyone was backed into a corner, the truth was the easiest way out, but the hardest choice to make.

Her gaze held fast on his as she said, "I fear it's a weakness I have, Your Grace."

His eyebrows rose with in a questioning expression, though his eyes continued to sparkle with humor. He moved still closer to her.

"Are you trying to tease me, Miss Tweed?"

"Certainly not."

His gaze stayed on hers. "I think you are."

"That would be foolish of me, Your Grace."

"What am I to think? You are much too strong, capable, and yes, sensible, to have or pretend to admit to any weaknesses."

He was so perceptive that it fascinated her. "Perhaps, in haste, I chose the wrong word. I only meant to imply that I have no patience or tolerance for things out of order."

"In that case you must agree with Lord Chesterfield that there is a place for everything, and everything should be in its place."

"I'm not certain Lord Chesterfield should be credited with that comment, Your Grace, but whoever said it was most correct."

"If you desire everything in its proper place, I'm wondering why this has slipped from your bun and is softly framing your face." As he said the words, he slowly pulled a long strand of golden blonde hair around for her to see.

By instinct, she reached up to secure the hair behind her ear, and as she did so, her fingers made contact with his. Chills of something she could only describe as delicious shuddered through her, and she quickly dropped her hand to her side.

Blakewell smiled and then proceeded to let the tips of his fingers glide along her cheek as he pushed the hair away from her face and behind her ear. His touch was warm, gentle, soothing, and strangely comforting. For an inexplicable reason, she closed her eyes and drank in the wonderful feeling of his manly touch, wanting it to last. She had the wildest desire to take hold of his hand and press it to her cheek. She didn't understand why, but she wanted to inhale his scent, taste his skin, and feel his strength.

Henrietta's lashes fluttered up, and she saw Blakewell staring down at her. His eyes were half closed; his moist lips were slightly parted. She felt his breath on her cheek. He was so near that their noses almost touched. His lips were not more than an inch from hers.

But, from somewhere deep inside herself, Henrietta found the presence of mind to realize that what she was feeling for the duke wasn't proper. Summoning all her strength, she took a deep breath and stepped back.

"I'm sorry, Your Grace; I didn't realize my hair had come down. I should have taken better care when I was arranging it."

His Grace took a step away from her as well and quickly said, "Perhaps you were so busy arranging my papers that you didn't notice."

He glanced down at his desk, and she saw that his gaze caught sight of the envelope she had been staring at when he came in.

"And what is this?" He reached down and picked up the letter.

"Oh, as luck would have it, Your Grace, as I organized your correspondence, I noticed the envelope from Mr. Conrad Milton, the solicitor I mentioned, and left it on top of the stack for you to read."

"Luck, you say?"

"Yes."

"As you arranged my mail, you just happened to see this? Are you sure you didn't come in here with the exact purpose of looking for it?"

"Yes, of course, I'm sure. I couldn't help but recognize the name the moment I saw it. I didn't open it, as you can see. I simply left it on top of the stack so you wouldn't have to search for it among the…" She stopped abruptly when she realized she couldn't say the word that was on the tip of her tongue.

"Among the rubble, the mess?" he finished for her.

"Actually, I was going to say clutter. The important thing for you to know is that I didn't read any of your correspondence."

"But you were tempted, were you not?"

She blinked rapidly. "No, no."

His eyebrows rose again, giving him that annoying, questioning look.

A frown flashed across Henrietta's face, and she was tempted to stomp her foot in frustration, but she would not let him reduce her to such immature antics. "Oh, all right! Of course I was tempted."

Suddenly, the duke folded his arms across his chest and laughed. It was a wonderful sound that immediately dispersed her aggravation at his accuracy. The man was very good at disconcerting her. Until she had met Blakewell, she'd never met a person who could.

"That was not a fair question, Your Grace."

With a hint of merriment still on his breath, he said, "It was more of a statement than a question, Miss Tweed. I already knew the answer."

"Your words felt like an accusation."

"Perhaps that was because of your guilty conscience. You didn't have to answer me, even if you thought they were. Thank you for your honesty, even if you did deny it twice before you admitted it."

"You are mocking me again, Your Grace, and I find that very unbecoming in a man of your rank."

"Perhaps I am, Miss Tweed, but really there's no reason for you to be miffed. As I mentioned before, you make it so very easy for me to do."

He put the letter on top of one of the neat stacks she had made and then walked past her to stand behind his desk. "You may take your book and go to bed now. As you have so obviously pointed out, I have work to do and you are keeping me from it."

Just like that, he was dismissing her as if she were a common chambermaid and the post from Mr. Milton as if it was of no importance at all.

Perplexed, Henrietta took a step toward him. "But aren't you going to open the letter from the solicitor?"

"Of course."

She waited, but he made no move to pick up the letter and open it. Their eyes met and held for a moment.

"May I wait here until you do?"

"You could, Miss Tweed, but there wouldn't be much point. I wasn't planning to read it tonight; as I've just said, I have other work to attend to."

She glared at him in surprise and took another step closer to him. "Why not? That letter can prove that everything I've told you about myself is true."

"It can only prove that Mr. Milton says the same thing you say. And I've already told you that I have little doubt about your story. It is so unbelievably strange that it must be true. Whatever needs to be done to settle the matter officially, I will do tomorrow—or, perhaps I should say, in due time. In any case, it's too late to do anything about your predicament tonight."

"But have you no natural curiosity about what the man wrote?"

"I have plenty of all kinds of curiosity, Miss Tweed, just not about this, not right now."

If she were in his place, she wouldn't be able to wait until morning to open the letter and see what it said. But she had already made note that she and the duke were very different in many ways. However, he was definitely too cavalier about her guardianship, and she couldn't allow that.

It wasn't her place to suggest anything to such a powerful man as a duke, a man who had already given her sanctuary without proof. She was being extraordinarily bold and brave when she said, "Then may I ask of you, for my peace of mind, that you look at it tonight so that I might sleep better?"

The seconds ticked by and he made no move. He simply stared at her with those dreamy eyes that seemed to nick her soul. For a moment she thought he was going to deny her request. But suddenly, he picked up the letter and the paper knife she had conveniently left on the right side of his desk and broke open the wax seal. Several sheets of foolscap had been folded together. He pulled the lamp closer and briefly read the top sheet before laying them all on the desk.

"Have no fear for tonight. Your slumber should not be disturbed. Mr. Milton confirms every word of your story. He has copied verbatim the part of your father's will about the list of guardians. He assures me that I am free to send my solicitor to view the original document or, if need be, he will bring it to me."

Henrietta breathed a sigh of relief and smiled gratefully at him. "Thank you for reading it, Your Grace. I do feel much better."

"Don't thank me yet, Miss Tweed. I will be looking into other arrangements that may be considered for your welfare."

The carelessness with which he spoke those words caused Henrietta to shiver.

"What kind of arrangements?"

"As your lawful protector, I'll do what most guardians do for their charges."

Hope surged within her that he might free her from the bonds of his guardianship. The thought was exhilarating that she might have a permanent home here in London. She could make friends, attend parties, take walks in Hyde Park, or wander the grounds of Vauxhall Gardens without fear that the curse would strike again.

"You'll consider letting me be my own guardian," she whispered almost breathlessly as hope flooded her chest.

His gaze searched her face for a moment before he said, "No, Miss Tweed."

"You will let me live here with you?"

"Only for a short time. To do otherwise, I fear, would be too danger—would be unacceptable. I am a bachelor, and you are a young lady."

"Then what will you do with me?" she asked, her hope fading as fast as it had risen, knowing there were few options open to her. "Are you considering sending me to a convent?"

"No, that never crossed my mind, unless that is your desire."

"No, I feel I'm much too opinionated for that kind of service."

"I agree wholeheartedly with that. What I intend to do is find you a husband."

"Over my dead body!" she exclaimed, saying the first thing that came to her mind.

He frowned. "I hope you wouldn't attempt anything so serious as to harm yourself, Miss Tweed," he said sternly.

Henrietta was so shocked by his statement that her shoulders flew back, her chin lifted, and her gaze pinioned him. His steely gaze stayed on her face, and she matched his intensity.

"No, of course I wouldn't. I am only making you aware of how grave I consider your suggestion of intending to find me a husband."

"But that is what young ladies your age do."

"I would sooner go to a convent than be forced to marry a man not of my own choosing—and especially one you might consider acceptable."

"I'm not heartless. Of course, you would have to agree to anyone I would suggest."

Henrietta knew she would have to marry one day. Most young ladies did. But it wasn't something she had reason to give much thought. She wanted a home she could call her own, but she had never considered that it might come with a husband.

In a rush of fretfulness that was hard to control, she said, "Sign my inheritance over to me, Your Grace, and allow me my freedom."

"I can't do that. If I'm to take seriously this debt of my father's that has been passed to me, what you suggest would be irresponsible. Your father, as would my own, would expect me to see you properly wed."

"I know my father never would have brought me to London one day and expected me to start looking for a husband the next."

Blake saw raw passion in Henrietta Tweed's eyes, and that alone kept him from telling her that, yes, he believed her father would have brought her to London one day and married her off the next. But all he could think was that he wanted to take her in his arms and kiss her until she melted against him and surrendered everything to his will.

If fate was going to send a tempting, young lady to his door, why couldn't she have been one he could ravish, rather than one he had to protect?

He shook his head and looked down at the stack of ledgers on his desk. He was weary.

"Go to bed, Miss Tweed. I have a lot of work to do, and you are hindering me."

For a moment, Blake didn't think she was going to leave. He thought she would insist on saying something else, but thankfully, after only a moment, she turned and walked proudly out of the room with her book tucked under her arm.

"Bloody hell," he whispered after he heard her footsteps heading up the stairs.

If all wards were as strong, outspoken, resourceful, and desirable as Miss Tweed, there wouldn't be a man alive who would accept the guardianship of any young lady. The hell of it was, the way she challenged him as if she were his equal appealed to him. How many young ladies had that kind of courage and self-confidence? The ladies he danced with at the parties and balls seldom said anything to him for fear of saying the wrong thing. Not so Miss Tweed. She rushed in where angels wouldn't dare tread.

He turned to the bookshelf at his back and poured himself a splash of brandy before taking a seat in the chair behind his desk. He sipped his drink and thought back to a few minutes ago. He had almost kissed her when he touched her hair. He had wanted desperately to do so. If she hadn't stepped away, would he have kissed her?

Blake chuckled quietly. Why was he berating himself? He was a man who loved beautiful, exciting women, and Miss Tweed was both of those things. And much more. Of course he had wanted to kiss her. She'd stimulated him more than any other young lady had in a long time—if ever.

But he wasn't supposed to kiss her. Whether he liked it or wanted it, for now she was under his protection. And that made her untouchable.

If all went well, Constance would be her chaperone and take charge of her. He wouldn't have to see her or come in contact with her—very much.

Plenty of bachelors would kill to offer for the hand of a beautiful, capable, and intelligent young lady like Miss Tweed.

But Blake would have to make sure the fellow was decent enough. He wouldn't want her to marry a man who couldn't hold his ale. And with the passion he sensed smoldering inside her, she surely didn't need one too old to keep her happy in bed.

Blake put his glass down, picked up the letter from

Mr. Milton, and glanced at the pages behind the letter. She could not be treated like a poor relation. Her inheritance was considerable. Obviously her previous guardians hadn't robbed her, and he couldn't let her husband do it, either. He couldn't let Miss Tweed marry a heavy gambler or wastrel.

Blake picked up his brandy and settled himself into his chair. Lord Chesterfield had said, "Women, in truth, have but two passions, vanity and love; these are their universal characteristics."

According to Blake's grandmother, Lord Chesterfield was seldom wrong about anything—and never wrong about women.

A slow, confident smile eased across Blake's face. He had a feeling Miss Tweed would take exception to that particular comment from his grandmother's friend.

Blake chuckled to himself. Perhaps he'd mention the quote to her one day.

Yes, and he would look forward to her reaction.

Five

My Dearest Grandson Lucien,

Here are more wise words from Lord Chesterfield: "A man of sense sees, hears, and retains everything that passes where he is."

Your loving Grandmother,
Lady Elder

BRIGHT LIGHT ROUSED HENRIETTA FROM A DEEP SLEEP. Reluctantly, her eyelids fluttered up and she turned toward the glare. She saw the back of a lady who was opening the draperies on a wall of windows, causing streaks of sunshine to spill into the darkened room.

The slender woman was expensively dressed in a dark rose-colored gown of lightweight velvet. Her dark auburn hair was arranged in a neat chignon at the back of her neck and held there with elegant, beaded combs that twinkled and sparkled when they caught the sunlight.

Henrietta rose to her elbows and rubbed her eyes with the backs of her hands as memories of the past two days flooded her mind: the long, bumpy coach ride, the formidable duke, and the uncertainty of what lay before her now that she was in the home of the last guardian on her father's list, a man who had made it quite clear that he didn't want her there.

She quietly watched the lady secure the drapery panels away from the windows on large brass hooks attached to the wall. The woman was too well dressed for a servant. She might be another guest in the duke's house. But what would she be doing in Henrietta's room?

No, that couldn't be, Henrietta thought as her mind cleared from sleep. She had been at the duke's home two days, and she would know if there was another guest in the house.

Perhaps the woman hadn't seen her lying in bed. Henrietta cleared her throat and said, "Excuse me, Miss, but who are you?"

The lady seemed to take a deep, steadying breath before slowly turning to look at her, which she did a little too thoroughly for Henrietta's liking. She stared at Henrietta's face as if she were trying to decide whether she approved or disapproved of her before she spoke. But at the same time, Henrietta took the opportunity to look over the stranger.

Her delicate skin and face were lovely. She had expressive, green eyes that were set off by thin, flared eyebrows and a flawless complexion. She didn't appear to be as tall as Henrietta, but beneath the high-waist dress she wore, her frame looked a little fuller. One thing Henrietta couldn't miss, in the tilt of her head and the set of her shoulders, was that she bore all the outward traits of a very self-confident woman.

Without smiling, the lady inclined her head slightly to the side and said, "First, I'm not a miss. I'm Mrs. Constance Pepperfield."

Henrietta would have felt more comfortable in front of this lovely, self-possessed lady had she not been in bed and wearing her night rail.

"Very well, Mrs. Pepperfield, would you please tell me what you are doing in my room?"

"I'm here to help you."

"That's very kind of you, but I already have a maid."

Mrs. Pepperfield looked stunned for a second, but then her lips relaxed into a knowing smile. "Though I might have been doing a servant's duties in pulling back your draperies, I assure you, Miss Tweed, that I am not a servant."

"My apologies. No offense was intended."

She nodded once. "None taken. There can't be much more than a dozen years of difference in our ages, Miss Tweed, so I suggest we start our relationship with you calling me Constance, and I should like to call you Henrietta."

That seemed a rather presumptuous request, considering there was no one to make proper introductions for them, and Henrietta still had no idea who this lady was or what she was doing in her room.

"All right, Constance," she answered reluctantly. "What can I do for you?"

"Nothing, my dear. It is I who will be doing something for you. I had assumed Blakewell or someone on his staff would have informed you by now that he asked me to be your chaperone for the rest of the Season."

Chaperone? For the Season?

Henrietta knew what the Season was for—finding suitable husbands for young ladies. That thought sent a chill through her. Obviously, the duke had been serious a couple of nights ago when he told her he wanted to find her a husband. Apparently, he'd wasted no time putting his plan into action after reading Mr. Milton's letter.

What was she going to do?

After living all her life in small towns and villages, attending the balls and parties of London's Social Season had appeal. She had always wondered what it would be like to drink champagne and dance until dawn. But… there seemed to always be a "but." She knew nothing about men and had no desire to be married. She didn't know why, as that was the dream of most young ladies. But then most young ladies hadn't grown up the way Henrietta had. She had no knowledge of courting or flirting with a gentleman. And the last thing she wanted was to be cast off to yet another man as ward or wife.

She hadn't spent the last few years thinking about love, a husband, and a family. She had dreamt only of having a home of her own that no one could force her to leave.

She would love nothing better than to be in charge of her own destiny and to stop the curse that had followed her for the past twelve years.

Feeling at a complete disadvantage, Henrietta threw back the covers, and as gracefully as possible, scooted off the bed and grabbed her wrap.

While slipping her arms into the garment, she said, "It was extremely nice of His Grace to think of such a lovely idea, but I feel compelled to say that, at my advanced age, I don't really need a chaperone."

Constance folded her arms across her chest in disbelief. "Advanced age? Surely you jest."

"I shall be twenty soon."

"That is not old, Henrietta."

"I'm old enough to be a chaperone, governess, or companion to others. I wish the duke had spoken to me before hiring anyone."

Constance uncrossed her arms and took several steps toward Henrietta, but not in a threatening way. Her dark eyes zeroed in on Henrietta's, and her voice was pointed as she said, "First, my dear, it is not a lovely idea; it is necessary. If you don't know that, I have more to teach you about London Society than I thought. Secondly, I am not employed by anyone, and I have never been for hire. I am doing this for you as a favor to Blakewell and only because of our close, long-standing friendship. Do I make myself clear, Henrietta?"

Her straight shoulders and tilt of her chin spoke volumes about what she thought of her station in life. And just by the way she said the duke's name, Henrietta was certain the two did indeed have a close relationship.

"Yes, of course, Mrs. Pepperfield—Constance. I'm sorry to have implied otherwise."

"I'm sure you don't know, as I understand you are new to Town, but it is best you remember that whatever Blakewell wants, he gets."

The duke wanted Henrietta out of his house, and obviously the easiest way to accomplish that was to marry her off to the first man who offered for her hand.

Henrietta bristled. How could the duke find her a suitable husband? He couldn't even keep his desk straight.

To Constance, she simply said, "I suppose that is true of most dukes. I'm told they are all very powerful."

"Indeed, that would be the logical train of thought, but I assure you that it is not true. Blakewell is different from most dukes, which I'm sure, given time, you will see for yourself."

Without waiting for a response, Constance turned, walked over to Henrietta's wardrobe, and flung the doors wide.

The first thing she pulled out was a pale blue traveling dress with a matching pelisse. She held it up and looked at it as she said, "I took the liberty of asking your maid to bring up warm chocolate and toast for you. She informed me that you don't usually rise before noon, but I knew we had a lot to accomplish today. She should be here shortly."

Henrietta didn't like to wake early because she usually read a book until the wee hours of the morning. She had taken *The Forbidden Path* to bed with her the past two nights, but she had spent more time thinking about the formidable duke and his idea of finding her a husband than she had reading the book.

"This won't do," Constance said and dropped the gown to the floor.

She reached inside the wardrobe for another dress. It was quickly discarded in the same manner. Not clear on exactly what was going on, Henrietta stood stunned for a moment and watched as Constance took out one garment after another, barely giving them a passing glance before tossing them on top of each other, creating a heap of clothing on the floor.

Peggy had pressed and put everything away properly over the past couple of days, and now this woman was making a complete disaster of her clothing and the room.

Coming out of her shock, Henrietta said, "Please stop! You have no reason to empty my wardrobe."

But Constance continued to pull capes, chemises, bonnets, gloves—everything—out of the wardrobe, giving them only a fleeting glance and then tossing them to the floor with the rest.

Henrietta rushed over to the pile of clothing and started picking them up as fast as Constance threw them down at her feet. She filled her arms until she couldn't hold any more.

"Stop this madness. This is ridiculous. Constance, please, I must insist that you leave my personal belongings alone at once."

Constance threw a glimpse over her shoulder toward Henrietta and said, "I wish that I could, my dear, but I'm afraid that none of these dresses or gowns—," she stopped and held up a pair of worn, but still serviceable gloves, before tossing them to the floor, too. "None of this clothing will do for London's High Society, and it's certainly not suitably grand enough for the ward of Blakewell to be wearing in public."

The clump of clothing in Henrietta's arms was so big she could hardly see over it. "What do you mean? These dresses and gowns were just made last year. They are lovely and perfectly good," Henrietta argued as she watched two black wraps and her only gold-colored velvet reticule hit the floor.

"And I'm sure that, dressed in these quaint gowns, you looked quite—fetching in whatever small village you came from, Henrietta, but let me assure you they will not do for the life you will be living in London. And you must think of Blakewell's reputation as well."

"What?"

"It will not reflect favorably on His Grace if his ward looks like a poor relation who is not well thought of. With clothing like this, you would not be allowed in any of the homes, balls, or parties to which you will be invited, and you would most certainly be laughed out of Town, if anyone ever saw you wearing these out-of-date and out-of-fashion clothes."

Constance pointed to the mass of clothing hanging out of Henrietta's embrace. "Besides all that..."

There was more?

"Most of the shades are either too pale or too drab for your coloring. And the styles are much too old-looking for someone as young and as beautiful you."

Henrietta looked at the pink dress Constance wore. The lightweight velvet looked as soft and as expensive as any of the finest silks Henrietta had seen. The lace trim on the neckline and sleeves was delicate, exquisite, and beautifully sewn onto the fabric. Suddenly, Henrietta knew what Constance was talking about. While she had new clothing made each year, none of the pieces were made from the finest of fabrics and lace or had the rich detail and fashionable styling of the dress Constance wore.

Henrietta had always thought she had more dresses

and gowns than she needed, with gloves, wraps, and bonnets to match them all. Each one of her previous guardians had insisted she be properly dressed, but obviously not expensively or fashionably enough for Constance.

The weight of the clothing pulled on Henrietta's arms, and they began to ache. She threw the heavy bundle onto her bed and said, "These are in excellent condition. I can't just throw them out."

Constance closed the door to the tall wardrobe and casually leaned against it. "Of course not. I wouldn't dream of suggesting you should. I know of a little shop in town that takes out-of-date clothing and remakes it for the less fortunate. Plenty of women can use your unwanted garments, and we'll see that they get them—but after you have new ones made, you can no longer wear any of these."

Knowing that the clothing wouldn't be thrown out with the rubbish was some consolation.

Constance kept talking, giving Henrietta little time to respond to anything.

"I see I'm going to have to dress you from the skin out. I hope Blakewell knows how much this effort is going to cost him."

Henrietta flinched. "There's no need for the duke to spend his money on me. I can pay for my own clothing. My inheritance is quite sufficient."

"I'm sure it is, and it will do nicely for your dowry. But that's not how things will work for you now. You are the duke's responsibility, and in case I haven't made it clear before, I'll remind you that whatever Blakewell wants, he will get. Besides," she smiled almost wickedly, "I shall have an enormously good time putting everything on his account."

With that, Henrietta knew further argument with Constance was futile.

"As soon as you've had breakfast and dressed, we are going to my modiste. I sent over a note telling her to expect us. I believe she should be able to start immediately on gowns for you. She'll want to please the duke. You need so many things so soon that I'll tell her to solicit all the help she needs from other dressmakers and milliners—as long as she has something for you to wear before the end of next week. We are already into the Season, and we don't have much time to get you out to the parties.

"I'm sure you will get a flurry of invitations once I let it be known you are Blakewell's charge. Of course, I'll select only the choicest of dinner parties and balls for you to attend and, at first, perhaps we'll only go to one party each night to keep the mystery surrounding you for as long as we can. I'll be very careful whom I ask to get you vouchers for Almack's where, as you probably know, only the most worthy of Society are admitted. Well, the list goes on, but enough of that for now."

Yes, please no more, Henrietta wanted to whimper.

Her head was spinning. This lady wasn't like any chaperone Henrietta had ever met. Constance was like a general in the Prince Regent's army. She could have single-handedly defeated Napoleon's army, had he not already met his fate at Waterloo.

"We will get along very well, Henrietta, if you follow my instructions. It is my job to see that you

make the best impression possible at all our engagements. You will meet some of the most handsome
and wealthiest gentlemen in London. You might even
catch the eye of a titled man. By now, some will have
made a match as the Season is under way, but I'm sure
we'll find you one that suits."

Henrietta tuned Constance out. Hearing once again
that the Season was under way and some gentlemen
already betrothed gave Henrietta a glimmer of hope. If
Blakewell kept to his promise that she had to approve
any gentleman who showed her interest, she could
rebuff them all and hopefully have until next Season
to get used to the idea of a husband.

Since Lord Palmer's death a few weeks ago, only
one thing had been on her mind: talking her new
guardian into signing over her inheritance.

Constance was still chatting when Peggy walked
into the room carrying a tray with Henrietta's toast
and warm chocolate. Peggy's eyes grew wide with
shock as she looked at the clothes scattered across the
floor and bed.

"At last, your breakfast has finally arrived,"
Constance said. "Good. It's half past noon. I'm going
to leave you to eat and get dressed. I don't mean
to rush you, Henrietta, but we don't have time to
waste. I'll be downstairs in the drawing room waiting
for you."

Constance walked over to the pile of clothing on
the bed and picked through it, finally pulling a light
gray morning dress trimmed with silvery-blue lace
from the heap and laying it aside.

"Wear this. It's not your best color, but it should do

for today," she said to Henrietta, turning to walk out with a flourish of rose-colored skirts swishing.

Peggy put the tray on a chest and her hands on her hips as she surveyed the scattered clothing.

"Who is that lady, Miss Henri, and what have you done to your clothes?"

"That was Mrs. Constance Pepperfield, my newly acquired chaperone."

"Harrumph," Peggy said. "What do you need her for? You have me."

"I'm afraid she's His Grace's addition for me. Don't pout, Peggy. She will not take your place, I assure you; your employment is secure."

"She came into the kitchen this morning and ordered me around like I worked for her instead of you. I told her you didn't like to be disturbed this early in the day, but she insisted I bring up your tray."

"It's all right, Peggy. I don't think anyone can stop Mrs. Pepperfield once she's made her mind up."

"Why did you take out all your clothes? Didn't you like the way I put them away for you?"

"Don't be a ninny. Of course I did. You did a superb job as always. I'm afraid this chaos was made by the General—I mean, Mrs. Pepperfield."

"What did you say to her to make her so mad that she did all this?"

Henrietta looked again at the gloves, capes, and gowns strung across the floor from the wardrobe to the bed, and she smiled. "She didn't do it in anger, Peggy. Constance claims my clothing is not good enough for London Society, and she is going to see to it that I get all new clothes."

Peggy's eyes grew wide once again. "You best be careful around her, Miss Henri. It looks to me like this lady has a mean temperament."

"She's not mean." Henrietta laughed. "She's just firm and thorough. And for now I have no choice but to do as she commands. Now, I'd best have my chocolate while it's hot and get dressed before she comes looking for me."

"We sure don't want that," Peggy said and started picking up the clothing. "That woman has no respect for a person's property."

Henrietta rushed through her breakfast and then dressed in the morning dress Constance had picked out for her. It wasn't her best dress, and Constance was right, it wasn't her best color, but Henrietta didn't think what she wore would matter much today since she was being fitted for a whole new wardrobe.

The vestibule was empty when she reached the bottom of the stairs, and the house was quiet except for the muffled sound of voices coming from a doorway farther down the corridor. Henrietta peeked into the drawing room, but Constance wasn't there. She looked down the corridor again and realized that the doorway was the entrance to Blakewell's book room. Not wanting to disturb him, should it not be Constance in conversation with him, she softly tiptoed closer to the open door and listened for a moment.

"I hope that Henrietta will be prompt and I won't have time for refreshment, Blake," Constance said, "But thank you for offering. She and I have a lot to accomplish today and a very short time in which to do it. Here is a list of everything I need from you."

Henrietta heard the rustle of paper.

"I need accounts set up in her name at the shops listed at the bottom of the list. She'll also need an expensive, yet not too fancy, carriage with four well-schooled bays. The driver and footman should be even-tempered, their livery dashing, and, of course, they should be dedicated only to Miss Tweed."

Henrietta almost gasped out loud. She took a soft step back, reeling from the things Constance was asking for. A carriage with four horses, plus a driver and a footman?

"All that seems fair enough; I'll see to it," the duke replied.

"And it will need to be done today, Blake. You mustn't tarry about this if you expect her to be at her first party by the end of next week."

"I understand, and I'll get it done."

It shouldn't have shocked Henrietta to hear that Constance knew Blakewell well enough to know he liked to put off doing things, and with any luck, that might work to her advantage when he was looking for a husband for her.

"I don't mind telling you that the price will be high to get her properly betrothed before this Season is out. Do you have a problem with that?"

"Not at all, spend whatever you need. I don't want anyone thinking I'm not taking proper care of her."

"Splendid. I'll expect you to be at every party we attend."

Henrietta heard a chair squeak. "Is that really necessary?"

"Absolutely, you should have the first dance with

her at whichever party we decide she should make her debut. Her suitors must know that she not only has your protection and guidance, but also your affection. You will need to treat her as if she were your very own daughter. This will show everyone that you won't tolerate anyone bringing the least bit of scandal to her reputation. You must work with me on this if you want her suitably betrothed by the end of the Season."

Betrothed by the end of the Season? That was mere weeks away. That sent a shock of reality through Henrietta.

As far as Henrietta was concerned, the only good thing about having a husband was that she would finally have a home of her own. She wouldn't be uprooted every couple of years and sent to yet another town, another house, another guardian. But being a wife was not something she'd ever had reason to give much consideration. None of her other guardians had ever suggested that she needed to marry.

"Now, are we set on everything?" Constance asked.

"Completely."

·"Good." She sighed. "You know, Blake, I've never been a chaperone to anyone, but since you visited me the other night and gave me some time to think about the idea, I decided I would like to do it. It will give me something to do rather than just attend the Season's parties looking for a match of my own."

"You, Constance, looking for a match? I thought you were enjoying your freedom and your pleasure as a young and wealthy widow."

Henrietta heard a soft, feminine laugh.

"I do. I have. And I will. It does have its advantages, as you know only too well. But sometimes I think it would be nice to have a husband once again to share things with. Though I would want a much younger husband than my last, God rest his soul."

"Constance, you are beautiful and intelligent. You could marry any man you wanted. I know of several worthy men who would offer for your hand, if you would give them the least sign you are ready to be courted."

"Perhaps next year."

Henrietta felt uncomfortable listening to this private conversation. When they were discussing her, she felt justified in listening, but not now. She slowly backed away from the door toward the drawing room.

She studied about what she should do. She could wait in the drawing room until Constance and His Grace finished their dialogue and Constance came looking for her, or she could go back to the book room and let Constance know she was ready to start their day.

Without further thought, Henrietta started down the corridor at a brisk pace and walked to the doorway and knocked. She looked over at the duke, who was sitting behind his desk, and her heart fluttered deliciously. He was so handsome with his light brown hair and brownish-gray eyes, chiseled features, and broad shoulders hidden beneath his crisp white shirt, beautifully tied neckcloth and dark expensive coat, that she almost forgot what she was saying.

Almost.

She hadn't seen him since the night he had caught her sitting at his desk.

She smiled confidently at them, though she'd never met two more intimidating people in her entire life. "I thought I heard voices in here. Good morning, Your Grace. Good morning once again, Constance. I'm sorry for interrupting you."

The duke rose immediately and said, "Good morning, Miss Tweed. Have you been enjoying your stay?"

"Very much, thank you."

Constance stood up, too. "Henrietta, I'm glad it didn't take you long to dress and come down." She turned to Blakewell. "I trust you will take care of the things I requested earlier without delay."

"It will all be arranged within the hour, Constance."

She gave a satisfied sigh. "Good. We'll be off then. Come along, Henrietta."

"Ah, one moment, Constance," the duke said. "I'd like a word alone with Miss Tweed before you go, if you don't mind."

Surprised, Henrietta looked from the duke to Constance. It was clear by the tight expression on her face that Constance had not expected Blakewell to want to speak to Henrietta alone, either.

"Certainly, Your Grace, I'll get my cape and gloves and be putting on my bonnet. I'll wait for her by the front door."

Constance left without further words or glances at Henrietta or the duke.

Blakewell moved from behind his desk and stood very close to Henrietta. He had a commanding presence that she had never sensed in any other man. Despite her efforts to stay calm, her breaths grew shallow, her heartbeat raced, and a fluttering filled her stomach. No other man had ever made her feel this way and she was baffled, yet intrigued, by all these new feelings.

He looked down into her eyes and, with a slight smile, asked, "Were you really sorry for interrupting us?"

"Of course, I—"

Suddenly the tips of his fingers landed on her lips. Henrietta froze. An unexpected thrill of desire flared through her, heating her cheeks and radiating through her entire body. The gentleness of his caress was soothing when it should have been egregiously shocking.

"Remember, we discovered that you are not very good at denying the truth, didn't we?"

His fingertips slowly, gently, outlined her lips as he talked, and his gaze stayed on her face. Unable to speak for the feel of his skin on hers, Henrietta nodded.

Of course she remembered telling him that she hadn't been tempted to read his letter when, indeed, she had been extremely tempted.

"You were very quiet, but I knew you were there."

His fingers left her lips and he cupped her chin, tilting her face toward his. She smelled the scent of shaving soap on his warm hand. She looked into his calming eyes, her labored breathing eased, and her shoulders relaxed. There was something strangely comforting about being this close to him.

"How did you know I was there?"

He let his thumb rake across her lips again before removing his hand and taking a reluctant step away from her. "I wouldn't be a good master of this house if I didn't know what goes on inside it, now would I?"

She shook her head and let out a deep breath. "I should have known you would know I was there, no matter how quiet I was."

"I wanted to thank you for reorganizing my desk and arranging my correspondence."

"Does that mean you're no longer angry with me for my presumption?"

He chuckled as his gaze took a sweeping glance down her face before racing back up to settle on her eyes. "No, I'm not angry. In fact, I've found it quite easy to sit down at my desk over the past couple of days and do the work I've needed to get done for quite some time."

Relief washed through her and she smiled. "I'm glad I was of help. It truly is difficult to know where to begin when there is such a jumble of papers. Order puts things in perspective, don't you think?"

He laughed. "Ah, that sounds too much like a quote from Lord Chesterfield to me, and I would never agree with that man."

"Surely you jest. He was a gentleman's model gentleman."

"All the more reason not to rely on anything he said. I would much rather be a lady's model gentleman."

"But he was a master on how to be the perfect man, was he not?"

"What lady would enjoy a perfect man?"

Henrietta smiled. Was she flirting with the duke? "You are a clever man, Your Grace. Perhaps you should write your own book about men," she answered honestly.

Blake laughed softly. "You know, Miss Tweed, sometimes you seem so innocent and at other times you seem so…"

"Old?"

"No, not old. Wise. Perhaps, I should try to find my way out of this conversation by simply saying that you seem well read."

"That is true."

"Now, you better go. I don't want to keep Constance waiting for you too long. She might think of more for me to do, and her list is already so long that I'll need the rest of the morning to accomplish all that she wants done."

"Your Grace, may I be at liberty to come to your book room again for another book? I've been reluctant to enter after our last encounter."

"Of course, come and borrow whatever you like."

"Thank you."

The duke turned his attention back to his desk. Henrietta looked at him for a moment longer before quietly walking out of the room, trying to understand all those strange and wonderful feelings brought on by Blakewell's touch.

Six

My Dearest Grandson Lucien,

Some of Lord Chesterfield's wisest words were the following: "One of the most important points of life is decency; which is to do what is proper and where it is proper; for many things are proper at one time, and in one place, that are extremely improper in another."

Your loving Grandmother,
Lady Elder

TRUE TO HIS WORD, WITHIN THE HOUR BLAKE HAD sent Ashby out to accomplish the numerous and time-consuming errands ordained by Constance for Miss Tweed. Blake was seated in his carriage, loaded with account books on either side of him, and on his way to deliver them to his solicitor, all thanks to the organized and efficient Miss Tweed. After he finished with his solicitor, he would find Gibby and see what the old man was up to, as he'd promised his cousins a couple of days ago.

Blake propped a booted foot on the opposite seat and laid his head against the cushion as the carriage rolled along the cobbled streets. He had hoped to clear his mind and enjoy the quietness of the ten-minute ride into the heart of the city, but troubled thoughts of Miss Tweed intruded.

He was attracted to her the way a man was fascinated by a woman he wanted to bed. She didn't flutter her eyelashes at him, hide her smiles behind a fan, or talk in a breathy voice like most of the ladies who tried to gain his attention. What kind of madness was this attraction he had to her? Was he more attracted to her simply because he shouldn't be?

Blake had carefully read Mr. Milton's letter and believed Miss Tweed was, indeed, his ward. Because of that, he couldn't have romantic feelings for her. His only role would be to protect her until she married.

It would be so much easier if she were merely a poor relation. If that were the case, he'd be quite content to bestow a few pounds on her, help her find suitable employment as a governess or a companion, and send her on her way. But Miss Tweed was no mere waif. Not only was she beautiful, she was quite wealthy, too. According to Mr. Milton's account, her father had been a shipping merchant who had a lucrative trade in the Eastern spice market. He had married late in life and settled in Dover. Henrietta was his only child.

Her father had chosen her guardians well. None of them had pilfered her inheritance and, quite possibly, some of them had increased it. She would be an excellent match for any man—any worthy man.

What twist of fate had brought him to this unexpected turn in his life that he must think about finding a husband for a young lady?

Blake laughed at the irony of it.

The thanks he'd given Miss Tweed earlier were genuine, though. He couldn't explain it, but seeing his desk in order had given him the incentive to settle down and do the work he'd put off for weeks. Over the past two days he'd read and answered every correspondence on his desk as well as checked the ledgers.

Miss Tweed had only been in his house for two days, and already she had changed his life for the better—and the worse. Yes, his desk was clean of paperwork, but he was also buying horses, carriages, and clothing for a woman who would never be his mistress.

Blake would do what was expected of him and take the position of her guardian seriously. That didn't mean it would be easy.

His thoughts drifted back to the tempting feel of her lips that morning. He rubbed his thumb and fingers together and remembered the touch of her lips on his skin. He had no idea what in the devil had made him do that, other than the fact he'd simply wanted to. After all, he had never needed further cause than that before.

When Henrietta had walked into his office with the self-confidence of an aging dowager, he'd been mesmerized by her. It wasn't so much her beauty that attracted him, though she was certainly lovely; it was the way she carried and conducted herself, the way she looked at him, the way she challenged him and tried to bend him to her will. He even found it appealing that she worried about his being in danger from a curse.

Still, he shouldn't have touched her—and certainly not her lips. They were soft and yielding beneath his touch. They were full, dusky pink, and beautifully shaped. He'd wanted to kiss her, just as he'd wanted to kiss her when he'd found her sitting at his desk sorting his mail. Thankfully, he'd come to his senses before he'd acted on his desire. He had needed all his willpower to put distance between them.

Blake opened his eyes as the carriage rolled to a stop. He needed to find Miss Tweed a fiancé fast. He wanted to get her off his mind and out of his house because the places his thoughts were taking him were dangerous for her reputation and his freedom.

A few hours later, Blake walked into Harbor Lights, the small, private gentlemen's club where he and his cousins had been members for years. White's was the most popular club in town, but some titled men belonged to smaller, more elite clubs, where they could go when they wanted more privacy and attention than the larger club afforded.

That wasn't the reason Blake was walking into the little-known Harbor Lights Club after having spent the better part of the afternoon with his solicitor. He was looking for Sir Randolph Gibson. Blake knew Gibby often came to Harbor Lights for an early supper before making his appearance at the evenings' parties. The old man loved the Season.

Long ago, Gibby had told the cousins that their grandmother, Lady Elder, was the only woman he had ever loved enough to want to marry. She had turned him down because she wanted to marry a viscount or an earl, and later in life she had. Gibby had remained her friend for the rest of her life, and a bachelor all of his.

Blake couldn't remember a time Gibby wasn't in his life. And it wasn't that Gib didn't have good and trusted friends other than the three grandsons of Lady Elder. He was extremely well liked among the ton, especially with the widows. They could always count on him for a dance at the balls, afternoon rides in Hyde Park, or much-coveted invitations to sit with him in his opera box.

After a quick look in the billiards, game, and book rooms, Blake found Gibby in the taproom, sitting by a window on the far side, with an empty plate and a glass of port on the table in front of him. A slice of sunlight streaked across his round face and robust shoulders. His full head of silver hair glinted in the late afternoon light, giving him the appearance of a much younger man. As usual, his dress was impeccable and dashing for a man well past his glory days.

Blake remained still for a few moments and watched Gibby smile as he stared out the window. Blake didn't want to disturb him. Something in the street had caught Gibby's attention, amusing him. Staring at him, Blake couldn't help but wonder if he had ever regretted not marrying and having a family. The three cousins were the closest people Gibby had to family, and they had always treated him like a favorite uncle.

Once again Blake was reminded of Miss Tweed and how she had no family to call upon for help of any kind. Blake was all she had.

When Gibby turned from the window, Blake started toward him. The old man's eyes sparkled and his brow wrinkled as Blake pulled out the chair opposite him and sat down.

"I don't suppose it would matter to you if I was saving that seat for someone else."

"It wouldn't matter at all."

"That's what I thought." With steady hands Gib pushed his empty plate aside and pulled his glass of port closer to him. "Since that's the case, what are you drinking?" He motioned for a server to come over.

"Ale."

Gibby mouthed the word to the server and looked back at Blake. "Are you here for something important or to mind my business again?"

"Don't you think someone needs to?"

"No, I can't say that I do."

"If what I'm hearing from Race and Morgan is true, it doesn't seem as if you know how to manage your affairs without getting yourself into trouble."

"Trouble? You know, every old man should be as damned lucky as I am and have three young fools looking after his business for him. I bet the three of you make London a lot safer for all of us simple-minded people."

Blake laughed. "You bloody ungrateful bastard."

He knew Gibby loved the attention he and his cousins always showed him, even if he always acted as if he wanted them to stay out of his business affairs.

Gibby smiled, leaned back in his chair, and puffed out his chest proudly. "I guess we both call them as we see them."

"If we didn't look after you, who in the hell do you think would?"

"Might I say again that I would be quite happy to look after myself?"

Blake let out a sound that was half chuckle, half sigh. He enjoyed bantering with the old dandy, whose father had made his wealth in shipping in the 1770s when England was still trying to keep control of its colonies across the Atlantic. The old sea merchant never got to enjoy the fruits of his labor and trade, but Gibby had certainly benefited from his father's sound business judgments. They had made his son a wealthy man, and by aligning himself with the king, Gibby had been knighted a few years ago. But of late, Gibby had turned his attention to risky business ventures that worried Blake and his cousins.

"Tell me, who the hell is this nasty knave who's trying to talk you into this half-brained idea of investing in a fleet of hot-air balloons?"

"I don't believe I will tell you."

"Don't get petulant with me, Gib. Damnation, the man must be daft to consider such an ill-conceived plan."

Gibby held up a finger and, with a glint in his eyes, said, "Ah, ha! Already your story has a flaw in it. I'm glad you and your nosy cousins don't know everything about my comings and goings."

Blake eyed him warily. "What do you mean?"

"Curious, are you?"

"You're damned right I am."

"That's comforting."

"Look, old man, you should appreciate having us watch out for you. We've saved your soul from the devil more than once and, for some God-forsaken reason, we're ready to do it again."

"Yes, yes, I know," Gibby grumbled. "I've heard the sad, pitiful story before. If not for my three guardian fools, I'd either be in debtors' prison or the poorhouse by now. Thank you kindly for saving me from riches beyond my wildest dreams."

Blake grinned. The old fogey was still sharp as an ax. "Guardian fools, are we?"

"It's one of my favorite titles from Lord Chesterfield."

Gibby knew that Lady Elder had sent her grandsons quotes from Lord Chesterfield until her death. He also knew how much they hated finding those quotations in her correspondence.

"Go to hell, Gib," he said good-naturedly.

"All right, perhaps it wasn't one of his enlightening terms. Who knows? Your grandmother attributed it to the man, and I will, too, since they are both dead and won't know the difference."

"Enough of this kind of talk, Gibby. Tell me about this man and his madcap idea of buying a fleet of balloons."

Gibby picked up his glass and nearly drained it before saying, "As I said, your spies are slacking in their duties. It's not a man who has asked me to fund the purchase of the balloons. She's a lady."

Blake managed to swallow the curse he wanted to

utter. His lips twitched slightly at one corner, but he hoped that was all that changed in his facial expression. He didn't want Gibby to know that he considered a female swindler the worst—and the hardest—kind to deal with. But deal with her he would.

He could only hope the woman didn't have Gibby thinking she was in love with him, or worse, if Gibby started thinking he was in love with her. That would be a disaster to have to deal with. Sir Randolph Gibson would be the perfect catch for an unscrupulous woman.

To hide his sudden unease, Blake leaned back in his chair and took his time asking, "A lady? That could mean a lady of Society, a lady of trade, or a lady of the evening."

"You are so cynical, Blake."

And worried.

"You give me reason to be."

"She's a lady of quality," Gibby answered as the server placed a tankard of ale in front of Blake.

Blake took a long drink. He didn't like hearing that Gibby was involved in this crazy scheme with a woman any more than he liked hearing he was Miss Tweed's guardian. But Blake could only handle one catastrophe at a time, and right now Gibby was sitting in front of him. He had to keep Miss Tweed off his mind.

"That tells me she's better known in trade than in High Society. Am I right?"

Gibby nodded and smiled with good humor. "You're not only right; I bet you're intelligent, too."

Blake chuckled. Gibby was difficult to beat. "I

am, not that it matters in this instance. Now tell me about this lady who is looking for a business partner among Society."

"She believes, and I've decided I agree with her, that hot-air balloons will be the next mass mode of travel, especially for ladies. They would much rather travel in the weightless, softly floating basket of a balloon than a stuffy, bumpy carriage that can so easily get stuck in the mud, lose a wheel, or fall prey to highwaymen and thieves. And with a good strong wind, a balloon can get to Kent in half the time of a coach because it can fly over clusters of trees rather than having to go through or around them."

Blake's thoughts of settling this matter with mere conversation were fading fast. He could just see a woman batting her eyelashes and feeding that line to Gibby and then him lapping it up like a puppy tasting warm milk for the first time.

"What about the perils of ballooning? Did she mention those? High winds can send a balloon hundreds of miles off course; the basket can tip over or crash into buildings, trees, water, or whatever."

Gibby's old eyes sparkled. "Certainly. She's intelligent, just as you are, and she's already thought of all that. Balloons don't fly if the wind's too strong or in bad weather, unlike carriages and coaches that take off even if it's raining like a winter gale off the northern coast of Scotland."

"There are other hazards," Blake insisted. "The flame that creates the hot air could go out. The balloon could come crashing to the ground, killing all on board, or the worst and most likely possibility is that the flames could catch the envelope on fire and the whole thing would burn up, as has happened on many occasions in the past."

"Not many occasions. Some. At the first sign of trouble, the operator of the balloon would start a hasty descent and land it safely, as you know has happened on many occasions in the past," Gibby said using some of Blake's exact words.

Blake decided against a condescending remark and instead asked, "Do you mind telling me the lady's name?"

"I doubt you've ever heard of her, but her name is Mrs. Beverly Simple."

"And it's my guess that Mrs. Simple is a widow, correct?"

"Yes. She's a lovely young widow and has been for a couple of years now."

"One last question, Gibby; have you given her any money yet?"

Gibby's face turned serious for the first time that afternoon. He remained silent.

"Gibby?"

"No. Not yet, but I have promised her my help. Breaking your word is folly because nobody will trust you afterwards."

Blake knew that was a variation on one of Lord Chesterfield's quotes, but Gibby had the decency not to reference it this time.

"I'm sure you know that a gentleman is only as good as his word."

And everyone in London knew Gibby was a gentleman. Blake decided to forgo asking if Gibby had agreed to give the woman a certain amount of money yet.

"I'm assuming you won't mind if I make a few inquiries about Mrs. Simple for you?"

"For *me*? Oh, you don't have to do it for me, Blake. I've already made all the necessary inquiries. But, if you want to spend some of your money and do it for *you*, go right ahead. You won't find anything in her background to suggest she's anything other than the fine lady she is, with a splendid idea. This is not like one of those schemes in the past to get money from me. This lady really wants to make this business happen."

"You're probably right," Blake said with more ease than he was feeling.

Suddenly Gibby's eyes brightened, all the seriousness was gone. "I have the perfect idea, Blake. Why don't we both go see her on Saturday? She has a barn on the outskirts of London where she keeps two balloons. She'll take you up for a ride and answer all your questions."

Blake hesitated. He didn't like being up in a balloon. He had taken a ride a few years ago, and it wasn't a pleasant experience. When he'd looked over the side of the basket, he had the sudden feeling that he was going to fall out of the basket. His two cousins had laughed, drunk champagne, and enjoyed the ride. Blake had only been able to stay in the basket by looking straight ahead and not down at the ground.

"What about it?"

"All right, Gib," Blake reluctantly agreed. "Arrange it, and I'll go with you."

"Good. The best time to go up is early in the morning. The winds are usually calm then. Because you get such joy out of taking care of me, pick me up in your carriage at four o'clock Saturday morning."

"Four? Damnation, Gibby, I'm usually just getting to bed at that time."

"So just stay up and don't go to bed. I'll send word to Mrs. Simple to expect us by sunrise. And don't forget to have Cook pack some of those fruit tarts she makes."

Gibby sat back in his chair and gave Blake a satisfied smile. Blake couldn't help but wonder if, somehow, the old man knew exactly why Blake didn't want to go up in the balloon.

Seven

BLAKE WALKED INTO THE FOYER OF THE GREAT HALL and stood at the entrance to the ballroom. Finding his cousins was not going to be easy, considering the bevy of lavishly gowned ladies and expertly dressed gentlemen, all drenched in the glow of candlelight. The opulent ballroom, with its crystal chandeliers, gilt fretwork, and carved moldings, was London's most famous hall, and every duchess and countess wanted to have at least one party in the grand building.

The crowd must be at over three hundred, Blake guessed. From corner to corner, he saw people dancing and laughing, smiling behind fans, and whispering behind hands. As he searched the faces in the crowd, he saw friendly smiles, loving looks, longing glances, and jealous stares flash across the ballroom, but there was no sight of Race or Morgan.

He was about to head into the middle of the crowd when, all of a sudden, Lady Pauline, Lady Windham, and the Dowager Duchess of Beaufort appeared before him, all talking at one time.

"We have just heard you have a ward," the old duchess said breathlessly.

"How did this happen, and is it really true or just a nasty rumor?" Lady Windham asked.

"When will we meet her?" Lady Pauline chimed in quickly with her question.

"We were told she's the most beautiful young lady in all of England. We can't believe you've kept her a secret. Is it true?"

"If it is true, Your Grace, her first appearance should be at my party next Thursday," Lady Windham said. "Remember, Blakewell, you owe me."

He owed her? Ah, yes, for that minor, compromising indiscretion a few months ago.

"Your Grace, please tell us who she is and where she came from."

"Why have we never heard of her before now?"

"We must be the first to know."

All Blake could think was that he was going to strangle whichever cousin had let it slip to the ton about Miss Tweed.

He waited silently and let the women wind down from all their questions. He then held up his hand and said, "I'm not spoiling the surprise. All in good time, ladies, all in good time." He stepped down into the ballroom and quickly melted into the large crowd.

Blake couldn't help but smile when he heard the shocked gasps from the women behind him.

Several more ladies and even a few men tried to approach him to ask questions, but Blake didn't stop for any of them. Being a duke had a few benefits, and one of them was the fact that no one pushed him to answer anything he didn't want to answer.

After a couple of passes around the ballroom, Blake finally found Race on the terrace talking with a young widow who was about to end her period of mourning. No doubt, if Race had his way, sooner than Society expected.

He waited for Race to acknowledge him and then gave him a right nod, which all the cousins knew meant they needed to assemble outside on the right portico for a discussion. He then searched through the crowd again and found Morgan chatting with a couple of men about horses. Blake gave his oldest cousin the same sign and then turned to head outside to wait for them. Instead, he came face to face with the Duke of Rockcliffe and his brother, Lord Waldo.

"You missed a good card game at your cousin's house," Rockcliffe said.

"Is that right?"

"It was a good evening for me and Waldo. Your cousins don't play any better than you do."

"Too bad you couldn't make it," Lord Waldo said, his pale brown eyes seeming to bulge more than usual. "We won plenty of their money and lined our pockets quite nicely before we left."

Blake looked at the younger Rockcliffe. Lord Waldo was a little taller than his brother and much leaner. He had a sharp nose and big round eyes that always looked as if they were about to pop out of his head. Blake didn't have anything against Lord Waldo. In truth, Blake had always felt sorry for the man because, rather than making his own way in life, he lived in his brother's shadow.

Turning his attention back to Rockcliffe, Blake said, "It's difficult to play cards with a snake. You can't see his hands."

Rockcliffe's victory grin turned sour. "Are you accusing me of something, Blakewell?"

Blake remained silent, letting his contemptuous expression speak for him.

"If you don't have any proof to back up your accusations, those are fighting words."

"Name the place and time whenever you are ready, and I'll be there."

Rockcliffe merely sneered and walked away with his brother following. Rockcliffe was no fighter, and every man in the ton knew it.

On his way outside, Blake walked past a buffet table filled with food. A tray of mushrooms topped with slices of figs looked good, so he picked one up and popped it in his mouth as he strode by, thinking he'd eat more later in the evening.

The night air was cool and damp when Blake stepped onto the stone portico to wait for his cousins. Rain was on the way. He could feel it. A slice of moon broke from behind a dark cloud to shed a little light on the misty evening. In the hazy distance, Blake could see smoke from the fire the carriage drivers had built to stay warm while their employers enjoyed the inviting merriment inside.

Within a couple of minutes, Race and Morgan walked up together—a sure sign to Blake that the two had begun their discussion before arriving.

When they stopped in front of him, Blake asked, "Which one of you gets the bloody nose for letting it slip that I now have a ward?"

"Why would we do that?" Morgan asked, looking at Race as if to make sure he hadn't said anything to anyone.

Race looked puzzled. "You have a ward?"

Blake didn't appreciate Race's humor. "Perhaps I should bloody both your noses. That way I'll be sure to get the right one."

"Damnation, Blake, don't be so riled," Morgan said. "We haven't told anyone anything about you or Miss Tweed. What could we say anyway? You told us very little about her."

"Though we are ready to hear more," Race said with a gleam in his eyes.

"I was asked questions about her tonight, but all I've said is that I can't speak for the duke," Morgan said, remaining serious.

Race held up his hand. "Wait a minute. You mean she really exists?"

"Most definitely," Blake said, "And well you know it."

"Quite frankly, old chap, I considered the idea that you made up the story to have an excuse to miss the horse race and card game. You have to agree that you have used outlandish excuses in the past for being late or completely missing appointments or events."

"He's right about that, Blake. You are known for failing to show on time—if at all."

Blake nodded agreement. He wasn't ever intentionally late or absent on purpose, and he believed them both when they said they hadn't told anyone about Miss Tweed.

"Sorry, Cousins. I didn't expect to be hammered with questions about her the minute I arrived tonight."

"Who, other than us, knew about her?" Morgan asked.

"Just Constance."

"And I assume your staff knows she's at your town house," Morgan added.

"Yes." Blake had forgotten about the staff.

"Well, there's your gossipmonger."

"Morgan's right, Blake. You know there are no secrets among servants. They have such a network that they can move gossip along the streets of London faster than one of Morgan's thoroughbreds runs."

"You're probably right. Now that I think about it, there are any number of people who could be the culprit. It could even have been one of the shopkeepers where Constance and Miss Tweed have been all week."

"Anyone, but not us; we stick together, right?" Race said.

Blake smiled and clapped both Race and Morgan on the shoulder. "Of course. I'm still trying to get used to the idea that I'm responsible for someone's welfare. I would rather have had a little more time to get used to the idea of being a guardian before the ton knew about her."

"What fun would that have been?" Race quipped.

"What do you intend to do with her?" Morgan asked.

"She's nineteen. The only thing I can do is find her a suitable match."

"If she's fair to look at, that should be easy enough. If not, you can bestow a large dowry on her, and then you'll have plenty of blokes who'll vie for her hand."

For some reason, Blake was suddenly uncomfortable talking about Miss Tweed and matchmaking with his cousins.

"She's quite lovely and intelligent, too." *Not to mention sassy and bold.* "And her inheritance is more than enough to satisfy any man I'd allow her to marry. But talk about Miss Tweed can wait for another time. There's another reason I'm here. Gibby. We have some work to do concerning this insane balloon idea."

"Did he tell you who wants his money?" Race asked.

"Yes. Mrs. Beverly Simple."

Race and Morgan said in unison, "A woman?"

Blake nodded. "It has always been my thought that there is usually a scoundrel of a man behind every treacherous woman."

Race grimaced. "Are you quoting Lord Chesterfield?"

"Blast it, I hope not."

"Does Gibby fancy himself in love with her?"

Blake shrugged. "You know Gibby as well as I. He's had his mistresses over the years, but I've never known him to be serious about any lady other than our grandmother."

"It will be nothing but trouble if some woman has finally laid hooks into him."

"Hence our jobs," Blake said. "Race, see what you can turn up on Mrs. Simple. Find out where she came from and anyone who's remotely connected to her by business or family relation."

Morgan held up his hand. "I know my job. You want me to find out all I can about anyone with interest in balloons—from who sells them to who's buying them. Consider it done. What are you going to do?"

"We can't let you off just because you are a guardian now," Race said with a smile.

Blake took a deep breath. "I'm going up for a balloon ride with Gibby and Mrs. Simple Saturday morning at daybreak."

"But I thought you didn't like ballooning."

"I don't."

"That's right," Race said. "I remember that it made you sick."

"It made me dizzy. There's a difference."

Morgan and Race looked at each other, and then at Blake. Suddenly they both started laughing.

"You two are bastards," Blake muttered.

"But amusing bastards," Race said. He clapped Blake on the back. "Let's quit this party and go to White's for a game of cards and a drink."

Later in the evening, Blake quietly opened his front door and stepped inside the dark house. It had taken him a few months, but he'd finally stopped Ashby from waiting up for him every evening. The last thing Blake wanted after a night of dancing, drinking, and cards was to have anyone other than a lady helping him undress.

Blake took off his hat, cloak, and gloves and laid them on a table. He paused as his stomach rumbled uncomfortably. Maybe he'd had too much to drink and not enough to eat. He shook his head. That couldn't be right. He couldn't have consumed much more than a tankard of ale and a glass or two of wine.

He turned to head up the stairs but stopped when he noticed a faint light coming from his book room. For a fleeting moment, he thought Ashby might have finally had a crack in his armor and left a lamp burning, but almost as quickly he remembered Miss Tweed was in the house. That's where he had found her a few nights ago. No doubt she was looking for a book or perhaps arranging his desk again.

Quietly he walked down the corridor and stood just outside the doorway to see if he could hear the rustle of papers. What he heard was humming. A flash of arousal streaked through his loins. She was humming a slow melody that he found not only enticing but soothing. He closed his eyes and listened to her soft, lilting voice drifting out of the room.

Somehow he knew she was walking toward the door, and he opened his eyes just before her head appeared around the corner.

She smiled at him and his stomach did a somersault. All his frustrations with the responsibility of her and with Gibby seemed to melt away. There was something about seeing her with that "welcome home" smile that made him feel better.

"You can come in," she said. "I'm only looking over your bookshelf again."

"So you knew I was out here."

"Yes. I was almost sure I'd heard the front door open and close a minute or so ago. I don't know why, but I sensed you were standing just outside the doorway."

"Just as I sensed you in the corridor that morning," he said.

Their eyes held for a moment before she stepped back into the room.

He joined her in front of the bookshelf and asked, "Have you found another book?"

"Not yet. I've finished and replaced *The Forbidden Path*. It was very good." Her fingers skipped along the spines of the titles as she spoke. "There are so many books here that I haven't read that I was finding it difficult to decide which one to borrow next."

"Perhaps I can suggest something."

She looked back at him. "That would be wonderful."

Blake stepped closer to her and looked at the titles. And looked some more. To his surprise, he realized he hadn't read many of the books on his shelves.

"I see you are having a hard time deciding, too."

"Yes," he said, not wanting to admit to the truth. Finally his gaze landed on one he remembered reading, some of it anyway. "If you like stories with ghosts in them, this one should satisfy you."

She smiled at him again. "I do like a good mystery with a ghost in it. Horrid novels are very popular right now. For some reason, people like to be frightened."

"As long as they know it's not real but only pages in a book."

"Yes. This will do quite nicely. And it's a thick

book, too, so it should keep me reading for at least two nights."

"You read fast."

"Not so much as I read for long periods of time. Mostly at night. Thank you for your suggestion."

"I'm glad I can return the favor since you helped me with my correspondence." He looked over at it and saw that more mail had been piled on top of it since he'd left that morning.

Henrietta's gaze strayed to the desk, too. "That's the thing about mail. It comes every day, and you have to start over again."

"It's a nuisance, for sure," he said, though the letters on his desk were the last thing on his mind. "I won't start on it tonight, but I should make a note in my appointment book that I have a balloon ride with Gibby early Saturday morning. I can't forget that."

Her eyes quickly clouded with concern. "Your Grace, I'm not sure it would be wise for you to go up in a balloon. I would worry about you."

His stomach cramped for the second time, and he paused before saying, "You would worry about me?"

"Yes. From what I've read, balloons can be quite dangerous, and I don't want anything to happen to you."

He gave her a knowing smile. "You're concerned about the curse, aren't you?"

"I have to be. It's real."

"If you are so concerned, then why don't you come with me and keep me safe?"

Her eyes questioned him. "Truly? You want me to come with you?"

Blake didn't know what in the world had made him ask her that, but now that he had, he couldn't take it back. What was he thinking? What would he do if he became light-headed like the last time he went up?

"Of course, I mean it."

"Oh, Your Grace, that would be absolutely thrilling. I would love to go up in a balloon. I saw one a few years ago. It looked so heavenly hanging in the sky. It floated along so quietly, so effortlessly, with no bumps or rolling from side to side like when you're in a carriage. It just sailed on the gentle breeze."

It struck Blake that she used a lot of the same words Mrs. Simple had used on Gibby. Could a woman actually look at a balloon as a safe, convenient mode of travel?

"So you're not afraid of the danger for yourself, only for me?"

"There is no threat to me because of the curse, and I don't think you will be in danger from the curse if I am with you. None of my other guardians died when I was with them."

Blake chuckled. "All right, since this is your game, we'll play it your way. Come along with me on the balloon ride and keep me safe."

"I shall be happy to, Your Grace."

Henrietta reached up and kissed him on the cheek. His hands caught her upper arms, imprisoning her with his powerful fingers. Henrietta was aghast at herself as her feet landed flatly back on the floor. Had she actually kissed his cheek? What folly overtook her good sense?

Not wanting to look into his eyes, she glanced down at his strong, capable hands on her arms. She felt power beneath the commanding grip of his masculine fingers. When she lifted her lashes, their eyes met and held. She experienced that same strange sensation low in the pit of her stomach as when he had touched her lips that morning.

As with a will of their own, her lashes fluttered upward. She gazed into his eyes and felt hot, breathless, and excited.

"I'm sorry; I shouldn't have kissed you. Please forgive me. That was extremely forward of me. I meant nothing by it other than my gratitude to you for offering such a wonderful experience and an opportunity to see to your safety."

Blake lowered his head toward hers. Despite knowing better, he was going to kiss her. He simply didn't want to stop himself.

His voice was low and suggestive as he whispered, "You don't need to apologize for kissing me on the cheek, Miss Tweed. I'm not going to apologize for kissing you."

She widened her eyes.

"You are going to kiss me?"

"Tit for tat."

"I don't think it would be in our best interest for you to do that, Your Grace."

"Neither do I, but I don't think you want to stop me. But please feel free to try, because unless you do, I'm going to kiss you."

His tone and the light of intrigue in his brownish-gray eyes made her stomach quiver deliciously. Teasing warmth tingled across her breasts as she tried to force herself to move away from him.

The duke leaned his body into hers. She sensed his strength; she felt his heat. He reached up and placed one hand on the side of her cheek and caressed her skin. Warmth flooded her at his touch.

A small gasp of wonderment was all that escaped her lips. She knew she should push him away, but she had no desire to do it. She stood there, barely breathing, and allowed him to captivate her with his compelling caress and provocative words.

His hand confidently slipped over to her ear, and his fingertips slowly outlined its shape before slipping behind her ear to tenderly caress the soft skin there.

Henrietta feared that, at any moment, her legs might go weak on her. She didn't understand why it felt so good when this man touched her.

"I'm waiting, Miss Tweed, giving you plenty of time to walk away."

"You were right, Your Grace. I find it's not easy to remove myself from your presence even though I know I should do so immediately."

His fingertips never left her skin as they traced from behind her ear and over her jawline until his thumb rested at the corner of her lips. His warm palm lay against her neck. She wondered if he could feel her pulse beating out of control.

He leaned in closer. Still, she didn't object. Heat from his body soothed her, and his breath fanned her cheek. The clean scent of his shaving soap stirred her senses.

With his mouth no more than an inch from hers, his gaze locked on hers. She was mindful of his every breath, and her heart thudded wildly against her chest.

He traced the curve of her upper lip with his thumb. The warmth of his touch sizzled through her. For a moment, she was afraid he wasn't going to kiss her, but then his lips came down to hers, lightly brushing across them. The contact was delicate, feathery, and enticing. Henrietta's stomach quivered.

The duke raised his head and looked down into her eyes. Her heart fluttered in her chest as her lashes blinked against his beckoning stare. He was questioning her, asking with the lift of his eyebrows if he should try his luck and kiss her again, or would she find the strength to deny him this time?

Henrietta had not even had a kiss on the cheek since her parents died, and she had had too few hugs the past twelve years. How could she withdraw from something that felt so wonderful and natural?

"Kiss me again," she whispered.

Blake smiled. He lifted her chin ever so slightly. The lace from the cuff of his sleeve tickled across her bare skin as the back of his arm rested softly, innocently, against her breasts.

Slowly he bent his head and kissed her again, moving his lips seductively over hers for a few moments before letting his lips caress down her chin, over her cheek, and along the soft warm spot of her neck. He breathed in deeply the scent of her before lifting his head and finding her lips once again.

His heated breath caressed her skin before she heard his whispered words, "You smell heavenly, and you feel so right in my arms."

Slow curls of unexpected pleasure came alive inside her and, without conscious effort, her chest lifted to feel more of the weight of his arm against her breasts. The warmth of his touch seeped inside her, and she gave herself up to the new unexplained feelings of wanting a man.

"You are very tempting, Miss Tweed. Do you realize how easy it would be for me to take advantage of you right now?"

"Yes," she whispered.

"Are you frightened?"

She looked up into his eyes and softly said, "No."

Another cramp grabbed hold of him. "Damnation," Blake whispered, and stepped away from her. What was happening to him?

"Did I do or say something to upset you?" she asked.

Blake raked the back of his hand across his lips. "No, you didn't do or say anything wrong."

"I think we were both suffering from some sort of spell and got carried away with fanciful notions."

"That spell is called desire, Miss Tweed. And I would venture to say it was a little more than fanciful notions. This is all the more reason why I should be the last person to be your guardian."

"No," she said, taking a step toward him. "Please don't send me to yet another house to live. You have been a very good guardian so far."

"Until just a few minutes ago," he stated flatly. "I'm afraid I'm not used to denying myself anything that I want, and I wanted to kiss you. I knew the minute I saw you that I wanted to hold you in my arms and kiss your tempting lips."

"Really? You knew you wanted to kiss me the first time you saw me?"

He chuckled ruefully. "Of course I knew. It doesn't take a man more than a glance at a woman to know whether or not he's attracted to her in that way."

"I didn't realize that. I'm afraid I'm not very familiar with men and kissing."

Blakewell smiled. "That doesn't help our situation, Henrietta. There are very good reasons I am considered a devilish rogue by the ton. Denying myself something I want is very new to me."

"You are correct, Your Grace. And I should have been more proper and sensible and not allowed you to kiss me."

"It is up to me to make changes. From now on, my sole responsibility will be to keep you chaste and find you a worthy husband. That is exactly what I'm going to do."

So he was back to wanting to marry her off to a suitable man.

"I understand. I hope you won't deny me the balloon ride with you because we kissed."

He looked at her for a long moment and finally said, "No, of course not, Henrietta. Remember, my safety will not be guaranteed if you are not with me."

"You are teasing me, Your Grace."

He smiled indulgently. "It's so easy to do. You'll have to be up early because we have to pick up Gibby at four."

"Gibby?"

"Sir Randolph Gibson. He will be going with us. He is the one who knows the lady who has the balloon."

Suddenly a fiendish cramp twisted Blake's insides,

almost buckling his knees. He could no longer ignore the pain in his stomach.

"What's wrong, Your Grace?"

"Nothing." He winced and turned away from her, wanting to hide the surprising agony he was in.

"Don't tell me nothing; I can see you are in pain."

"Hell's gate!" he murmured, and took in a deep, shuddering breath. An unusual feeling of weakness in his legs seized him and drenched him in a cold sweat.

Henrietta grabbed hold of his arm and forced him to face her. "Please, tell me what is happening to you!"

Blake hated seeing the fear in her eyes, but all he could do was gulp in air, trying to quell the quaking in his stomach.

"I'm going to get Ashby."

"No, it's stomach cramps," he said through clenched teeth. "I ate a mushroom earlier. I think it might have been poisonous."

"Poisonous mushrooms! Heavens above! Did you eat more than one?"

"No."

"Good. Come with me," she said, holding tightly to his upper arm. "There's no time to waste."

Henrietta rushed him down the corridor and into the kitchen. He leaned against a table while she quickly fumbled through the cabinets and found a glass and a tin of salt. She scooped about half a cup of salt into the glass and then filled it with water and quickly stirred.

"Drink this," she said

"I can't," he said, gasping for breath.

His stomach was already churning like a swollen

river about to crest its banks. Had he been one to panic, this might have been the time for it. But panic had never been his weakness.

"You must drink it, Your Grace. Mushrooms can be deadly. Do it now."

He saw terror in her bright eyes. She was frightened for him, and truth be told, he had no choice but to drink it.

He took the glass from her hand and said, "Don't follow me."

Blake threw open the back door and stumbled down the steps. On shaky legs he made it to the side of the house, where he fell to his knees and drained the glass in one swallow. Within seconds the salty water came back up, and everything else in his stomach as well.

He fell back onto the cold, damp grass, too weak to move. He didn't know how long he lay in the darkness, waiting for the worst of the pain to go away.

After a few minutes of being completely still, he was stronger. What a hellish thing to endure. His insides felt as if they had been burned.

On steadying feet, he rose and headed for the back door. Henrietta sat on the steps waiting for him. It made him feel better just seeing her there with her arms wrapped around her knees. He didn't know what to think about this young lady who didn't wilt in the face of a crisis. She knew exactly what to do and took charge of the situation. His admiration for her was growing.

He cleared his throat and sat down on the step just below her.

"I told you to stay inside," he said

"I don't follow orders very well."

"So I've noticed."

"Do you feel better?" she asked.

"Yes," he said, even though the cramps had only just subsided, not gone away.

"Now do you believe me about the curse?"

"Curse?" Blake chuckled lightly, and then grimaced at a remnant flash of pain. "Please, Henrietta, don't make me laugh. My stomach is too sore. I ate a poisonous mushroom, and it made me sick. Nothing more, nothing less. I'm not dead or dying. Anyone could have picked up that bad mushroom at the ball tonight."

"But it was you. Have you ever eaten a poisonous mushroom before?"

He sighed. "No, but Morgan has, and I don't believe he's ever been cursed."

"You are teasing me again."

"No," he said softly. "I'm not up to that. Would you do me a favor?"

She placed her hand gently on his shoulder. Her touch stilled him.

"I'll do anything for you, Your Grace."

He looked up at her. "Good. Say good night to me and go to bed."

All sympathy left her face and Henrietta huffed. "That's a fine thing to say to me after I saved your life."

"Perhaps it is, but you did say you would do anything for me, and that is my request."

Her expression turned serious, and her eyes glimmered through the darkness. "I'm reluctant to leave you. I feel I should stay longer and make sure you are going to be all right."

"Thanks to your quick thinking, I am fine, now. Good night, Henrietta."

"Very well, Your Grace, good night." She reached down and kissed him softly on the top of his head, and then quietly slipped back into the house.

Eight

AT THE APPOINTED HOUR ON SATURDAY MORNING, Henrietta was dressed and waiting below stairs by the front door with cape, gloves, and bonnet in hand. She heard talking and the tinkling of pots and pans coming from the kitchen at the back of the house, but she didn't venture to see which servant was up at this uncivilized hour to prepare the food basket for their journey.

She had been too excited about the balloon ride to sleep for more than a few minutes at a time. And not even the intriguing book with the ghost in it could take her mind off Blakewell. She could not forget the emotions that had stirred inside her when his lips had

touched hers two nights ago. During her wakeful-
ness, she had relived his kiss, his touch, and his words
over and over in her mind, willing all those new,
wonderful, and astonishing feelings to resurface and fill
her senses once again with inexplicable pleasure.

Henrietta had never expected to have a guardian as
young, as handsome, and as pleasing as Blakewell. And
she had never expected that the first man to awaken
her womanly desires would be not only her guardian,
but a duke! But then fate had always seemed to deal
unsympathetically with her, starting with her parents'
deaths when she was seven, and then to the curse Mrs.
Goolsby spoke of coming true over and over again.

She understood perfectly why Blakewell was
keeping a safe distance between them after their lapse
in good judgment when he kissed her. She knew he
was committed to protecting her, and that included
shielding her from himself.

She had seen the duke only once since the night he
had eaten the bad mushroom. He had looked as fit and
handsome as ever when she met him coming out of his
book room the next afternoon.

"How are you feeling, Your Grace?"

"I am well, thank you," he had replied coolly. He
pulled a sheet of folded newsprint from under his arm.
"Have you seen this?"

"No, what is it?" She took the paper from him and
opened it. The headline read "Poisonous mushrooms
at the Great Hall: More than fifty people taken ill."

Her eyes widened, and she looked up at him. "So
it wasn't just one mushroom?"

"Apparently a whole tray of them was bad. Happily,

there have been no deaths reported." A quirky grin lifted one corner of his lips. "Do you still think a curse was responsible, or was this simply a careless scullery worker who doesn't know a good mushroom from a bad one?"

"I think you are a formidable opponent, no matter what you are up against, and I'm glad you are suffering no ill effects. May I keep this and read it?"

He nodded. "I hope this puts your mind at rest."

Perhaps the fact that the duke was not the only person to become ill from the mushrooms left the incident open to interpretation, but it was not enough to persuade Henrietta that the curse did not exist. She could not escape her conviction that His Grace was in constant danger.

The sound of a door shutting above her roused Henrietta from her reverie, and a few moments later she saw Blakewell descending the stairs. He wore a black wool coat over a white ruffled shirt and a white-and-red striped waistcoat. His neckcloth was tied in a simple bow, and the legs of his fawn-colored riding breeches were stuffed into shiny, black knee boots. He was dashing. For a fleeting moment, she had the feeling that he might rush down, grab her up tightly in his strong arms, and swing her around while kissing her madly.

But that thought quickly faded when he failed to give her an enthusiastic smile after seeing her waiting by the door for him.

Henrietta swallowed the disappointment, gave him a hesitant smile, and said, "Good morning, Your Grace. I trust you slept well."

He mumbled something that sounded like a greeting and hurried down the rest of the stairs.

"Very well, Henrietta. How about you?"

"The same," she answered, not wanting him to know the truth of her restless hours in the bed. "I trust you are feeling well with no lasting effects from the bad mushroom."

"Thank you for your concern, but I feel fine." He looked down at her hands and, in a more formal tone than she would have liked, he said, "Is your wrap heavy enough? The ride will be long and cold."

"Yes," she said, placing her bonnet on her head and tying the ribbon under her chin. "It's quite warm. I should be fine."

The butler must have heard the duke come below stairs, because he suddenly appeared from the kitchen holding a basket and Blakewell's cloak.

"Good morning, Ashby," Henrietta said.

"Good morning, Miss Tweed," the perfectly dressed butler answered politely, but like his master, he had no early morning smile for her.

After she pulled on her gloves, Blakewell took her cape from her hands, and she turned her back to him so he could help her with it. The heat from his body, as he stood behind her, calmed her. His fingers briefly caressed the back of her neck as he fitted the cape around her shoulders. His warm touch soothed her. She was sure she felt him hesitate before stepping away from her.

"Would you like me to take the basket to the carriage, Your Grace?"

"That's not necessary, Ashby. I will do it," the duke

said, putting on his long black cloak and then taking the basket from his servant.

Blakewell turned to Henrietta. "If you are all set," he said, "the carriage is waiting for us."

Their gazes caught and held as she pulled her gloves up farther on her arms.

"I'm ready."

He opened the front door, and they stepped out into the darkness of the early morning chill. A footman dressed in fashionable red and black livery opened the carriage door, and His Grace took her hand and helped her step into the plush cab. Through his gloves and hers, she could feel the strength and the heat of his fingers. The warmth stayed with her like hot coals from a banked fire as she settled onto the upholstered seat.

"Keep your feet and skirts away from the iron pot on the floor by the far door," he said as he climbed in behind her. "It has hot coals in it that will help keep your feet warm on the ride."

"Yes, I feel the heat from it already," she said, though in truth she knew the heat she felt came from being so close to the duke, not from the container of hot coals sitting beside her feet.

His Grace sat on the velvet-covered seat opposite her, and the carriage took off with a jerk and a clank. The thick brown curtains that hung over the small windows were tied back, and a yellow glow from the lanterns attached to the outside of the carriage gave a little slice of light inside the cab. She could see half of Blakewell's chiseled, cleanly shaven face, and she tried to discern from his expression if he wanted to talk or if he wanted to be alone with his thoughts.

Perhaps the best way to find out was to see if he frowned when she spoke to him. "How often do you take these early-morning balloon rides?" she asked.

"Not often at all. This will be only the second time I've been up in one."

He answered and he didn't frown. Henrietta's confidence grew.

"You must have enjoyed it to want to go again."

"I'm going because of Gibby."

"Oh, the gentleman you mentioned the other night just before you became so ill," she said. "I'm sure I shall enjoy meeting him. Is he a relative, friend, or business acquaintance?"

"There's no blood relationship between us, though it wasn't for lack of trying on his part. I've known him all my life. He was my grandmother's devoted friend for many years. They met when she was widowed from her first marriage. He loved her and wanted to marry her. She rejected him but married three more times."

Blakewell seemed to be more than willing to talk, so she said, "My goodness, that seems like a lot of husbands. But you say she never married Sir Randolph?"

"I don't think she ever even considered marrying him."

"That must have been hard for him—to see her marry three times when he loved her. I've read in books about unrequited love."

"He coped. He always thought she'd marry him one day, but she never did."

"According to most of the poetry I've read, we can't make ourselves love someone or make anyone love us."

Blakewell half-laughed under his breath. "Love was not the problem, believe me. My grandmother loved him madly, but a mere knight was not impressive enough for her social passions. All she ever wanted was to be the wife of a titled gentleman. With her fourth husband, she managed that and became the Countess of Elder."

"It's wonderful that your grandmother realized her dream of marrying well, but how sad for Sir Randolph."

Blakewell laughed, and Henrietta loved the pure, genuine sound of his laughter. She was enjoying their easy conversation and being alone with him in the chilly but cozy carriage.

"Take my word for it, you have no reason to feel sorry for Sir Randolph Gibson. He can be an ornery old man. He would be much easier to look after if we had some legal claim to him. I'm convinced he has more friends than anyone in London. Right now, there are more than half a dozen women who would marry him immediately if he would just offer for their hand. Besides that, he thrives on getting himself in trouble, as with this balloon venture, just so my cousins and I will have to spend extra time with him."

"What do you mean by 'balloon venture?'" she asked as the carriage rolled to a stop.

"I'll have to save that explanation for another time. We've arrived at his house. I'm going to move over and sit by you to give Gibby more room."

"All right," she said and gathered her skirts closer to give him more room beside her.

Sir Randolph appeared in the doorway of the

darkened cab and climbed inside with a grunt and a groan. He was a distinguished, older gentleman with a head full of beautiful silver hair. His chest had the robust filled-out look of a much younger man, but as soon as he sat down and faced her, Henrietta saw the telltale signs of advanced age around his eyes and mouth.

He spotted her as he settled into the cushioned seat, and his surprised gaze darted between her and His Grace a couple of times before his attention settled on the duke.

"I didn't know you were bringing a young lady with you, Blake," he said as the carriage started its bumpy rolling once again. "You always were the sly one of the three cousins."

"Really? Is that how you see me? Sly?"

"As a fox."

"Thank you for the compliment." Blakewell smiled craftily at the ageing dandy. "Let me see, what is it you've always said to me in similar situations as this: 'I'm sorry, ole chap, there wasn't time to send a note and let you know about that.'"

Sir Randolph chuckled. "You should have better manners than to use an old man's words against him. Besides, what's there to be sorry for? I'd much rather look at her pretty face than yours."

"I do like it when, on the rare occasion, I do something that pleases you. Sir Randolph Gibson, may I present Miss Henrietta Tweed, my ward? Miss Tweed, my oldest and dearest friend, Sir Randolph Gibson."

The old gentleman smiled broadly at her and dipped his head in acknowledgment. "It's my pleasure to meet you, Miss Tweed."

Henrietta nodded and said, "I'm delighted to make your acquaintance, Sir Randolph."

"Perhaps you are the only person in London who hasn't heard about my new ward."

He looked at Blakewell again and said, "No, I've been hearing rumors for almost a week now that you were given guardianship over a young lady. I am constantly questioned about the ward of the duke. But luckily I didn't know anything to tell anyone. I guess when we were talking a few days ago, you forgot to mention Miss Tweed to me."

Blakewell leaned back comfortably in the seat and confidently folded his arms across his chest. With a wry grin, he said, "Forgive me. I had other things on my mind when we spoke."

"I know. You were too obsessed with my business to think about your own."

Blakewell took off his gloves and tossed them to the seat beside Sir Randolph. "At the time, I thought yours was more pressing."

"You always do, but that doesn't say much for your abilities as a guardian, does it? Are you sure you're up to the task?"

"I'm not sure at all, but for the time being, I'm prepared to do what I can."

Henrietta felt a pang of envy. She could see in their faces and hear in their voices that these two men had a long-standing and comfortable relationship. She had never had a close friend with whom she could be so carefree.

"Sir Randolph," Henrietta said. "So far, His Grace has taken excellent care of me."

"I can see that."

"And nothing else needs to be said about that subject," Blakewell injected. "I suggest that the two of you get acquainted while I see what Cook put in the basket for us to eat."

"Did you remember to tell her about the fruit tarts?"

"Yes, because I knew you would send me back to get them if I forgot."

"That's what I wanted to hear."

Blakewell turned to Henrietta. "There's a possibility that Gibby might have known one or more of your past guardians, even if they didn't live in London. I'm assuming that most of them were close to the same age as Gib. Why don't you tell him about them?"

"Most of them?" Sir Randolph asked.

"She's had five since her parents died, but that story might be too long for this trip."

Blakewell started digging through the food basket to find something to eat.

Anticipation rose inside Henrietta at the thought of exchanging stories with Sir Randolph about her former guardians.

"It's not a long story at all. It's a wonderful idea. If you don't mind, Sir Randolph, I would love to tell you their names to see if you knew any of them."

"I don't mind at all. I can't think of anything that would entertain me more on a long journey than to be engaged in conversation with a young lady as beautiful and charming as you."

Henrietta smiled with graciousness at his compliment. "Thank you. Perhaps we should start with the last one, Lord Palmer."

"Palmer, yes, I knew him, knew him well. We went on several hunts together with the Duke of Norfolk. Of course, that was many years ago."

"Don't tell any raucous stories, Gib. Remember you are talking to a young lady."

"I think I can tell the difference between a young lady and a blade without any help from you."

And so the conversation went.

Time passed quickly as Sir Randolph was, indeed, acquainted with two of her former guardians and he had heard of two others. Henrietta found him to be a clever and charming man with a quick wit and a discerning mind.

The three of them drank warm chocolate from pewter cups and ate scones filled with plum preserves as they discussed people from long ago, poetry, books, and Lord Byron's latest scandal. All the while, Henrietta was conscious of the duke sitting inches from her. At times she was convinced she could feel his touch, though he never actually made contact with her person.

The coals in the iron pot had cooled, and the pitch darkness of night was slowly replaced with dawn. Henrietta looked out the small window in the carriage door and saw sunrise spreading across the wide expanse of morning sky. Slashes of pink, blue, and dark gray lay on the horizon.

Nine

WHEN THE CARRIAGE ROLLED TO A BUMPY STOP, Blakewell pushed open the door and stepped down. He waited for Sir Randolph to exit the cab before reaching inside to help Henrietta. Instead of taking her outstretched hand as she expected, he grasped her waist with his strong, firm hands and lifted her out of the carriage and set her on her feet. He gave her waist a little squeeze before turning to his driver and giving him instructions.

Cold air nipped at Henrietta's cheeks as she surveyed her surroundings. They were in what appeared to be a large clearing. Not far from where she stood, she saw a large building with what looked like barn doors thrown wide open. Near the building, several people were milling around a large wooden basket with smoke rising from its center. The outside of the basket was elaborately decorated with pink and yellow flowers and blue ribbons. Stretched beside the basket lay a huge piece of colorful fabric that resembled a discarded drapery blanketing the dew-moistened ground.

From the corner of her eye, Henrietta saw a woman approaching them so she turned to look at her. The woman appeared to be at least twenty years older than Henrietta, maybe more. She wore a friendly smile and moved with a quiet demeanor that seemed more practiced than natural. Her black cape, gloves, and bonnet were all trimmed with a narrow band of expensive-looking fur.

"Sir Randolph," the attractive woman said, extending her hand to him and staring directly into his eyes. "How lovely to see you again so soon, and you brought guests. It's so wonderful of you to do that."

The old man's dark brown eyes sparkled with pleasure from the verbal and visual favor the woman bestowed on him. She definitely wanted Sir Randolph to know she was happy he had arrived.

He kissed the back of her hand before complimenting her on how lovely she looked. He then made the introductions smoothly and quickly, as only a man who had spent many years in Society could do.

Mrs. Beverly Simple smiled at all three of them,

but her gaze lingered on Sir Randolph as she said, "I'm pleased you could come and go up with us this morning. My employee in charge today tells me that it is an exceptional day to go up, and that sunrise will be beautiful." She turned to Henrietta. "I'm especially pleased you are here, Miss Tweed. Have you been on a balloon before?"

Henrietta returned the woman's smile. "No, first time."

"How about you, Your Grace?" Mrs. Simple asked. "Have you ever been up?"

"Yes. Once," he said with no enthusiasm in his voice or his manner.

"Then you know how lovely it can be." She looked at Henrietta again. "I'm sure you'll find it exciting, and you will get to see how safe and practical ballooning can be for travel between London and its surrounding counties. But, of course," she stopped and smiled at Sir Randolph. "I'm really hoping ladies will use our balloons to travel between London and their summer homes. You're not afraid of heights, are you, Miss Tweed?"

Henrietta's stomach tightened with anticipation. "Ah, no, I don't think so. I've probably never been higher than the fourth floor of a house, though. How far up will we go?"

Mrs. Simple laughed, and once again Henrietta had the feeling it was more practiced and forced than natural. Henrietta considered the possibility that Mrs. Simple might be nervous about taking them up. After all, she was entertaining a duke.

"We'll go quite a distance farther up than you've

been before, Miss Tweed. As long as you don't have a fear of heights, you will love it. It truly gives you the opportunity to ride the wind and feel completely free."

"It sounds absolutely thrilling. I don't think I'll have a problem."

She winked at Henrietta. "Good. I've never had a lady faint on one of my balloons."

"And, Henrietta, I'm sure if you feel sick or frightened of the heights we reach, Mrs. Simple will have the balloon lowered back to the ground immediately," Sir Randolph said in a solicitous voice.

"Of course, and it does happen on rare occasions," Mrs. Simple said in a tight voice. "I do like to warn everyone that floating can be such an unexpected sensation that some people do have slight difficulties. You seem very confident, Miss Tweed, and I don't expect you to have any."

Henrietta was too excited about this adventure to have any trouble. To be up in a balloon with the duke was too heavenly to even dream about. She turned and looked at him. He didn't appear as excited as she, but then he had been up in a balloon before. She couldn't expect him to show as much enthusiasm as she felt.

"Why don't we go watch the inflating," Mrs. Simple said as she deliberately positioned herself by Sir Randolph so she could walk beside him. "My maid will be serving our refreshments of champagne and fig tarts after we are aloft. This, I might add, is the kind of personal attention you will never find on a hired carriage or a mail coach," she said, throwing a self-satisfied glance in the direction of Blakewell.

"I believe it's tradition to have a bottle of champagne or wine onboard, is it not, Mrs. Simple?" the duke asked in response to her smug expression.

"Yes, you are quite right about that, Your Grace."

"Why is it that you always have it onboard?" Henrietta asked as they walked toward the basket.

"I could answer that for you," Mrs. Simple said, "but Sir Randolph has such an eloquent speaking voice; perhaps I can impose on him to tell you." She looked over at him. Her eyes sparkled. "Would you mind relating the story for me?"

He beamed with pleasure at her compliment. Despite his advanced years, he had no trouble keeping up with the pace they were walking.

"I don't mind at all. I'd be honored to repeat the story you've told me." He turned to Henrietta. "As you probably already know, the first balloon was made in France."

"I do remember reading that about balloons, but little else."

"Yes. Concerning the French, I happen to agree with what Lord Chesterfield said about them."

"Did you have to mention that man's name?" Blakewell muttered.

"I knew it was a sure way to annoy you," the old man answered, though there was no mischievousness in his tone.

"Consider your mission accomplished and continue your story," the duke said.

"Thank you, Your Grace. As I was saying, ladies, Lord Chesterfield always said, 'There are really only two things the French are good for: one is fashion and the other is wine.' However, the French do take great pride in ballooning as one of their gifts to mankind, along with the finest of wine and the best of fashion. The French actually call the balloon an aerostat, but we prefer to use the word 'balloon.' When the early balloonists started flying great distances from their homes, naturally they traveled over various towns and villages. At first, they met with all kinds of misfortunes. Most of the people in the villages had never seen or even heard of a balloon big enough to carry people from place to place. There were accounts of balloonists being shot down out of the sky because people didn't know what the hot-air balloon was. Frightened villagers attacked some balloonists with weapons or threw others immediately into prison."

Henrietta gasped in shock. "All that sounds appalling. Why did the villagers behave so dreadfully?"

"A lot of people thought the balloons carried creatures that had come from the heavens to harm them."

Henrietta was enthralled with the story. "Creatures from heaven?" Henrietta asked. "That's absolutely shocking."

"But true," Sir Randolph answered.

"No one can tell the story like you, Sir Randolph," Mrs. Simple said. "You make it come alive for everyone."

Henrietta watched how Mrs. Simple doted on Sir Randolph. Was the woman truly besotted with him? Henrietta wasn't sure. For some reason, Mrs. Simple's smiles and compliments didn't feel genuine.

"Fine Frenchmen that they were, balloonists started taking along a bottle of champagne or wine from their region of France. They could give this to the locals when they landed to prove they were human—not creatures from the heavens, but actually people from faraway villages."

"That's a fascinating story," Henrietta said.

They stopped a few feet from the wooden basket, and Henrietta peered inside. She saw a metal fire ring. Using bellows, workers caused the ring to smoke and fill the balloon with hot air. She watched with awe as the colorful fabric started to swell. With each swish of air she heard, the balloon became fuller and bigger until it slowly started to lift off the ground.

"The balloon part can be made of any lightweight material. This one is made of taffeta," Mrs. Simple told them. "I had each panel sewn in a different color so the balloon would look like a big bouquet of colorful flowers floating in the sky." She paused and sighed contentedly. "I wanted it to be so beautiful that ladies would want to ride in it."

"It is truly magnificent," Henrietta said as the balloon continued to swell until it stood erect directly above them.

Mrs. Simple looked at the duke and said, "As you can see, as part of our plans for producing balloons for travel, we've made a larger basket that will hold up to six travelers comfortably. We've installed bench seating for those who may want to sit down on some of the longer journeys."

"Ballooning is fine as a way to spend a Sunday afternoon or as a hobby, Mrs. Simple, but I don't see it as a safe or practical way for anyone to travel on a daily basis, as do coaches, carriages, and horses."

Mrs. Simple's shoulders lifted, and her gaze seemed

to freeze on the duke's. "I disagree with you about that, Your Grace. I think ballooning will be especially practical through the summer when the roads are heavy with freight traffic and boggy from rain. This will be the perfect way for ladies to get from London to Kent or Dover, or wherever their summerhouse might be, without the worry of falling prey to highwaymen or accidents. It will be easier and faster to move travelers from one city to another. But, let's go onboard, shall we, and you can see for yourself," she said with her practiced smile.

Mrs. Simple opened a gate that was built into the basket and the four of them boarded.

"I understand the hot air making the balloon rise, but what makes it come down?" Henrietta asked.

"That's an excellent question, Miss Tweed," Mrs. Simple said. "Look straight up. There is a circle cut in the fabric at the very top of the balloon. It's attached to this rope hanging in the center of the basket. When we are ready to land, my employee will pull smoothly on this rope. That will make the top of the balloon open. The hot air will escape, allowing us to slowly and safely descend to the ground for a very gentle landing."

"Exactly how far have you flown in a balloon, Mrs. Simple?" the duke asked.

"Oh, goodness, distance-wise it would be hard to say, but from town to town, perhaps from London to Dover. It could be that Dorset is farther. I've flown to every county in and around London. I'm not really sure of the distance between each, but I am happy to tell you that I landed perfectly each time, and nothing dreadful has happened to me yet."

"That's comforting," he said dryly.

Henrietta didn't know why, but she was certain Blakewell had taken an instant dislike to Mrs. Simple. "In 1785, a French-made balloon successfully crossed the English Channel for the first time," Mrs. Simple continued. "Ballooning has only gotten safer since then. I have been flying in balloons for over three years, and I've never been in an accident. Now, if everyone is ready, I think the inflating is finished."

The workers on the ground let go of the ropes, and the balloon lifted off the ground with a shake, a shudder, and a swing. Henrietta almost lost her footing. She grabbed hold of the rim of the basket to steady herself as the balloon tilted to one side before smoothing out into effortless floating as it lifted higher into the air.

Henrietta's stomach did a flip but, just as quickly, she looked at the horizon and the beautiful colors in the sky. Her stomach settled. She felt peaceful and serene.

She stood beside Blakewell and watched the ground get farther away. Their carriage and the barn became smaller as they sailed above the treetops. The wind blew strong and cold against her face as they floated effortlessly across the air.

Enjoying the experience, she turned to the duke and her eyes widened. Something about him didn't seem right. His gaze was transfixed on the ground below. His hair blew wildly in the wind, and his face was ashen. The knuckles on his hands had turned white from the death grip he had on the rim of the basket.

"Your Grace, are you all right?"

He didn't respond. He stared blindly at the ground.

She looked behind her. Mrs. Simple had Sir Randolph engrossed in conversation, and the two workers were busy. Blakewell leaned so far over the edge of the basket that she feared he might fall out.

Could he be afraid of heights, as Mrs. Simple had talked about? Surely not. The duke was much too self-confident for that, but what was the matter? She grabbed his upper arm and forced him to turn around and face the inside of the basket.

"Look at me, Your Grace," she whispered, but realized the wind took her words away. She squeezed his arm and gave him a little shake. "Look into my eyes, Your Grace," she said in a stronger voice and then quickly glanced back to see if anyone had heard her. Thankfully, they were all otherwise engaged.

"Don't look out or down. Just look at me. That's right," she said in a softer voice.

His gaze caught hers, and he blinked rapidly. His breaths were shallow and fast.

"Henrietta," he whispered, and ran his hand through his tousled hair.

"Yes." She took a deep breath and smiled at him. "Are you feeling better now?"

He nodded. His breathing slowed and color slowly returned to his face.

"Your Grace, I was so worried about you. What happened? Did you feel faint or dizzy?"

He shook his head as if to clear it and raked his hand through his hair again. "Damnation," he cursed softly under his breath. "Don't worry about me. I'm fine. I don't know what happened or why, but when I looked down, I suddenly felt as if I was going to fall out of the basket, and I couldn't stop myself."

Breathing easier now that he was back to himself, she let go of his arms and, with a teasing smile, said, "I think you would have fallen out if I had not been here to take hold of you."

He cleared his throat, rolled his shoulders, and grinned at her. "You jest, Henrietta."

Continuing to give him an easy smile, she said, "I do not, Your Grace. I think I may have just saved your life. And for the second time."

"Second time?"

"Don't forget the salt water and the mushroom."

"How could I forget that?"

"You can't. I believe that means you owe me."

"Don't be preposterous. I became a little dizzy for a moment."

"And you were about to fall out of the basket."

"I was not," he said not too convincingly. "You want to believe that because of that blasted curse you talk about."

"The curse is just as real as your fear of heights."

"But I don't have a fear of anything, just as there is no curse. It must be the motion of the balloon that bothers me. The same as if I were on a big ship and became seasick."

"Rubbish. This balloon is floating along as smoothly as a weightless bubble on the air." She threw her arms wide and let the chilling wind catch her face, tugging strands of hair from beneath her bonnet. "I think this is glorious. Breathtaking. The colors on the horizon are simply beautiful. I don't think I ever realized just how magnificent the sky is. The sun has risen above the horizon."

He started to turn around, but she grabbed his arms again and said, "No, no, don't look out." She smiled and let go of him. "I'll do the looking for both of us, and I'll tell you how beautiful everything is."

He smiled so warmly at her that Henrietta felt as if her heart melted in her chest.

"All right, courageous lady, I'll allow you to do that for me, this time."

At that moment, Henrietta wanted nothing more than to reach up and kiss his lips. She wanted to explore more of the wonderful feelings that she had discovered the night he had kissed her.

"Well, what do you say, Miss Tweed?"

Henrietta spun around. Sir Randolph and Mrs. Simple stood right behind her. She prayed they couldn't read her thoughts and know that she was just wishing she could kiss the duke.

"Isn't this the perfect way to travel?"

"Oh, Sir Randolph, I seldom travel, so I can't speak to that. But I can tell you being up here is enchanting. To be above the trees and to fly with the birds is a heavenly experience."

"Before we have champagne, I would very much appreciate your opinion. Is there anything about it you don't like, Miss Tweed?" Mrs. Simple said.

"Perhaps the most disagreeable thing is that it's very windy and cold," Henrietta answered honestly. "I don't think I could stay up here for long."

"I agree it's much more pleasant in the summer than late spring."

"What about you, Blake?" Sir Randolph asked him. "What do you think about it? Are you ready to give your stamp of approval?"

Henrietta looked at him. His color was good, but she could tell he was not completely over whatever spell had gripped him.

"The view is—breathtaking. The colors on the horizon are beautiful. I don't think I ever realized just how magnificent the sky is at this time of morning," Blakewell said, using Henrietta's words to his own advantage.

Sir Randolph harrumphed.

Henrietta gave the duke a mischievous smile, letting him know his secret was safe with her, so he added, "But, Gib, this is not a way I would ever want to travel."

Ten

Dearest Lucien,

Lord Chesterfield says that: *"When one is learning, one should not think of play; and when one is at play, one should not think of one's learning."*

Your loving Grandmother,
Lady Elder

THE CARRIAGE ROLLED TO A STOP IN FRONT OF BLAKE'S town house, but he didn't move. When his footman opened the door, Blake waved him away. Henrietta slept so peacefully beside him that he was reluctant to wake her.

She hadn't taken long to fall asleep on the ride back to London. Gibby had slept most of the way, too, after he had lulled Henrietta to sleep with his incessant talk about the charming attributes of Mrs. Beverly Simple, the new Lord Mayor's political woes, and the financial scandal involving three elderly members of the House of Lords. Henrietta hadn't even roused when the carriage had stopped to leave Gibby at his house.

Now Blake had to wake her, and he would, but first he wanted to watch her sleeping for a few moments longer. Her black bonnet with ribbed trim perfectly framed her lovely, heart-shaped face and acted as a pillow against the velvet seat cushion, preventing her head from falling onto his shoulder. Wispy strands of shiny, golden blonde hair had escaped her headpiece and lay across her forehead and delicate-looking cheek.

Afternoon sunlight filtered through the window of the carriage door and fell across the bottom half of her face, highlighting her beautifully shaped lips. They looked so pink and kissable against the smooth, creamy shade of her skin. She was all wrapped up in her black cape, which hid the definition of her breasts, but he could see the slight rise and fall of her chest beneath her wrap.

He closed his eyes against the sudden remembrance of the balloon ride and his irrational fear of being so high above the trees. The ride in the balloon certainly hadn't troubled Henrietta, Gibby, or Mrs. Simple and her workers. So why had it bothered him so badly that it left him feeling light-headed? He couldn't imagine what made him feel so vulnerable once the cords were untied and they had left the ground and floated freely through the air. It was like no other experience he'd ever had.

Blake was not without bravery in his heart. He had once stared without flinching down the barrel of a pistol held by a man who meant to kill him. He had grabbed the reins of a wildly bucking stallion, never fearing he'd be trampled beneath the horse's hooves. But for some reason, both times he went up in a balloon, that gripping fear of falling took hold of him and would not let go.

This time he might have fallen out of the balloon, had it not been for Henrietta's quick thinking and forcing him not to look down. Thankfully, she'd been perceptive and had kept the others onboard from knowing. He'd never forget that she had done that for him. The flight had been bearable only because he'd kept his gaze on her and not the ground below or the heavens above.

She looked so beautiful and happy to be floating on the wind and gliding through the clouds that keeping his gaze on her had not been difficult. He had quite enjoyed keeping his attention on no one but Henrietta.

He smiled to himself as he remembered seeing the wonderment in her eyes when Gibby handed her a glass of champagne, and she took her first sip. Her whole face lit up with delight as the bubbles burst on her tongue and she swallowed the cold liquid for the first time.

Blake opened his eyes and looked at her again. Her eyelids twitched and he wondered if she dreamt. And if she did, what did she dream about? Did she dream of a handsome beau, or something else?

What he really wanted was to wake her with a kiss on her beautiful lips, but should he chance it? It might frighten her. What would he do if she screamed and brought the neighbors running?

But what if she just slowly opened her eyes and wound her arms around his neck and kissed him back? He leaned in close to her.

"Henrietta," he whispered, but his voice was so soft, her slumber so deep, that she didn't stir at all. That was all the prompting he needed.

Ignoring the warning bells going off in his head, Blake reached over and placed a soft kiss on the corner of her mouth. She stirred a little and made a sighing noise. That made him more courageous. He placed a quick, soft kiss on her lips, and then a longer lingering kiss. She stirred again, her hand coming up to rub her nose, but her eyes didn't open.

He smiled to himself. He knew it wasn't fair of him to watch her sleep and steal kisses from her lips without her knowing, but he was enjoying every moment of it. After all, what kind of rogue would he be if he didn't, from time to time, do a few things beyond the pale?

With no further thought of stopping himself, he kissed the corner of her mouth again and breathed in the warm, womanly scent of her. He slowly moved his lips across her soft, cool cheek and back to her lips again. She made another sighing sound and stirred to the point of raising her arms and stretching them above her head. He wanted to gather her into the fullness of his arms and pull her close. He wanted to feel the soft heat of her yielding body against his, but warning bells went off in his head once more, and he dared not go that far.

Not this time.

Suddenly, Henrietta's lashes fluttered upward. She saw him leaning over her. At first she smiled at him, but then just as quickly, as if startled, her eyes opened wider. She sat up straight and started rearranging the folds of her cape.

"My apologies, Your Grace. I must have dozed off for a moment," she said.

There was something especially desirable about a woman just waking from sleep. He wanted her right now, right here in the carriage stopped in front of his house in the middle of the afternoon.

Blake groaned silently. What was wrong with him? That was no way to be thinking about any innocent young lady.

Especially his ward.

"A long moment," he said, trying to clear his wayward thoughts. "We're home."

"Home?" She looked disbelievingly around the cab. "Sir Randolph?"

"We dropped him off at his house not more than ten minutes ago. You were sleeping so peacefully that I didn't want to wake you to tell him good-bye."

"I really didn't mean to be such a bore and sleep all the way home. I do hope that you and Sir Randolph slept as well?"

He grinned. "If it makes you feel any better, yes, Gibby fell asleep not too long after you did. I tried to, but found that I couldn't rest for all the little snoring sounds you made."

Henrietta gasped. "Snoring? Me, Your Grace? I do not."

Blake laughed when he saw the horror in her eyes. He was having such fun teasing her that he didn't want to stop. "Don't tell me you are one of those people who think you don't snore because you stayed awake one night to see if you snored and you didn't."

Her perfectly shaped eyebrows shot up. "Of course not, Your Grace; that's a ridiculous thing to say. And you are dastardly for even implying such a thing about a lady."

He laughed again at her umbrage. "Well, pardon me. Perhaps you weren't making the snoring sounds. Maybe it was Gibby."

She eyed him warily, finally catching on to his humor. "You are a scoundrel, Your Grace."

"So I've been told."

"You are teasing me, aren't you? I don't think you heard snoring noises from either of us."

Grinning, he said, "You're right, I didn't, but you are so easy to tease, it was too appealing not to do it."

"You are a rake."

"Sometimes."

"More often than not would be my guess."

"Probably." Blake turned serious as he looked into her beautiful sky-blue eyes and said, "Thank you, Henrietta."

Her lips parted in surprise at his words and her gaze held his steadily, as if she were searching for answers to an important question.

"Why are you thanking me?"

"For what you did for me when we were up in the balloon this morning."

"Oh, you mean for saving your life."

Now it was her turn to tease him.

"I'm not admitting anything," he said, picking up her gloved hand and giving her fingers a soft squeeze before releasing her. "I had those same feelings the last time I went up in a balloon, and you were not there to save me; yet somehow, I managed to hold on and live to go up another day."

"All right, I'll concede for now that I didn't save your life. However, I think I've figured out what bothers you about being up in a balloon."

"Really? Tell me."

"I think it's your lack of control. Being a duke, you have control over so many things, especially concerning your own life. But up there, in the sky, other people are in control and you are completely dependent on them. I'm sure that's not something you are used to. Perhaps that causes you to have the strange feeling of falling when you are so high up in the balloon."

He thought about her words for a moment. Could that be his problem? On a horse, in a carriage, or even the few times he'd been on a ship at sea, he had known what he would do, should trouble arise, but high up in the sky in a balloon, he would be powerless to do anything.

"That could be a logical explanation for what happens to me," he agreed.

"Surely I have no right even to suggest this, but perhaps, if you took lessons and learned how to fly a balloon so that you could be in control, that would clear up your problem."

The trouble with the idea of learning to operate a balloon was that he had absolutely no desire to do so. The last thing he wanted to do was go back up in a balloon. Ever. And learning how to handle one of the blasted things held no appeal for him. He was happy traveling by coach, horse, or sea. Or, if nothing else was available, he'd just use his feet and legs and walk.

"Perhaps we should plan an outing and go up—"

"Perhaps I should ask you something I was thinking about on the ride back home."

She moistened her beautiful lips and said, "You want to drop the subject?"

"I do."

"Very well, we'll talk about whatever you want."

"Tell me, what did you think of Mrs. Simple?"

Henrietta gave him a questioning look. "I'm thinking you mean other than that she was lovely, solicitous, and strong-minded."

"Yes," he said, not wanting to prompt her any further than necessary. He wanted Henrietta's true assessment of the woman.

A wrinkle formed between her eyes as she studied what to say. "May I speak forthrightly?"

"That's what I'm asking of you."

"I noticed that she was very attentive to Sir Randolph and, while she said and did all the right things to make one think that she adored him, I noticed that her smile didn't reach her eyes."

Blake sat back in the cushion. "I think I know what you mean, but perhaps a little more explanation would help me understand your analogy better."

She smiled at him and his loins tightened. His body always seemed to go crazy when she looked at him with that understanding expression.

"When I was at Lord Brembly's house in Dorset, he taught me many things. He was a very kind and knowledgeable man. I learned from watching and listening to him as well as from doing the studies he gave me each day. In the summer, his grandchildren would come for visits. I would watch him light up with excitement as they bounded from the carriage and ran to him. His smile and laughter reached all the way to his eyes. But when their stepfather stepped off the coach, the smile stayed on his lips but left his eyes."

"Interesting."

"Yes. I asked him about this one day. He praised me for being perceptive and then told me that his love for his grandchildren was genuine, but not so for his daughter's second husband. He said his smile didn't reach his eyes because the smile wasn't true."

Blake nodded. "I can see the validity in what Lord Brembly said. And I felt the same way you did about Mrs. Simple. I sensed she was putting on an act with her flattery of Gibby."

"Something tells me that you don't think Sir Randolph saw what we saw."

"I'm fairly sure he didn't, but whether that's because he doesn't want to see it or he *can't* see it, I'm not certain."

"Are you trying to decide if you should tell him of your suspicions? That her attentiveness seems false and forced?"

"Yes. She's wooing him because she wants him to invest in her balloon business. I think the idea is downright madness."

"So that's what you meant earlier about a balloon venture."

He nodded. "I'm trying to figure out if she's trying to get money from him and then disappear, or if she's actually foolish enough to think she can open a travel business." Blake smiled at her. "Thank you for your insight and Lord Brembly's as well. Come on, we better go inside."

He opened the carriage door, jumped down, and reached back for her. Ignoring her hand, he grabbed her waist and helped her down. He knew it was devilishly improper. That was one of the many reasons the gossip pages occasionally referred to him as the 'devilish duke.' Helping a lady exit a carriage by circling her waist was far more exciting than merely holding her gloved hand while she stepped down.

"Your Grace," she said as they walked toward the front door, "thank you for the most wonderful day I have ever had—and a day I shall never forget."

Her words sent a flare of desire shooting through him. She looked so pretty gazing up at him with the cool wind caressing her cheeks. He would have given anything if he could have kissed her right then. But he knew the perils of doing so. If anyone saw them, her reputation would be ruined. Instead, he lightly pressed his hand to the small of her back and guided her toward the front door.

"Between Gibby's loud snoring and your strange little sleeping noises, believe me, I will never forget the day either."

With that, Henrietta responded with a faked look of horror. "Your Grace, if you had been a proper host, you would have gone to sleep first so that you would have no idea if your ward and your oldest and dearest friend Sir Randolph snored, sighed, or even talked in their sleep."

Blake laughed as he opened the door. "I should have known you would twist my words around so that I was the one at fault."

"Absolutely, and with good reason. You were trying to amuse yourself at our expense, and I can't allow that to happen."

"You play the injured damsel very well, Henrietta," he said, helping her with her cape.

Her eyes sparkled with merriment as she peeled off her gloves and said, "I was speaking the truth."

Constance walked out of the drawing room and joined them in the vestibule.

"Good morning," Blake said. "I didn't know you would be here today."

"Obviously," she said with a tight expression on her face. "And it's afternoon, by the way, Your Grace, not morning."

Constance was unhappy about something, but he had been having such a good time with Henrietta that he really didn't care.

Blake looked at the tall clock standing in the corner behind him. "So it is."

"Good afternoon, Constance," Henrietta said as she took off her bonnet.

Constance gasped in surprise and her expression turned grim. "My heavens, Henrietta, what happened to your hair? And yours, too, Blake, you both look like you've been caught in a windstorm. You're disheveled. Where have you two been, and what have you been doing?"

Henrietta's hand went immediately to her hair and she tried to smooth it.

Blake didn't like Constance's accusatory tone. "Nothing improper, Constance, I assure you," he said as he combed through his hair with his fingers. "We've been on a balloon ride and, as you can imagine, it was windy so high up in the sky."

"And quite cold," Henrietta said. "If the two of you will excuse me, I would like to go to my room and freshen up."

"Of course," Blake said.

"I think that's an excellent idea," Constance added.

Henrietta said good-bye to them both and headed up the stairs.

Constance folded her hands across her chest in a disapproving manner. "A balloon ride, Blake? What were you thinking?"

"I didn't know that I had to be thinking anything. Come, let's finish this conversation in my book room."

He left his cloak and gloves on the newel post for Ashby to put away and walked down the corridor with Constance beside him.

"What can I do for you?" he asked, stepping aside so she could enter the room before him.

"The first thing I need to know is if you still wish me to be Miss Tweed's chaperone and have her ready for her first party next week. I've decided that must be at Lady Windham's house because she will have only the cream at her soirée."

Did he want that?

"Yes, of course. My thoughts on that haven't changed."

And Lady Windham's was the best choice because she had already reminded him that he owed her for not tattling on him last year when she saw him in a passionate embrace with Miss Barbara Camden. That could have been a disaster. Blake certainly hadn't wanted to be forced to marry Miss Camden, whose kisses had left him feeling like he'd jumped into a cold river in the deep of winter.

"Then please tell me: how I can possibly get her ready in time if you are running off with her to ride in balloons or engage in some other mindless frivolity that will in no way enhance her qualities to make a suitable match?"

"I must say that I didn't give a thought to the possibility you might need her today, Constance. She has been out with you every day for a week. If I had thought about it at all, I would have assumed the two of you had finished with whatever you needed to do. It's Saturday."

"Men!" she exclaimed in an exasperated voice. "As if we could do all that we needed to do in a week! You have no idea what goes into having dresses, gowns, and everything else properly made."

Thankfully.

"Blake, we have to pick fabrics, styles, trimmings. Several women are working around the clock to get dresses, gowns, capes, gloves, and even unmentionables, made for Henrietta in time for Lady Windham's ball next Thursday. Henrietta will need to be at fittings all next week, and probably much longer than that, to get all her clothing finished."

"I leave all that up to you," he said, becoming quite bored with the conversation and Constance's harangue.

"Not only does she need to be fashionably clothed and coiffured, but I need to quiz her on manners to make sure she knows how to present herself and what to say and what not to say when she makes her debut in Society next week."

"Is that necessary, Constance? She seems quite well mannered to me."

"I need to make sure she knows that she can dance only once with a gentleman in any one evening no matter how charming he might be or how much he might engage her. I want to make sure she knows that you must approve anyone who asks to pay her a visit or take her to the park. I need to know—"

Blake held up his hand to silence her. "You've made your point, Constance. Do whatever you need to do."

"I need you to not claim her attention."

"Consider it done."

"Thank you, Blake. You know some women in the ton absolutely live to find fault with young ladies, especially if they or their close friends have no connection to the young lady. And no one will have a connection to Henrietta, except you."

"I am not without friends in the ton, Constance."

"Of course you're not." She smiled. "And while you are extremely well liked, Your Grace, keep in mind that you have rejected all their daughters through the years and have remained a bachelor. In other words, you are considered a rake who has amused himself with their tender affections and broken their hearts. Take my word for it, these ladies will be looking for any slight imperfection in Henrietta and will pounce on the smallest detail. If I'm to be her chaperone, you must stand aside and allow me to work with her all day, every day, and into the evening, if necessary."

Blake started to tell Constance that he didn't like being reprimanded by his former lover but, at the last second, decided against the reprimand. He had, after all, asked for her help.

"Is that all?"

"Yes, as long as we understand each other."

"We do."

"Good. With your permission, I'll go find Henrietta and we'll get started on what we have left of the day."

"Please, by all means, she's yours."

For now.

Eleven

My Dearest Grandson Lucien,

Read this splendid quote from Lord Chesterfield: "Never hold anybody by the button, or the hand, in order to be heard out; for if people are not willing to hear you, you had much better hold your tongue than them." This one might possibly give you a smile, as well as the sage advice offered in these words.

Your loving Grandmother,
Lady Elder

AS SOON AS CONSTANCE LEFT THE ROOM, BLAKE walked over to his desk and sat down in his chair. The first thing he saw was the pile of mail and papers on his desk. It had gotten bigger since last night.

A lot bigger. What a nuisance.

Blake continued to stare at the messy desk and knew that Henrietta would not approve of the clutter. But why in the hell did he care what she thought? She was his ward, not his keeper.

Why in the bloody hell had he turned off his

father's secretary? Why had he not taken the time to find another? And why had it only started to bother him since Henrietta arrived? He had to make a priority of getting a secretary. Soon. Maybe Race or Morgan, or even Gibby, might know of someone.

In frustration, he swiped the jumble of envelopes, documents, and papers to one side of his desk with the back of his hand, sending two or three of them so near the edge that they fell off. He would deal with all that correspondence later. He didn't have the patience for it right now. He had too many other things on his mind. Gibby's plight and his own attraction to Henrietta were at the top of his list. Not that he could do anything about either one of them at present.

He was certain Mrs. Simple intended to get her hands on Gibby's money—and quite possibly him, too. But did she want to abscond with it or actually pour it into a balloon business? Either way, the money would be lost.

He was baffled by the unexpected feelings he had for Henrietta. But why? He was a man; he was supposed to be attracted to beautiful, intelligent, desirable women. But, somehow, it just seemed wrong for him to want to bed his legal ward.

A shadow crossed his vision, and he looked up and saw his housekeeper standing in the doorway. He could only hope she hadn't seen his little display of irritation with the mail.

"Yes, Mrs. Ellsworth?"

"Begging your pardon, Your Grace," she said. "I was wondering if you'd be wanting something to eat. I can prepare a tray and bring it to you."

"No, thank you, but please prepare a tray for Miss Tweed and take it up to her room right away. She'll be leaving again soon."

"Yes, Your Grace, I'll see to it immediately," she said and disappeared as quietly as she had arrived.

With the frame of mind Constance was in, she wouldn't think about getting Henrietta anything to eat before she whisked her away to do whatever ladies did. Who would have thought being fitted for dresses would be such an ordeal? A man only had to be measured once, maybe twice, and then he was finished until his clothing was ready.

Blake leaned his head against the back of his chair and closed his eyes. He remembered how soft and pliant Henrietta's lips had been beneath his, and how lovely she looked in sleep.

"No," he said aloud as he opened his eyes. She was his ward. He was her protector, and he would keep her safe from every man with improper intentions, including himself.

What he needed to do was get away for a few days and clear his mind. Maybe then he could look at his predicament with a fresher eye. Or maybe the easiest way to do that was to get another woman on his mind. He should go out tonight and dance, drink, and gamble until dawn and then find a woman to bed.

He had turned off his last mistress about three months ago. At least she would have been able to ease his frustration and calm the eagerness that raged in his loins every time Henrietta smiled at him. A number of young widows would welcome a rendezvous with him. Maybe he would make some inquiries at the parties tonight.

Blake sensed someone in the doorway again. He looked up and saw Ashby. Blake groaned silently.

What now?

Servants could be a hell of a bother. They constantly wanted to ask him something, tell him something, or do something for him. Sometimes, he wished he lived completely alone.

It was hell being a duke.

"Yes, Ashby. What can I do for you?"

"Sorry to disturb you, Your Grace, but I thought you might want to see the cards of the gentlemen who called on you today."

Ashby placed a silver tray in front of Blake.

Blake looked down at it. There must have been more than a dozen cards. Receiving one or two a day hadn't been unusual since he became a duke, but why so many today? That was odd. He usually had half a dozen or so cards by the end of the week, mostly from members of Parliament—all wanting to know when he would take his rightful seat as the Duke of Blakewell and fulfill his political duties. Blake had not set a time to join the Parliament in any capacity—even if the duty and honor came with his title.

Rubbing his chin, he looked at Ashby and asked, "This many men stopped by to see me just today?"

"Yes, Your Grace."

Blake was puzzled. "Have I forgotten anything important?"

"Not that I'm aware of, Your Grace, but I'm not privy to all your engagements."

Blake pushed papers aside and moved things around until he found his appointment book. He had recorded several entries when he went through his mail a couple of days earlier. Only one looked interesting. He had made a note that Lady Houndslow was in Town. She had sent him a note saying she'd like him to pay her a visit.

He had forgotten about that invitation. The young widow had just finished her time of bereavement and was accepting visitors and invitations. He hadn't seen her in over a year because she had decided to spend her mourning at her estate outside London. Maybe this was the perfect time to reacquaint himself with the voluptuous widow. She might be just the woman he needed to take his mind off the alluring Henrietta.

"Thank you, Ashby. I think I'll make an unannounced visit to Lady Houndslow today. Make sure I have a bouquet of flowers to take with me."

"I'll have them ready and waiting for you at the front door."

"Good. Add a basket of Cook's plum tarts." A plate of those sweets would melt any woman's heart.

"Yes, Your Grace."

Ashby remained standing in front of Blake's desk.

Blake asked, "Is that all?"

"No, Your Grace. Lord Raceworth and Lord Morgandale are here to see you. Should I send them in?"

By the saints! What next?

"Yes, of course, Ashby. Have them come in."

The butler left and Blake fingered through the cards on the tray. What the devil were all these visits for? Some of the men he knew well, like the pretentious fop Lord Snellingly, and others were names he recognized, but he couldn't say he knew the blokes. That was puzzling.

Blake rose from his chair as Race walked in with his usual swagger. Morgan was right behind him with his regal strut. Both cousins wore all the self-confidence of a mighty king. Mother Nature had blessed his kindred with splendid looks, easy charm, and more intelligence than they deserved. And just as their grandmother had instructed them from an early age, they never failed to take advantage of their good fortune.

"Don't tell me you two have already found out all we need to know about Mrs. Simple and whoever in London has interest in balloons."

"All right, we won't tell you," Race said with a smile. When Blake didn't return his good humor, Race continued by sheepishly saying, "Sorry, not me. I haven't done a thing yet to check on Mrs. Simple's past, present, or future, but I do have an appointment to meet this afternoon with a man who will assist me."

"I've done a little better," Morgan said. "I have a man making discreet inquiries for me. I plan to meet with him later today to hear what he has to say. I'll stop in some of the smaller clubs as well to see if there is any chatter about balloons."

"I'll get my solicitor to hire someone from Bow Street to make discreet inquires about Mrs. Simple and her past," Race added.

Blake walked over to his side table and took the top off a crystal decanter. He didn't have to ask his cousins if they wanted a drink. They always appreciated a glass of the expensive port he had shipped in from Portugal each year. His father had began that ritual years earlier when France wouldn't export wine to England.

"If you have no information, why are you here?" He poured splashes of the wine fortified with brandy into three glasses and then replaced the decanter's top.

"Do we need a reason to visit you?" Race asked.

"Usually," Blake said, giving a glass to Morgan and one to Race.

"We wanted to see how it went for you this morning," Morgan said.

"Yes," Race added. "We were worried."

Blake picked up his own glass and took a sip of the slightly sweet, yet strong wine. "There's no need to worry about Gibby. He knows exactly what he's doing. He loves the attention Mrs. Simple gives him. But you know, the more I think about Mrs. Simple, the more I believe she is serious about a business. I'm beginning to think she doesn't want to take his money and run. I think she truly believes she can start a transportation business with balloons and get people, women mostly, to buy passage to travel from place to place."

"Ah, Blake, thank you for telling us what you think of Mrs. Simple. I think we will have to wait for more information about her before we proceed. But what we really wanted to know was how well you fared when you went up in the balloon this morning."

They tried to keep straight faces, but Morgan's lips twitched from wanting to smile and Race's lips puckered like a fish because he was trying so hard not to smile. They were both about to burst from holding in their laughter.

If they thought he was going to give them the satisfaction of details, they could think again. Blake's lips were sealed about what happened on the balloon ride. He wasn't telling them anything, especially that the bewitching Henrietta had gone with him.

Maybe Gibby was on to something by calling them Guardian Fools. Blake was beginning to feel like Race and Morgan were watching his every move.

"I was fine," Blake said innocently and took another sip of the port.

Race and Morgan looked at each other.

"Are you sure? You're still looking a bit pale to me, Cousin," Morgan said, trying to goad him into saying more. "Yes. Your hair is still standing straight up on your head, and your hands look a bit shaky to me."

It was not only hell being a duke; it was hell having two inquisitive cousins!

Blake raked his hand through his hair. He should have paid attention to it when he first got home. He forced himself to remain collected and calmly said, "It was bloody cold so high up in the sky, and the wind blew like the devil, but I've never witnessed a more beautiful sunrise. Wish you could have seen it and enjoyed the champagne with me. It has never tasted better than it did this morning." Blake ended by giving them a crafty smile.

"Come now, you can't blame us for worrying about you," Morgan said.

"Worrying?"

What a laugh.

"Yes, considering how strange you acted the time you went up with us. Remember, you went ghastly white and felt like you were going to faint. Did you feel that way again?"

"Damnation, Race, what are you talking about? I have never felt faint in my entire life. I said I felt like I was falling. There is a big difference between that and feeling faint. Leave it to you to muddy the facts."

"Oh," Race said in a voice that let Blake know he didn't believe a word of what he'd just heard.

"This time was better, much better," Blake lied without compunction. Some times he just couldn't be completely truthful with his cousins. "The devil take you both. You weren't worried about me. You want to make fun of me."

Race chuckled. "Of course we do. Can you blame us for wanting to have a go at you?"

"Yes," he grumbled, and then immediately said, "No, of course not. I suppose I would do the same. But I've said all I'm going to say on the subject. Now, was there anything else you two Guardian Fools wanted? If not, I have a lot of work to do."

"Guardian Fools, are we?" Race said with a huff. "What kind of name is that to call us?"

"Yes, Blake, if we didn't look after you, tell us who would," Morgan said with indignation.

Blake smiled and then laughed. He had said something very similar to Gibby when he had called the three cousins Guardian Fools.

"What's so funny?" Race asked.

"Nothing that I want to discuss with the two of you," Blake said and walked over and picked up the decanter and refilled all their glasses.

"Well, there was one other reason we came to see you this afternoon."

"Or two," Race added and then sipped his drink.

Blake knew something was up, but they were taking their own sweet time telling him about it.

"That's right. One is that we were hoping to meet your ward," Morgan said. He walked over to one of the wing-backed chairs and sat down.

"She's all the rage," Race said, taking the other chair. "You certainly know how to stir up gossip and set the scandal sheets on fire. I can't remember there being such a furor over a new young lady coming to London as there has been with Miss Tweed."

Blake leaned a hip against his desk and crossed his booted feet at the ankles. He could just imagine what the tittle-tattle must be among the ton. It was still a shock to him, too.

"I'm afraid that you won't be able to meet her today. She's with Constance doing whatever ladies do to get ready for balls."

"Don't tell me you're going to make us wait and meet her when everyone else does."

"As a matter of fact, I hadn't given it a thought at all, but I think I will make you wait, as that's all you two devils deserve. Make your plans now to make Lady Windham's first party next Thursday night. That is where Henrietta will make her debut."

"He's going to hold a grudge because we were teasing him about the balloon ride."

"So it seems," Morgan said and glanced down at the silver tray Ashby had brought in and left on the desk.

He picked up some of the cards and looked at them. "Looks like you are a very popular fellow, Lucien."

Blake jumped on the opportunity to change the subject from Henrietta, even though Morgan had called him by his first name.

"It appears that way, but I don't know why all these gentlemen came to see me."

"Really," Morgan said. "I'm surprised you don't know why."

Blake didn't like the sound of that. "I don't even know some of them, but something tells me you know what's going on and that you're going to tell me what this is all about."

"Better us than someone else, right?" Race said.

Blake's uneasy feeling grew.

Morgan took a sip of his port and then said, "It's already out among the ton that you are trying to find a suitable husband for your ward."

"I don't know how that can be. She's only been here a week. I haven't made any inquiries of anyone yet."

"You don't have to. The servants are talking to their employers, and shopkeepers are talking to everyone who comes into their shops. It's already all over Town that your ward is beautiful, intelligent, and kind. That is all a man needs to know about a woman if he's looking for a wife."

"And it doesn't hurt that her guardian is a duke," Race added. "Everyone assumes you'll place a handsome dowry on her."

"That's enough to bring out the men who aren't even looking for a wife."

"There's no more you need to say. The Season is for young ladies to make matches, and Miss Tweed is joining the Season. It's my guess all these men stopped by to tell you why you should choose them to be Miss Tweed's dearly beloved."

Morgan pushed the silver tray aside. "Looking at some of these names, I'd say that most of them could do a lot worse for themselves than marry the ward of a duke, and I'm sure they know that. Even Lord Snellingly has called on you."

"That popinjay," Race said. "He has been looking for a wealthy woman to marry for years. He thinks he's another Lord Byron. All he wants to do is write poetry."

Having men vying for Henrietta's hand was only Society taking its natural course, a course he put in motion by asking Constance to help him introduce Henrietta to Society. But for some reason, his stomach tightened at the thought of fops like Lord Snellingly vying for Henrietta's hand in such an impersonal way.

"There's more," Race said.

Blake leaned heavier against his desk for support. "More? What more could there be? I have every rakehell and fortune hunter in London calling on me."

Morgan and Race looked at each other, and then back to Blake.

"Spit it out, you two."

"You tell him, Morgan. You're the oldest."

Morgan took a deep breath. "As of this morning, there's a new wager on the books at White's."

That couldn't be good news.

"And already it has become the most popular wager to bet on."

"And?" Blake held his breath.

"You can place a bet that you think Miss Tweed will be properly engaged by the end of the Season, or you can place a bet that she won't. Or you can bet on whether you think she'll snag a titled gent or not."

"Hell's bells!" Blake hissed.

"Sorry, Blake, we knew you wouldn't like the notoriety of this."

"It's distasteful. What the bloody hell are the outrageous members of White's doing betting on the future of a young lady none of them have met?"

"You can't blame Society. It's all a game with them. Always has been. You know they mean no harm to you or Miss Tweed. The more outlandish the bet, the better men like it. We've certainly wagered on our share of shocking bets."

That was true. But now that the tables had turned and Henrietta was the subject of a wager, he had a different attitude about the betting.

"Besides," Race said. "You, of all people, suddenly becoming a guardian is big news and worthy of a wager at White's."

"But cheer up," Morgan said, reaching over and clapping Blake on the back. "We have come up with a plan for you."

Blake eyed them warily. "A plan for me?"

Morgan rose from his chair, pushed the scattered mail aside, and set his empty glass on Blake's desk. "Yes. I need to go out to Valleydale. I have some new thoroughbreds that are going to be delivered there in the next few days. I want to check them out and make sure I get the horses I've paid for. Race and I were thinking this would be a good time to get you out of London and let things calm down."

"And it will give the three of us the opportunity to spend some time together riding, hunting, and other things," Race added.

"If you'll remember," Morgan said, picking up the conversation, "the village has a lively tavern and a couple of wenches who would love for us to pay them a visit."

Race grinned. "What do you say about the idea of getting away from London for a few days?"

Blake looked from one cousin to the other. Constance had told him she needed Henrietta to herself; Gibby was on notice not to do anything about Mrs. Simple; and he was looking for a woman to ease his recent celibacy. And he did remember the wenches. Morgan was right about the tavern. It was a lively place, and it could be just what Blake needed to get his mind off Henrietta.

"When do we go?"

"Meet at my house at first light," Morgan said.

The widowed Lady Houndslow could wait for another day. Blake set his glass down, walked to the doorway, and called to Ashby. Seconds later the dour man appeared.

"Cancel the flowers and tarts. I won't need them today."

"Yes, Your Grace."

"Tell Mrs. Pepperfield and Miss Tweed when they return that I've been called away for a few days.

I will be back in time to take Miss Tweed to Lady Windham's ball next Thursday night."

"Yes, Your Grace."

Blake turned back to his cousins, and with a smile on his face, said, "I'll meet you at dawn."

Twelve

My Dearest Lucien,

Here are a few more good words to live by from my favorite friend, Lord Chesterfield: "To ride well is not only a proper and graceful accomplishment for a gentleman, but may also save you many a fall hereafter; to fence well may possibly save your life; and to dance well is absolutely necessary in order to sit, stand, and walk well."

Your loving Grandmother,
Lady Elder

IT WAS HALF–PAST NINE IN THE EVENING. BLAKE STOOD stiffly in his drawing room, staring out the window into the darkness and waiting for Constance to bring Henrietta below stairs so they could make the short carriage ride to Lady's Windham's house.

His shoulder was killing him. He desperately wanted a glass of port or brandy—or anything to take the edge off the pain, but he dared not take a sip of anything until he had seen Henrietta through her first ball. If he started drinking now, he was afraid he wouldn't stop until the spirits eased the ache in his shoulder as they had done right after he was thrown from his horse.

The days at Valleydale with his cousins had been good until his mare stepped in a hole during a hunt and he and the horse went down hard. Blake's left shoulder had taken the brunt of his fall, knocking his arm out of the shoulder joint. Morgan had put the arm back in place for him, but the pain had been excruciating. And it still pained him.

Much to his consternation, he had to ask Ashby to help him tie his neckcloth because certain movements were still too painful to accomplish alone. He didn't like the feeling of not being in control.

When he'd returned to London earlier in the day, he had gone straight to see a physician. Not that it had done him any good. The ornery old fellow had simply looked at his shoulder, told him to keep the arm still, and said it would be better in a few days, which was exactly what Morgan had told him. Blake had refused the laudanum the physician offered him for the pain. He knew that would put him to sleep. Tonight belonged to Henrietta, and he wanted to make sure he attended her first ball.

He wanted everyone in the ton to see that he was a proper guardian for Henrietta, though he couldn't feel any less like one. Every time he thought about her, he felt more like a seducer than a protector.

He hadn't seen Henrietta since the balloon ride last week, but that didn't mean he hadn't thought about her. Often. He had stayed busy with Race and Morgan during the day riding the new horses, hunting wild boars, and practicing archery, but at night, when he lay down to sleep, Henrietta always invaded his thoughts. Even after his evening with the tavern wench.

He had hoped the lusty woman would ease the ache in his loins and make him forget his ward, but that hadn't happened. The brief, unfulfilling encounter with her had left him more unsatisfied than ever. He still desired Henrietta. Maybe he was cursed. It was the first time he had ever failed to have a good time with a doxy.

When he had returned home earlier in the afternoon, Constance told him Henrietta was already in her room preparing for the evening. Blake didn't fully understand what he felt for Henrietta, but he was eager to see her.

He chuckled to himself as he remembered Constance waiting at the front door for him when he had arrived. She was beside herself with worry. She had been pacing in fear, thinking he wouldn't return in time to attend the ball with Henrietta.

His shoulder had hurt like the devil, and he'd been in no mood for her theatrics and scolding about how Henrietta would have been ruined forever if he had failed to arrive and escort her to Lady Windham's ball. But remembering he had asked for Constance's help, he had held his tongue and listened quietly to every word.

He was damned happy Constance wasn't upset about the wagers at White's. He was worried she might think he had something to do with that and be outraged. He was astounded that she seemed thrilled that the outcome of Henrietta's future was the latest bet on the books at White's and that Henrietta was being discussed in the gossip columns.

Women.

It was difficult to know what was going to upset them and what was going to help them flourish.

Blake heard footsteps on the stairs and the slight rustle of taffeta. Suddenly his breath shortened and he felt a way he hadn't felt in years—eager and expectant. He turned away from the window, and Henrietta appeared in the doorway.

His loins thickened in anticipation as he looked at her. She was stunning. The neckline of her dress was cut wide and astonishingly low with small strips of lace holding it on her shoulders. The soft swell of her breasts peeked temptingly from beneath layers of the gossamer-thin fabric of her ivory bodice. A ribbon of lavender silk banded the gown's high waist and connected to the ruffled, taffeta skirt.

She wore a choker of three strands of pearls and teardrop earrings to match. Her shiny, golden blonde hair was arranged in curls, with strands of small pearls woven through each ringlet, making her look like a princess. She looked so enticing that Blake wanted to pull her into his arms and lose himself in the feel of her body close to his.

Henrietta smiled at him. Blake smiled, too. Why did just seeing her cause funny feelings inside him? He had been attracted to beautiful women since he was a young lad, but what he felt when he looked at Henrietta was different. And he knew the feelings had nothing whatsoever to do with her being his ward and he her guardian. They all had to do with him being a man and her a woman.

"Well, Your Grace, are you pleased?" Constance asked.

Blake cut his gaze to the side and, for the first time, realized that Constance was standing right beside Henrietta. He hadn't even seen her. He had eyes for no one but Henrietta.

Clearing his throat, Blake walked over to Henrietta and bowed stiffly, trying not to move his shoulder any more than necessary.

He took her gloved hand in his, kissed the back of her palm, and then said, "Miss Tweed, you are the most beautiful young lady I have ever seen. None at the ball will outshine you tonight."

Henrietta smiled and curtseyed, saying, "Thank you, Your Grace, and might I be so bold as to say you are very handsome."

He acknowledged her compliment with a nod and then turned back to Constance. "You look lovely, Constance," he said as he took her hand and kissed it. "Job well done. I have no doubt that Henrietta will find favor with everyone who meets her tonight."

Constance beamed with appreciation for his comments as she curtseyed. "Thank you, Your Grace. We worked very hard so that you would be pleased."

Pleased? He was thrilled.

Blake's gaze locked onto Henrietta's again as if they were the only two people in the room. Very quietly he said, "I could not be any more pleased than I am."

Henrietta smiled again. "Constance was a wise choice for the duties you gave her. Her knowledge and taste in fabrics, colors, and styles to suit me were remarkable."

"I agree."

"May I also say welcome home, Your Grace. This house was big, dull, and empty without your presence."

A warm, contented sensation filled Blake at her words. He was happy to be back and damned happy to see her again.

Blake acknowledged Henrietta's words with a nod and glanced up to see his butler standing in the shadows of the doorway. "Yes, Ashby?"

"Sir, Lord Raceworth and Lord Morgandale are here and would like to be given permission to join you."

Blake chuckled lightly. He was not surprised that his cousins had arrived. They had hinted that they would not wait until Lady Windham's party to meet Henrietta. They were curious as cats about her, and he couldn't blame them.

"Show them in."

Henrietta was still fighting the feeling of butterflies in her stomach when two of the most handsome and impressive-looking men she had ever seen walked into the room. Her eyes widened, and her breath caught and held in her lungs as the Marquis of Raceworth and the Earl of Morgandale walked up to her.

One was only slightly shorter than the other, but both were tall, powerful-looking men with broad shoulders and narrow hips. They both resembled Blakewell in the way they carried themselves with a wealth of confidence and a little arrogance, too. They were fashionably dressed in formal evening wear of black coats with long tails. Their shirts, waistcoats, and trousers were buff white and shiny gold buckles adorned their black shoes.

Henrietta didn't remember hearing much of the formal introductions that are always necessary for titled gentlemen, but she heard enough to know that Lord Raceworth was the gentleman with light-brown hair like Blakewell and grayish-green eyes. Lord Morgandale was the taller of the two with darker and longer hair. Both men had the same strong and handsome features of the duke.

Clearly Lord Raceworth and Lord Morgandale were friends with Constance. The three of them talked together without awkwardness or pretense.

"It was good of our dear cousin to insist that we come and meet you here in the privacy of his home rather than wait until Lady Windham's ball, don't you think?" Lord Morgandale said as he turned from Constance to Henrietta.

"We can always count on him to know just when to do the proper thing," Lord Raceworth added with a twinkle in his eyes.

"You rakes are lucky I didn't disown you years ago and that I still allow you to enter my door," Blakewell said, and they all laughed.

Henrietta smiled as she enjoyed the banter among the three handsome cousins. She could see they had great fondness for each other. She felt a moment of envy. She had never had such closeness with anyone her own age and had never developed a deep friendship that carried over from one home to the next. She couldn't even remember what being part of a family felt like.

With the cousins, she sensed the mutual respect and admiration that sizzled between them. One day, maybe she would find someone with whom she could be as close as these men were to each other. Perhaps she and Constance could become close if she were allowed to stay with the duke. "What do you think of London, Henrietta?" Lord Morgandale asked.

"Forget London," Race said, "We want to know what you think of Blake."

"Race, please," Blake said.

"I don't mind answering," Henrietta said with a comfortable smile. "I find London huge, busy, and exciting as I ride along the streets with Constance each day in the handsome carriage the duke has provided for me. I'm awed by how much there is to see. There is so much life to the city that it amazes me. In most of the places I've lived, the only day that the High Street is busy is Market Day. I'm astounded by things as simple as the number of lamps on the streets here."

She stopped and looked at Blakewell. "As for His Grace, I've found him to be cautious, respectful, and fair. All the things a proper guardian should be."

"I'd say you've sized up London and Blake quite well," Morgan said.

"I'm delighted to finally be presented to you both. Constance has told me how close both of you are to His Grace."

"We are fortunate in that we get along well together and seldom fight among ourselves."

Henrietta smiled at the earl. "Now that I've met you both, I'm certain you have fun even when you fight among yourselves."

"For sure, though each of us always fights to win, be it at gaming or racing or to coax a smile from a pretty miss," Race said with a wink.

"As it should be, my lord."

Her attention settled back on the duke, and her heart grew full of emotion she didn't wholly understand. She was impressed with Lord Raceworth and Lord Morgandale. They were handsome, appealing gentlemen, but the feelings she had for Blakewell were very different from what she experienced when she looked at his two cousins. And what she felt for him was very different from what she'd felt for all her previous guardians. It was almost as if she yearned for his favor, his attention, for him.

Standing in the drawing room with Constance and the three extraordinary men in front of her, for the first time in her life Henrietta was looking at the duke the way a woman looked at a man she desired, a man she wanted to marry.

Candlelight, candlelight, and more candlelight. Henrietta had never seen so many candles lighting a home in her life, nor had she ever seen so many people in one place. This had to be what the Society Pages meant when they said a party was a crush. All she could see before her were ladies dressed in beautiful, colorful gowns and gentlemen clothed in richly detailed evening coats with elaborately tied neckcloths. Every lady's gown was adorned with feathers, flowers, or lace—and some had all three. Large jewels hung around their necks, dripped from their ears, and graced their arms, hands, and fingers.

The main party room at Lady Windham's house was hot, even though the spring evening was cold and damp. The air was filled with a mixture of scents ranging from perfume to food to candle wax.

In an adjoining room, a buffet table with a starched white cloth had been covered with beautifully arranged platters of fowl, fish, and lamb. A host of fruits and vegetables from every season and in every color were piled high in expensive china bowls. Henrietta had never seen such lavishness. It looked so delicious she wanted to sample everything on the table—except the mushrooms—but she couldn't touch one bite of the food. Constance had insisted she eat before she dressed, saying that a young lady would never eat at her first ball.

Some of the people danced to the lively music, while others talked in small groups or as intimate couples in faraway corners. The opulence of the house with its gilt fretwork, carved moldings, and velvet draperies was so magnificent that Henrietta felt as if she were in one of the many chateaux she had read about that had been built in France.

Henrietta didn't know how long she had been at the ball, and time didn't seem to matter to anyone. She had done nothing but be presented to a steady stream of people, so many that her head was spinning with all the names and faces of the people she had met.

Hours earlier she had realized there were way too many viscounts, earls, and barons to keep straight, though some would be easy to remember. Lord Waldo because he always followed his brother around the room, Lord Snellingly because he quoted poetry to her while Blakewell rolled his eyes in contempt, and an Italian count who tried to kiss his way up her arm but was stopped when His Grace pulled her hand out of his clasp, causing Henrietta to hide a smile behind her fan.

"Do you feel all right, Henrietta? You are looking tired," Constance said with a sudden wrinkle of concern creasing her brow.

"Me? Of course, I feel fine," Henrietta said, thinking Constance was entirely too perceptive. "The ball is all that I expected it to be with the grandeur, the glamour, and the excitement."

"Good. I'm sure the small village dances you attended at your last home cannot compare to something as magnificent as this party."

"Only in the gaiety of the people."

"Perhaps she is as bored as am I," Blakewell said.

"I am not bored, Your Grace."

"You've done nothing but stand in this stuffy, over-crowded room and meet people," he countered.

"That is true, Your Grace," she said, giving him a grateful smile. "This is a lot to take in at one time, and I'm afraid I wasn't prepared for so many people."

"I understand your frustration," Constance said, "but it's best to get all the introductions out of the way. With that done, all future parties and balls should be more entertaining for Henrietta." She looked at the duke. "Perhaps it is time for the two of you to dance."

Henrietta glanced over at Blakewell. He was the one who looked pale, though Constance obviously hadn't noticed with all the flurry of people. He'd been too quiet the entire evening. She couldn't help but wonder if he were completely over the bout with the bad mushroom.

Blakewell looked at Constance and said, "It has been a tiring evening for all. Perhaps we should wait until tomorrow night to dance, Constance."

"Nonsense, Blake, you must not wait. There are gentlemen here champing at the bit, just waiting for you to give the signal that they can ask Henrietta to dance. You need to introduce her on the dance floor so they will feel free to ask. Don't you see how everyone is looking at her as if she were a precious jewel?"

He looked down at Henrietta, and she saw admiration in his eyes. It thrilled her that she pleased him.

"Yes, I have noticed how everyone is admiring her," he said. "There's a dance starting now. Henrietta, may I have this dance?"

She curtseyed with all the warmth she had for him filling her heart. "I would be honored, Your Grace."

He raised his right arm, took hold of her fingertips, and led her to the dance floor. They took their places in the long line of other dancers. When the music started, the duke winced as he moved his left arm behind his back. She watched him carefully as the dance continued. With all the moves using his left arm, he grimaced, but his right arm seemed to be fine. The dance was a quadrille. The music moved fast, but Blakewell didn't. He was rigid and had none of the joy on his face that she saw in the other dancers' expressions.

Something was wrong with his left arm, and she intended to find out what had happened.

Earlier in the evening, she had wondered if something was wrong as they climbed into the carriage. He seemed stiff, but she had been a bit nervous herself, so much so that she'd forgotten that until now. As she twirled beneath his right arm, he was careful not to lift or move his left arm behind his back any more than necessary.

From the corner of her eye, she saw Lord Morgandale walk up behind His Grace, and as easily as if they were moving as one, Blakewell handed her over to Lord Morgandale, and suddenly she was dancing with the earl. Henrietta was stunned by this maneuver. She missed a couple of steps. Lord Morgandale smiled and gave her an approving nod. They danced until Lord Raceworth smoothly replaced the earl. Before the dance ended, Sir Randolph Gibson changed places with Lord Raceworth, and suddenly she was dancing and laughing with the dapper old gentleman.

Henrietta's chin lifted a little higher. She didn't know if they knew something was wrong with the duke's arm or if they were following their usual pattern, but she felt wonderful. No matter the reason, these men were letting Society know that the Duke of Blakewell's family accepted her. Her chest swelled with warmth and gratitude. She felt the prickle of tears in her eyes, and she blinked them away. For the first time since her parents' death, more than twelve years ago, Henrietta felt as if she had a family.

This realization was so overwhelming that she didn't remember the rest of the dance. She curtseyed to Sir Randolph when the music stopped, and he escorted her back to where the others were standing.

"Henrietta," Lord Morgandale said as she and Sir Randolph approached the others, "you will need to be patient with Blake. He doesn't know anything about being the guardian of a young lady. He will probably make many mistakes."

"I shall do that, my lord. I am well versed in this as I have had five previous guardians. I promise I will treat him gently and with the utmost care while he learns."

Everyone laughed at her remarks, including Constance and the duke. But Henrietta saw tightness around his eyes and mouth and once again worried that something was wrong.

"By that comment, I have no doubt that you will keep him well in hand," Lord Morgandale said.

"And I, for one, can't wait for you to begin his schooling," Race said.

"Bravo, gentlemen," Constance said as she lightly clapped her hands. "Morgan, Race, and Sir Randolph, it was a touch of genius for the three of you to dance with Henrietta before Blake finished his dance."

"I'm glad someone finally recognizes our genius," Race said.

"Geniuses?" Sir Randolph asked with a grin.

"You can't believe anything Constance says tonight," Blake said in a teasing voice. "She's had far too much champagne to drink and can't be trusted. She doesn't know what she's saying."

"I beg your pardon, Your Grace," Constance said in mocked horror. "I haven't left your side all evening. You know well that I've had nothing to drink but punch, just like you. We needed all our wits about us tonight. And, thankfully, I think we passed the test. Gentlemen, I'm sure Blake won't forget your support tonight."

"If I know these two blades standing beside me, they'll see he doesn't forget," Sir Randolph quipped.

"Seriously, gentlemen, all of you have let everyone in Society know Henrietta not only has the duke's protection, she also has yours."

"That was our intention," Morgan said.

Constance gave them all a satisfied smile. "Everything is working out perfectly." She beamed. "Now, Blake, we can go home. We won't attend another party this evening, nor will we let any other man dance with her tonight. We'll keep the mystery surrounding her at the highest level if we leave now. Everyone will want to know what parties she will be attending tomorrow night, and everyone will be watching to see who gets the first dance with her."

While Constance was talking, Henrietta watched as the Italian count she had met earlier, make his way toward them. He was a short, rotund man with black, curly hair and small dark eyes. He would be difficult to miss because of his regalia. He wore a full military uniform complete with a sword strapped around his waist. One side of his black coat was crowded with military medals, and large gold epaulets topped each shoulder.

The proud, strutting man walked up to Blakewell and said, "Ah, ha, good evening again, Your Grace. I see that Miss Tweed is now *accettare i balli*. I have been waiting *tutta la notte* for this opportunity."

The duke looked at Henrietta. She was trying to tell him with her eyes that she didn't want to dance with this flashy man. The duke smiled at her, and she relaxed.

"I'm sorry, Count Vigone, but Miss Tweed is tired and we were just leaving. Another time, perhaps." He turned to Henrietta and said, "Let's go."

Thirteen

My Grandson, Lucien,

Study on this by Lord Chesterfield: "In business a great deal may depend upon the force and extent of one word; and in conversation, a moderate thought may gain, or a good one lose, by the propriety or impropriety, the elegancy or inelegancy, of one single word."

Your loving Grandmother,
Lady Elder

A HARD STINGING RAIN WAS PELTING THE GROUND by the time Henrietta and Blakewell dropped off Constance at her home and returned to his house. The footman opened the carriage door for them, holding out an umbrella. The duke jumped out and took the umbrella from him before reaching back to help Henrietta down the two steps. Taking hold of her arm, he ran with her through the rain to the front door, pooled water splashing all over Henrietta's velvet slippers and the hem of her dress.

As they neared the door, Ashby opened it and immediately took the umbrella from Blakewell when they entered the warmth of the vestibule.

"It's not fit outside for man nor beast, Your Grace. Would you like me to prepare you a cup of hot tea?"

"None for me. How about you, Henrietta?"

"No, thank you," she said untying the ribbon of her new, fur-trimmed cape.

Henrietta noticed how Blakewell didn't use his left arm as he threw his rain-sprinkled cloak off his shoulders and handed it to Ashby. Lifting his left arm only slightly, he carefully helped Henrietta with her cape and handed it to the butler, too.

"You had best hurry to your room, Henrietta, and get out of your wet shoes," Blakewell said.

Not yet, she thought.

"If you don't mind, Your Grace, may I ask you something before I go to my room?"

His brow wrinkled with annoyance. "You don't need permission to ask me a question, Henrietta. You are always free to ask whatever you desire."

The tightness around his forehead, eyes, and mouth seemed more pronounced than it had been earlier in the evening. He looked tired for the first time since she had met him.

She remained quiet for a few seconds, hoping Ashby would excuse himself, while she took time to peel off her long gloves and lay them on the side table with her reticule.

When Ashby continued to stand with them, she breathed deeply and took the liberty to say, "May I speak to you alone, Your Grace?"

Blakewell looked at Ashby, who stood solemnly beside them holding the wet cloaks. "Thank you for your assistance tonight, Ashby. You're free to go to bed now."

"Yes, Your Grace."

Henrietta waited until the stiff butler had left the vestibule. She then steadied her breathing and calmly said, "I wanted to ask about your arm, or maybe it's your shoulder, but you have been favoring it all night. I know something is wrong."

He lowered his lids over his eyes and curtly said, "It's nothing."

"I don't believe you, Your Grace."

"You are too bold for your own good, Henrietta."

She nodded once. "It's one of my weaknesses, Your Grace."

He let out a half chuckle. "Only you would look at it like that."

"You might have fooled Constance and duped your cousins, Sir Randolph, and all the other people at Lady Windham's party tonight, but you have not been able to hide your injury from me. When we were dancing, you grimaced and winced every time you had to lift your arm higher than your waist or put it behind your back. I know you have been in pain all evening."

"Damnation," he muttered, rubbing the space between his eyes. "Sorry for swearing, Henrietta, but I had hoped no one would notice."

I notice everything about you.

"I'm not sure anyone else did," she answered in a reassuring voice.

He sighed. "You see far too much for someone so young."

"Age has nothing to do with my intuitiveness."

It has to do with how I feel about you.

"All right, yes, I hurt my shoulder while I was at Valleydale with Morgan and Race. Now are you happy that I've admitted it?"

The curse!

Her eyes filled with concern, and she took a step closer to him. "I'm not happy that you've been hurt. I knew something was wrong when I first came below stairs and saw you standing in the drawing room. How serious is your injury? Did your cousins not know?"

"Yes, of course, they knew. Morgan took care of my shoulder at Valleydale. That's probably why they came to my rescue and relieved me when I was on the dance floor with you, though they'd never admit to doing anything nice to help me."

A pang of disappointment stabbed Henrietta, even though she had thought that might be the case. Still, for a few moments tonight, when his cousins and Sir Randolph had stepped up to take his place dancing, she had felt as if she was part of their family.

"I've tried to tell you that you are in danger, Your Grace. First, you eat a poisonous mushroom, and then you almost fall out of the balloon, and now this."

His gaze slowly swept up and down her face. "My life was never in danger in any of those incidents, Henrietta. I saw a physician today. He said my shoulder is fine, and I should be feeling better in a couple of days. Now, if you don't mind, I really need a glass of wine to help ease the pain."

"Why haven't you already had one?"

"I didn't want anything to keep me from protecting

you in case some rake like that fake Italian count decided he wanted to get fresh with you."

"He's not really a count?"

"I don't know for sure."

"Well, in any case, you shouldn't have denied yourself a glass of wine, Your Grace. It wasn't likely anyone would accost me with you, Constance, Sir Randolph, and your cousins standing guard over me all evening. I was lucky I could breathe. Let's go into your book room. You can sit down, and I will pour you a glass of wine."

"You don't have to do that. I'm not helpless."

The way he looked and the huskiness of his voice caused a quickening in her lower abdomen.

"I can see that. I can't imagine you ever being helpless. I want to do this for you."

"You need to get out of your wet shoes. Constance will never forgive me if you get sick and can't finish the Season."

"It would not bother me if I didn't finish the Season."

His eyes locked on hers. "It would bother me."

She felt a stab of pain at his words and swallowed hard. Every moment she spent with him made her want to stay with him all the more and never leave his house or his side. She wanted to be with him. He might not need her help tonight, but she needed to help him.

"I understand, Your Grace. I am very healthy and not given to sickness, but to ease your mind, I will take off my shoes."

She lifted the hem of her skirt to just above her

ankles and stepped out of her wet velvet slippers. She picked them up and put them on the bottom stair so she wouldn't forget them when she headed up to bed.

"Henrietta."

"Come, Your Grace, you've done so much for me these past few days. Please, let me do this simple task for you by pouring your drink."

"Very well, I'm in no mood to argue any point with you tonight."

She walked ahead of him into the book room. Once inside, Blake sat down in one of the two wing-backed chairs in front of his desk. Henrietta lit the wick of the oil lamp that sat on the desk in front of him. A soft golden light filled the room while raindrops pitter-pattered against the windowpanes.

From the side table, she poured a generous amount of the dark burgundy-colored wine into a glass. When she returned to Blakewell, he was trying to untie the complicated knot in his neckcloth with one hand. His injured arm lay still at his side.

"Here, you drink this and let me untie that for you." She placed her hand on top of his to stop him. His skin was smooth and firm. She immediately felt as if a blanket of enticing warmth covered her. It was unforgivably bold of her to touch him without his permission, but she had no desire to stop herself.

He let go of the neckcloth and took the wine from her. "You must be feeling very brave tonight," he said.

Slowly, she untied the knot, carefully unwound the three-foot-long piece of starched cloth from around his neck, and dropped it on the desk behind her. She then detached the stiff, stand-up collar and deposited it on top of the neckcloth.

A few raindrops glistened on top of his head. They sparkled and twinkled as they caught light from the lamp. She smoothed her hand across his light-brown hair, melting the droplets of water with her palm. Once, twice, three times. Each instance, she deliberately let her fingertips caress his forehead before she brushed down the length of his hair. With the pads of her fingers, she gently massaged the area just above his ears in a circular motion, using a tiny bit of pressure. She wanted to erase every line of pain from his brow.

The duke closed his eyes, settled his head against the chair back, and breathed deeply. "Your hands are gentle and your touch is soothing, Henrietta. You are caring for me with the tenderness of a glorious angel. Somehow you knew just what I needed tonight."

She smiled happily to herself. She was the one who needed this. It was heavenly to be able to touch him all she desired.

The rain beat a steady cadence against the window and the side of the house. The oil lamp bathed the room in a soft glow and gave a hint of warmth to the chilled air. Henrietta continued massaging his temples, dipping behind his ears and trailing down the side of his neck with the slightest of pressure.

Blakewell sighed contentedly. "You have done much more to ease my pain than the wine could ever do."

His praise pleased her. "Your shoulder probably pains you because you haven't rested it since you were hurt."

"There is no rest when I am with Morgan and Race. They constantly have something going on."

"Perhaps I should keep them away from you tomorrow and for the next few days to give you time to heal."

"I won't see them tomorrow anyway. I made arrangements tonight to meet with Gibby late in the afternoon at the Harbor Lights Club. He and I need to have a serious talk."

"About Mrs. Simple and her balloons?"

"Yes."

"Do you expect the conversation to go well?"

"That depends on how deeply Mrs. Simple has sunk her claws into him."

"They seemed quite comfortable with each other to me."

"I agree with you."

Without asking, she picked up his injured arm from where it lay by his side and carefully laid it across his chest. "That looks like it would be more comfortable. Is it?"

"I find that, wherever you touch me, it feels better. You can come to my rescue any time you want to. I believe there are healing powers in your touch, Henrietta."

Her chest swelled with tenderness and she smiled gratefully.

"You should know by now that your welfare is very important to me."

"I do know that, and your welfare is of utmost importance to me."

"I have to admit that I have never done this for a man before," she whispered to him.

"I'm glad to hear that. It's not something you really should be doing for anyone save your husband."

"But tonight, it seems the natural thing to do under the circumstances."

He chuckled softly, and some of the pain dissolved from the corners of his wide mouth and heavy-lidded eyes. It made her feel exceptionally wonderful to know she was helping him, but it also gave her a strange kind of pleasure to be touching him so intimately. She was feeling things she had never experienced before, tightness between her legs and a yearning in her breasts.

She massaged his temples and neck for a little longer before moving to the front of the chair and stepping between his parted legs.

His eyes popped open. "What are you doing, Henrietta?"

She didn't answer him or look at him. Instead, she started humming softly, and as casually as if she had done it a thousand times, rather than for the first time, she deftly started unfastening the shiny brass buttons on his waistcoat one by one.

She felt his hot gaze on her, but she was careful to keep her attention on the buttons, not on him. She was giving him an inappropriate view down the front of her low-cut dress, but instead of it shaming or embarrassing her, it excited her. She wanted him to look at her and find favor with her. If she looked into his eyes, the mood of the evening would change from comforter to seducer, and while there was nothing she would like better at the moment, she knew it wasn't what His Grace wanted.

When the last button was undone, she stopped

humming and said, "Rise a little and I'll help you take off your coat."

His Grace complied and gave her the glass of wine to put on the desk. Henrietta helped him slip his good arm out of his evening coat. He winced silently and moved stiffly as she gently pulled the sleeve off the injured arm. With the same care to move his arm as little as possible, she removed his brocade waistcoat.

It seemed decidedly intimate to be touching him and helping him come out of his coats, but she had never done anything in her life that made her feel as special or as needed as helping Blakewell tonight.

When the clothing was off, he settled back against the chair again. She gave him the glass of wine and studied him while he took a sip.

He looked comfortable and yet still so handsome and powerful in his collarless shirt and buff-colored trousers. Her gaze settled on his neck. She had never seen it before because it was always hidden beneath his high collar and expertly tied neckcloth. He had a strong, masculine neck and, for reasons she didn't understand, she wanted to kiss him there.

The cut of his shirt showed how broad his chest was and how narrow and lean his hips were. The fabric of his trousers stretched tightly over impressive, muscular thighs and lower legs.

Henrietta had an overwhelming urge to crawl up in his lap and snuggle against his chest. She wanted to bury her face in the crook of his neck and drink in the heady scent of him. Never, since her father had died, had she wanted to be cuddled in a man's strong arms, but right now she wanted that more than anything.

She wanted to melt against his chest and be cradled in his arms so desperately that her heart drummed in her chest.

"Do you think perhaps you should take off your shirt and let me look at your injury to see if it is healing properly?"

Blakewell looked up at her and smiled so disarmingly that her heartbeat slowed and she relaxed.

"Do I amuse you?" she asked, still standing between his powerful legs and looking down at him with curiosity.

He let out a half chuckle. "Yes. I wouldn't take my shirt off in front of you even if I was bleeding to death. You are already on dangerous ground by standing between my legs. Henrietta, I'm straining to keep from compromising you further than I already have with my kisses and caresses. But just so you know, there is nothing to see but a few bruises. My injury is in the joint of my shoulder. It's going to hurt like the bloody devil until it heals, but heal it will."

"All right, if you are sure."

"I am."

He continued to grin at her, a handsome, breath-taking grin that made her want to throw her arms around him, hug him close, and kiss him solidly on the lips.

"You don't really want to see my injury. You just want to see me without my shirt, don't you?"

Henrietta blinked rapidly. Had he been able to read her thoughts?

"No, no. Of course not, I thought you might have an open wound that needed a clean bandage."

"Henrietta."

"Oh, all right," she said, with a light stamp of her stockinged foot on the floor. She clasped her hands together in front of herself for fear she would reach down and touch him. It was impossible to hide the truth from him. "I admit I am curious about how you look without your shirt."

With a satisfied smile, he drank from his wine again and then whispered, "You tempt me, Henrietta, but I must resist."

She took a deep, steadying breath and looked into his intriguing eyes. "I truly don't mean to, Your Grace. I swear I have never wanted to see any other man without his shirt."

His gaze held fast to hers. "I believe you, but as it is, it's taking all I have not to take advantage of your generous help tonight."

Henrietta took a step away from him and away from the chair, thankful he wasn't throwing her out of the room for speaking what she felt deep inside. In truth, she not only wanted to see his chest, she wanted to touch him and feel the firmness of the muscles beneath his taut skin. And God help her, for some reason she didn't understand, she wanted to kiss his strong neck and broad chest.

But she couldn't tell him any of that. She shouldn't even be thinking it. Her guardians had raised her to be a lady of quality.

She should leave him now. She had done all she could to make him comfortable. But how could she force herself to leave him, when she wanted nothing more than to be with him, in this cozy room with golden light and rain gently tapping the windowpanes?

Henrietta looked around the room and saw a small brocade footstool. She retrieved it and brought it over to his chair, set it down at his legs, and then sat on the stool.

"What are you doing? You don't have to sit on a stool at my feet, Henrietta. Please sit in a chair."

I want to be closer to you than the chair will allow me to be.

"I'm all right here," she said, looking up at him with all the passion she was feeling for him.

He seemed more relaxed with his head against the back of the upholstered chair. It pleased her that the pain that had been etched in his features when they arrived had lessened.

"The wine must be making you feel better. The strain is gone from your face, and you are looking more comfortable."

"It's not just the drink that has me feeling better. It is you, too."

She smiled at him. "I am glad."

"I love the low-cut neckline of your dress tonight, Henrietta. I've only seen you in your very prim clothing. You look very womanly. Constance knew exactly what design to pick for you to show just enough to make every man's mouth water tonight. Your skin is beautiful, tempting, and the swell of your breasts beneath your gown has me thinking things that I should not think."

Henrietta's breaths quickened at his words.

"Only you have control over your thoughts."

"Point taken. We must talk about something else." He cleared his throat. "It appears you stayed busy in the evenings while I was at Valleydale. No doubt I owe my organized desk to your ministrations."

"It was such a small thing to do for you. It took no time at all to come in here in the evenings and organize your mail and documents. I hope you don't mind that I did."

"I don't. I'm glad. That will help me immensely when I sit down to go over it."

"Your solicitor certainly sends a lot of papers over for your signature. It's no wonder you stay backed up on your correspondence."

"It is hell being a duke and in charge of so many properties and accounts. Perhaps I will look over some of it tomorrow before I meet with Gibby. Right now, I feel too much like a bird with a broken wing."

She laughed softly. "Not just any bird, Your Grace; you remind me of an eagle. An eagle with a bent feather, not one with a broken wing."

He chuckled. "I like your analogy better than mine."

"That is because mine is more exact. Tell me how your injury happened."

"We were riding over the lands of Valleydale, an estate my grandmother left to Morgan. He keeps most of his thoroughbred horses there."

"And you were riding one of those horses?"

"No, just one of his best mares. We were racing as we often do late in the afternoon before the sun sets and it gets too dark and cold to be out. My horse stepped in a hole, and we both went down."

"The horse?"

A wrinkle of disquiet formed between his brows. "We had to put the mare out of her misery. She broke her leg, and there was nothing to be done."

Henrietta leaned forward, almost touching his knees with her breasts. "I'm sorry about the horse. I'm sure it was dreadful for Lord Morgandale to have to put his horse down, but I'm more worried about you. You could have been killed."

His gaze searched her face. "I was never in any danger of dying, Henrietta. What happened was an accident. That is all." He rose and placed the wine on the desk by his clothing. He reached down and caressed her cheek with the backs of his fingers. "I want you to hear me well on this. What happened to me had nothing to do with a curse. Not the mushroom, not the balloon, not the shoulder. All of them could just as easily have happened to someone else."

She cupped his strong, warm hand in both of hers. "But it was you."

"Yes, because I was the unlucky one. Tell me, who told you there was a curse on you or your guardians?"

It was such an abrupt departure from what they were talking about that, for a moment, Henrietta was stunned. She noticed his glass was almost empty, so she said, "Can I get you more wine?"

"No, not now, and don't try to change the subject. I want to hear more about this curse that plagues you. Who told you about it?"

She let go of his hands and folded her own in her lap. "Her name was Mrs. Goolsby."

"Somehow that name seems fitting. How and when did she tell you about the curse?"

Henrietta had been completely comfortable talking about his injury, and she had loved helping ease the pain in his shoulder, but just thinking about the time she spent with Mrs. Goolsby chilled her.

She lowered her head and hooded her eyes with her lids. "I don't want to bother you with this when you are in such discomfort."

"Thanks to you, I am feeling much better than when we arrived. I want to know everything about this woman and what she said to you."

Henrietta remained quiet, refusing to look at him. She didn't want to remember anything about that woman or the time she spent with her.

"Henrietta?"

His tone was soft and persuasive, yet she still wasn't willing to respond to him.

He leaned forward and cupped her chin with his fingers, lifting her face toward his and holding her captive with the merest pressure. "Tell me," he said softly. "Look at me and tell me everything this woman said to you."

Henrietta lifted her lashes and stared into the duke's calm, reassuring eyes. She loved this man with her whole being. She loved him, and she could trust him with her past.

Fourteen

My Devoted Grandson Lucien,

Here are a few sober and sensible words from Lord Chesterfield: "Do not be seduced by the fashionable word 'spirit.' A woman of spirit is mutatis mutandis; *the duplicate of a man of spirit—a scold and a vixen."*

Your loving Grandmother,
Lady Elder

REALIZING THE DEPTH OF HER LOVE FOR HIM AND feeling his gentle strength gave Henrietta the courage she needed to confide in him. She wanted to turn and bury her face in the palm of his hand and slowly drink in the musky scent of him, but instead, she kept her sanity and managed to say, "All right, what do you want to know?"

"Everything. This woman, did she put the curse on you and your guardians, or did she just tell you that it was there?"

"I—I don't know. I was only seven at the time. I

remember her holding me by the shoulders and saying to me that I was cursed. I would have many guardians and they would all die."

Blakewell moved his hand and let the backs of his fingers caress down her cheek and across the crest of her shoulder and then glide trippingly down her arm.

"All right, maybe you should start by telling me about your parents' death. Do you mind?"

Yes. Don't make me remember.

The concern in his eyes and the tender expression on his face were sincere and comforting, but still her throat tightened, and she swallowed hard. "I haven't talked about them in a long time."

"I can imagine why. It's not too painful for you to talk about them tonight, is it?"

Yes. Don't make me, please!

She shook her head. "I don't think so. For so long now, I've tried to forget the memories of that night. It serves no purpose to remember the accident. I found out a long time ago that I couldn't change the past."

He picked up her hand and covered it with his while his other hand stroked her arm softly, repetitively.

"I'd like to know what happened. Why don't you start with the day of the accident?"

Suddenly, as if a curtain was slowly, dramatically rolled back, Henrietta allowed her memory to open and reveal the dark, stormy night many years ago that lay heavy with fog, and smelled of damp clothing and wet horse.

"My parents and I were on our way home from a visit with my father's half-brother, Lord Phillip Bennett. Though the journey between our houses was a good day-and-a-half carriage ride, my father made the decision that we wouldn't stop for the night, but continue home." She paused, and moistened her lips. "We had two drivers and a footman with us, as well as my mother's maid. My father said we were well protected from highwaymen, and we were safe from them, but not the weather. It had turned ghastly late in the afternoon. I remember that the driver stopped the coach twice and said he couldn't see through the rain and fog. Papa ignored his warnings and told him to continue."

"That was dangerous. Did he have good reason for such action?"

The duke's warm hand continued to move up and down her arm, warming her with his touch. It was as if he knew that thinking about that night had always chilled her.

"He told my mother he had a horrible pain in his chest and was desperate to get home to his own bed."

"Was the pain near his heart?"

Her hand flew to her chest. "Yes, I remember watching him throughout the evening. His hand constantly rubbed the area of his chest over his heart. We must have traveled for hours in the slashing rain, and I must have fallen asleep because I remember waking up and thinking someone had lifted me up and was throwing me from one side of the coach to the other and back again. I heard my mother's screams, my father yelling for the driver."

Henrietta stopped, not wanting to go farther into the darkness of that night.

Blakewell lifted her hand from her chest, carried it to his lips, and kissed the back of her palm. His touch was comforting and reassuring. His grayish-brown eyes were dark with sympathy and concern.

"It sounds as though perhaps the coach went over an embankment? Is that what happened?"

She nodded and swallowed hard once again. "I will never forget the sounds of the horses screeching and screaming. There was terrible screaming from my mother and her maid. I heard wood splintering and cracking as the carriage broke apart, and then nothing. Nothing, but blackness and silence."

"You were knocked unconscious?"

"I woke to rain hitting my face. It was dark, so dark, and I was so wet and cold. I started trembling, and I couldn't stop. I called to my parents, but they didn't come to me."

Henrietta felt tears pool in her eyes, and then spill over and run down her cheeks. She didn't want to cry. She hated crying from anyone. It was a weakness she never allowed herself, but now she was powerless to stop the tears from falling as freely as they had that black night.

The duke leaned forward and gently tugged on her upper arms. "Come sit here on the chair with me. Let me hold you."

He scooted over, giving her enough room to fit beside him in the large wing-back chair. He drew her into his embrace. Heat from his hard body soothed and comforted her at once.

Henrietta stared into the flickering flame of the lamplight as her story continued to tumble out. "I lay there crying until first light, praying my parents would find me, but they didn't. No one came for me. When I crawled to my feet and saw the chaos the wreck had caused, I started screaming."

A sniffle escaped past her lips. Blakewell's arms tightened around her. "I don't know when I stopped. The coach had been completely destroyed, broken into hundreds, thousands of pieces, strewn over a wide area. The horses lay halfway up the embankment, as still as the people."

"Your parents and the others?"

"I found my father first and tried to wake him. I shook him, but he wouldn't wake up. And then I found my mother. Her eyes were open, but she wouldn't respond to me. She was wet and cold. I hugged her close, but I couldn't wake her."

A heaving sob broke from Henrietta's throat, and she suddenly was wrapped in the duke's strong embrace. She buried her face in the crook of his warm neck and cried. Her body shook as she wept for the loss of her mother, her father, her guardians who might have lived longer if only the accident hadn't happened, if only there was no curse on her.

"Cry all the pain out," the duke whispered against her ear as he held her close. "I'll hold you. I won't let go of you," he whispered.

"I hate crying," she said between gulping breaths. "I hate fear."

"Ssh, Henrietta, it's all right to cry sometimes. It will make you feel better. And you don't have to fear anything. You are safe here with me. Everything is going to be all right."

Blakewell murmured reassurances to her as his hands ran up and down her back. She snuggled deeper into his strong arms. He was broad and powerful. She felt small, safe, and content in his protective hold. She wanted him to hold her like this forever. Her sobs quieted.

When her tears were spent and her sniffles silent, she raised her head and rubbed the last of the tears from her eyes. "I'm sorry, Your Grace. I had no idea I would still be so moved talking about the accident."

He pushed a strand of hair away from her face and dried a streak of wetness from her cheek with the pad of his thumb. He gave her an understanding smile. "Don't apologize for crying, Henrietta. It's all right. There is nothing wrong in crying over the loss of your parents. That kind of hurt never goes away."

With his good arm, he reached over to his desk, pulled a handkerchief out of his coat pocket, and gave it to her.

"Feel better?" he asked.

She nodded. "I've never been able to get that scene out of my mind. There was such a horrible jumble of brokenness. I started gathering the pieces of the carriage that I could carry or drag. I laid them out like pieces of a puzzle so I could sort them. I wanted to put the pieces back together. I wanted to make the carriage whole so everything would be right again."

He wiped her damp cheek again with his fingertips. "So that is why you hate disorder. You are still trying to put the pieces of the carriage back together, still trying to make your life whole again."

She put the handkerchief aside. "You would think

that, by now, I would know that I cannot do that, but I've wanted to so many times."

He kissed the tip of her nose. "Some lessons are hard to learn. I wish I could make the pain of the past go away as easily as you relieved my pain tonight."

"You have helped me by holding me close. I have seldom been hugged or even touched since my parents died. Thank you."

He gave her a reassuring smile. "I'll have to remember that and hug you more often. Tell me, when you couldn't wake your parents, you started gathering pieces of the carriage, right?"

She nodded.

"What else do you remember?"

"It was cold. I was wet. My hair, my shoes, my clothing. I kept moving, taking pieces of the carriage to one place. My mother looked so cold. I found a blanket that we had used in the carriage and covered her."

"My heart breaks for you, Henrietta. What a frightful thing to have happened to any little girl. But I need to know more about Mrs. Goolsby. Was she the one who found you?"

"Yes."

"That morning?"

"I don't remember the time of day, but I glanced up and saw an old woman standing some distance away, looking at me. She seemed to have appeared out of nowhere. We just stared at each other for a long time. She was dressed all in black. When she walked closer, I could see she was very thin and her shoulders were hunched. She had sharp features and a pale complexion, and her eyes looked like small dark beads.

"I can't remember every detail, but I know I walked with her back to her house. We climbed into an open carriage, and she took me to a man's house. He questioned me about the accident. I told him my uncle's name and where he lived. The man asked the old woman if she could keep me until they notified my uncle and he came for me. She agreed only after they offered her money for my care."

"That doesn't surprise me. So did you stay with her until your uncle arrived?"

"Yes. Mrs. Goolsby was a disagreeable woman, muttering to herself all the time. When we got back to her house, she took me upstairs to the attic and told me I had to stay up there because that was where the ghosts lived in every house."

He brushed another errant strand of hair from her face. "That was cruel of her," he said.

"She said I had been cursed, and she couldn't have me living in her house or she would die, just as my parents had. I told her I wasn't a ghost and I wasn't cursed, that I was a girl. She laughed and said, 'Of course you're cursed.' She took hold of my shoulders and shook me. Her long nails bit into my arms as she said, 'I can see it in your eyes. That's why your life was spared when all the others in the coach were killed.'"

"That makes her more than just a disagreeable old woman, Henrietta. That makes her sound like a wicked witch. How could that man, whoever he was, have left you in the care of someone so insane?"

"Perhaps he didn't know her. I remember I tried

to run away one day, but she caught me before I got out of the house and marched me back up to the attic. That's when she told me that I would have many guardians in my lifetime, but none of them would be with me for long. She said that anyone who had charge over me would die before I left their care, just as my parents had died."

"And you believed her?"

"I don't think I did, not at first. But how could she have known I would have many guardians? My father's will hadn't been read at that time. And it's as if he, too, had some kind of premonition, or why else would he have named so many guardians? Mr. Milton told me it was highly unusual to specify that many guardians in a will."

"I'm sure he just wanted his only child well taken care of, should anything happen to him, and you have been well cared for, haven't you?"

"Yes, except for the short time I was with Mrs. Goolsby."

"So she didn't actually put the curse on you; she just said you were cursed?"

She looked deeply into his eyes. "Yes. It was so long ago, I'm sure I don't remember everything exactly as she said it. I'm telling you the way I remember it."

"I'm sorry you lost your parents when you were so young and in such a horrific manner." He reached down and kissed her softly, briefly on the lips. "You never have to think about that old woman and what she said to you ever again."

Henrietta inhaled deeply, loving the smell of him, the taste of him, and the feel of him so close to her.

"But I do think about what she said, Your Grace. The curse is real, and my fear for your life is great."

Without asking permission, he bent his head and kissed her softly on the lips again. "I want to erase any more thoughts of the past from your mind. Did that help?"

"Yes," she whispered.

She wound her arms around his neck, reached up, and kissed him with all the passion and hunger she was feeling for him. The duke matched her kiss for kiss as he positioned her body so that she was pressed into the hardness of his lap.

He raised his head a little and his eyes questioned her.

Did she want more?

Henrietta's lips found his in an instant. She opened her mouth, and his tongue darted inside to tease hers. His lips moved smoothly, confidently, and effortlessly over hers, and she savored the sweet taste of wine in his kiss as her body melted closer to his. She was swept away with the new sensations twirling and curling inside her.

His hand slid down to her buttocks and cupped her against his hardness. His other hand slid up her waist to cup and caress her breasts. Henrietta gasped at the sheer desire that flooded her entire body. She moaned softly at the exploding pleasure filling her. It was as if she had been yearning for his magical touch since she first saw him.

Henrietta's stomach, her abdomen, and between her legs tightened at the thrilling rush of need cascading through her. Sensations that she had never experienced before shot to the core of her being, and she was filled with a tingling warmth.

Their kisses became more passionate with each second that passed. His tongue lightly stroked in and out of her mouth, teasing her. His kisses filled her with a hunger she didn't understand, but she knew only the duke could satisfy.

His hot, moist lips trailed down her neck and along her chest to the swell of her breasts. His lips and teeth nipped softly at her skin as his hand kneaded her taffeta-covered breast, sending delicious shivers of ecstasy to the center of her womanhood.

With urgency, his hand slipped inside her dress and beneath her undergarment to caress her bare breast. With his thumb and finger, he softly rolled her nipple back and forth, driving her mad with desire.

"I've wanted to touch you like this all evening."

Henrietta wasn't sure if she moaned a "Yes" aloud or in her mind. She only knew she wanted the wonderful feelings the duke was creating inside her to last forever.

Blakewell lifted her breast from the confines of her clothing and covered it with his warm mouth, teasing it and wetting it. Her arms tightened convulsively, and she pressed closer to him.

She felt as if she were ready to explode when suddenly the duke tore his lips away from her breast and buried his face in her chest.

Gasping for breath, he lifted his head and whispered, "We must not do this. You tempt me to the breaking point."

Henrietta felt bereft. She was overflowing with

sensations that needed a release she didn't understand. She didn't want him to stop kissing her, touching her, and making her feel as if she would burst from all the pleasure building inside her.

"Why?" she whispered against a ragged breath.

"I must keep you pure for your husband. I can't let this go any farther between us."

Henrietta went limp. Nothing had changed between them. He still wanted to find her a husband.

"I understand," she said, though it broke her heart to say it. "You are right. I didn't mean to tempt you."

"Don't move," he whispered. "I need to remain in control of myself, and to do that, I need you to be very still."

Not fully understanding, but not needing to, she nodded, sighed, and slowly melted into his strong embrace and went still.

She cupped his head to her chest and ran both her hands through his thick, beautiful hair. She wanted to stay this close to him for as long as he would allow.

Henrietta closed her eyes and gloried in the feel of being so close to the man she loved. As the seconds ticked by, his body relaxed and his breathing slowed to normal. As the minutes ticked by, she once again remembered the fear, the pain, and the desolation she had felt the night the coach toppled end over end down the soggy embankment.

Though she'd never admit it to His Grace or anyone else, there were still times she'd wake in the night silently screaming. She would never forget the horrifying sounds of the splintering wood and the screams of her mother, or her own.

And she would never forget this night when she brought comfort to the duke and, in turn, he held her close, kissed her passionately, and calmed childhood fears that never seemed to go away completely.

Fifteen

IT WAS ALMOST DARK WHEN BLAKE CLIMBED INTO HIS carriage the next day and told his driver to take him to the Harbor Lights Club. He was supposed to meet Gibby for a light supper before returning to his town house to escort Henrietta and Constance to the ball being held at the Great Hall.

There were really only two reasons for London's Season: to see, and to be seen. If a match happened to occur between an eligible gentleman and an expectant young lady, it was considered a successful Season for the couple.

A light rain misted the air, and a heavy chill settled

over London. Spring was late coming to the city. Twilight was just dreary enough to match his mood. He was restless, and he really didn't know why. It was unlike him to be so unsettled. He had always been the most carefree of Lady Elder's grandsons. Responsibility wasn't a word he'd ever paid much attention to, until Henrietta showed up at his door.

He had come so close to saying to hell with convention, to hell with what was right. He had been desperate to take their loving all the way and make her his lover. Fortunately, he had come to his senses in time to stop.

His shoulder felt better today, but there was still enough pain in the joint to let him know it was by no means healed. Blake had spent most of the day in his office attending to his correspondence and the mountain of papers his solicitor had sent for his suggestions, approval, or signature. Fortunately, Henrietta had made the long and tedious task much easier by arranging his mail in order of importance.

She seemed to know what needed immediate attention and what letters were mere idle ramblings that some poor soul wanted him to read. She had even mastered the mountain of invitations he had received by putting them in order of who he least needed to offend by not attending their function, be it a party, a tea, or the opera. Had Constance helped her with that?

Several gentlemen had called on him at different times during the day, obviously wanting to solicit him about Henrietta. He told Ashby to tell them all he wasn't available for a visit but to leave their cards.

He certainly wasn't ready to talk with any man about making a match for Henrietta. Just the thought of that wrenched his gut.

Especially when he saw cards from men like Count Vigone and Lord Snellingly, as if he would ever consider letting her marry either man! Did they think him a dolt? He had heard gossip around the clubs that both men were looking for a wife with a large dowry.

Blake shifted in the carriage seat. Thinking of Henrietta had his loins stirring with desire and longing. Longing? Blake winced. When had he ever longed for a certain woman?

Never!

However wrong or perverted it was, because he was her guardian, he still wanted her. He had desperately wanted to comfort her with all the kisses and loving she'd wanted last night after her tears. But he couldn't take advantage of her when she was so emotional from reliving the tragedy of her parents' deaths. She would have let him, but she was an innocent young lady. He couldn't change that no matter how badly they had both wanted to finish what they had started.

It was a good thing he had been in a hell of a lot of pain last night, or he might not have been able to hold himself in check when he pulled her onto his chair and cradled her in his arms. She had made him desperate to make her his.

He breathed in deeply and remembered the heavenly, womanly scent of her. He smiled just to think about her. It amazed him that he couldn't get her off his mind.

She had felt so good, so right, snuggled warmly against his chest, her legs and stocking-covered feet curled on top of his lower body. When she first lay against him, he felt her breaths coming fast and hard. He could tell she had never been that close to a man's desire before. She didn't understand how close he was to the edge when he asked her to be still. But within moments, she realized he only wanted to hold her close and offer comfort. She had slowly turned her face into the crook of his neck, her body relaxed against him, and her rapid breathing had returned to normal.

Even now he ached to hold her close and pull the tight bud of her breast into his mouth again.

Blake shook his head and stared out the small window into the misty, early evening as the carriage rolled and bumped along the streets. The pane was foggy, but he could see that several businesses had already lit their gaslights for the evening. The rain reminded him of what Henrietta had told him last night about her parents' deaths. What a terrifying ordeal for a child to go through! He had known by the look in her eyes as she related the details of the accident that she was reliving the horror and the terror of that dreadful night.

It was difficult for her to talk about, and he had hated to put her through that, but he needed to understand her fears. He wanted to understand this curse she talked about. Obviously, she was spared in the crash by an act of God when all others, including the horses, were killed. So why would anyone say she was cursed or put a curse on her or her guardians?

One thing was certain, Henrietta was brave, confident, and resilient, even as a little girl. His stomach knotted at the thought of a little blonde-haired girl trying to wake her parents, gathering pieces of a broken carriage in the rain, and wanting to put her life together again.

Henrietta had been so gentle, her hands calming, when she helped him take off his neckcloth and coats. Blake smiled to himself as he remembered every touch. Had she actually hummed a soothing melody for him?

She had known just what he needed to relax and rest his shoulder. When he pulled her into his arms, he had only meant to offer her some of the comfort she'd so generously given to him. He hadn't intended the passion that flared between them. His good sense, along with the wine and the previous sleepless nights, had proved too much for him, and he'd fallen asleep shortly after her breathing slowed to an easy rhythm.

He had no idea how long she had stayed with him or when she had left him. He had awakened in the predawn hours slumped in the chair, covered by his coat, his neck stiff and his arm paining him once again. But what bothered him the most was Henrietta's absence. It made him feel lonely.

That was a new feeling for him. It was as if someone or something was missing in his life. Blake couldn't remember feeling lonely, not even when his parents died. How could he? He was a duke. He was always surrounded by people. He was never alone. But he didn't want just anyone with him. He wanted

Henrietta. He wanted her touch. He wanted to touch her. And worst of all, he wanted to make love to her.

Blake quickly brushed that thought aside. That wasn't a feeling he wanted to examine too closely. Perhaps he wouldn't feel so frustrated, so in need of Henrietta, if he bedded a woman. His time with the tavern wench in the village near Valleydale had been the briefest, most unsatisfying romp he could remember experiencing. Maybe he would have better luck tonight finding a willing widow who would make him forget the growing desire he had for Henrietta. He had to do something since he couldn't seem to find the time to make inquiries about a mistress.

He laid his head against the velvet squabs and let the clinking and clanking of the carriage and the clip-clop of the horses' hooves drown out his thoughts of Henrietta. He had to concentrate on Gibby and his involvement with Mrs. Simple.

Blake looked forward to the quietness and the exclusivity of the private club. It was early enough in the evening that none of the regulars would be around—so, with any luck, he should have plenty of time alone with the old dandy.

A few minutes later, Blake gave a shudder as he shrugged out of his wet cloak and hat and handed them to the servant inside the Harbor Lights Club. Blake walked toward the taproom, thinking a tankard of ale and a bowl of chicken stew sounded good. He stopped in the doorway and saw that Gibby had already arrived, sitting in his usual place by the window and enjoying the last shards of twilight. Blake couldn't help but wonder if Gibby ever felt lonely and, if so, how he handled it. Blake didn't know Gib's exact age, but the man had to be in his seventies.

Gibby had had his share of mistresses over the years, some of them quite famous. There was the gorgeous actress who stunned the audience by waving and blowing him kisses from the stage; King George's scandalous, married cousin who flaunted convention and openly cavorted with Gibby in public; and then Blake's own infamous grandmother, Lady Elder. But even with the excitement that came with those women and others, had he missed not having a wife and children?

Blake walked over, pulled out the chair opposite the old man, and sat down.

"You are late."

Blake frowned. "Am I? I don't think so."

Gibby pointed to the tall clock standing in the far corner. "By half an hour, at least."

"Don't complain, old man. Half an hour is not late."

"It is to anyone but you. Now tell me, did you want me to meet you here so you could mind my business yet again?" Gibby asked.

"Mind your business is exactly what I want to do," Blake said in a matter-of-fact tone. "I've been doing it for so many years that it would be a shame to stop now, don't you think?"

"Not really. Contrary to what Lord Chesterfield said, you can teach an old dog new tricks."

"I'm not so sure the arrogant bastard said that, but if he did, I'm sure he would have finished the quote with, "You're not old, and you're not a dog.""

Gibby grinned. "Well, somebody said it."

"My grandmother always attributed every quote

she ever heard to Chesterfield, and in your old age, I think you've fallen into the habit of doing the same."

"Your grandmother taught me a lot of things. I remember one time we were—"

Blake held up his hand and leaned back in his chair. "Don't go any further. You obviously spent too much time with her when she was alive, and the last thing I want to know is all that she taught you."

Gibby's aged eyes sparkled with memories. "I loved every minute I ever spent with her."

"I have no doubt about that, or about the love she had for you."

Gibby shrugged. "You know, you're intelligent enough to find something better to do with your time than worry about what I'm doing."

"Sure, I could find something better to do, but it wouldn't be as much fun or as time-consuming as aggravating the devil out of you."

"But I'll be glad when it happens. I'm looking forward to some time alone with my own thoughts."

"You wouldn't enjoy it. I've tried to spend time with your thoughts, and they're boring as hell."

They both laughed.

"God loves a simple mind," Gibby quipped.

Blake breathed in deeply. It felt good to banter with the old geezer. "Have you ordered anything yet?"

"No, just got here."

"I thought you said I was late?"

"You were. I was late too, but I still got here before you did."

"Damnation, Gib, I don't know why I bother with you."

"I don't know either, but since I can't get rid of you, what are you drinking?"

"Ale."

Gibby motioned to the server and told him to bring a bottle of champagne and two glasses.

Blake wrinkled his forehead and leaned back in his chair. "I asked for ale, and you order champagne? Proof you are fast losing your sanity."

"Don't get too excited; my mind is splendid. I'm going to propose a toast to the next successful mode of travel, and I need champagne to do it."

Blake tensed. "I think you would have more success with the new steam locomotive George Stephenson is working on at Newcastle than with balloons. Mark my words, Stephenson's invention is an idea that has merit."

Gibby dismissed the idea with a wave of his hand as he said, "He thinks he can power a huge chunk of iron and make it go faster than eight horses. Nothing can go faster than the wind when it starts blowing."

"Stephenson has made great progress."

"So has Mrs. Simple. What did you think of her?"

"I thought her pleasant enough."

"Only pleasant enough?"

"Yes." Blake's eyes narrowed. "Gib, I can only be honest with you. Mrs. Simple is very nice, lovely, in fact; she seems intelligent enough to me, but the idea of ballooning as a way to develop travel is downright ludicrous."

"It's achievable," Gibby argued.

"It's madness."

"It's going to happen."

"You saying it won't make it so," Blake argued.

"Mrs. Simple wants to set up a schedule where she'll have balloons traveling to all of the ten counties nearest London. She figures she'll need at least thirty balloons to get her business started."

"Thirty? Bloody hell, Gib, that is a lot of balloons and will cost a damned fortune."

"Not so many when you think of it as three balloons for each county. They'll only make one trip a day. She needs one for the people, one for their luggage, and an extra in case one is broken and unable to go up."

"You mean in case one of them crashes?"

"No, I don't mean that at all. I mean in case the fabric gets ripped or something like that happens."

"This worries me, Gibby."

"I know it does. But you saw the way Henrietta loved floating above the trees, high in the sky. I think all women are going to enjoy it and appreciate that it's faster than a coach."

"I still say it's too risky. There is no way you could get enough people interested in flying to run a business of ballooning people from London to other villages and counties. And at best, you can only do it a few months out of the year because of the weather."

"You are just a naysayer."

"Damnation, Gibby, I'm trying to find out if the woman's just trying to get her hands on your money and abscond to who-knows-where with it, or if she is foolish enough to truly believe she can make a prosperous venture out of this preposterous idea."

"If I didn't know you so well, I'd take offense at what you just said."

Blake sighed, realizing he had sounded angry. He wasn't. "You know I mean no offense to you. Will you give us more time to look further into this before you give her any money?"

"I'll hold off a little longer, but I must help her. I gave my word."

"I know. But, there's no hurry, is there? I mean if she's legitimate?"

"Well, you know what Lord Chesterfield said: 'Time can be a blessing or a curse, depending on how you use it, wisely or foolishly.'"

Blake knew that only too well.

"The balloons have to be made, and that takes time. Mrs. Simple only has the two at the barn. She's afraid someone else might hear of her plans and start a business before she has time to do it. There's no room for competition in this business."

Blake sat back in his chair and laughed. The thought that someone might steal this idea was just too humorous.

"I know you get yourself wrapped up in ridiculous projects like this just so one of my grandmother's grandsons will bail you out."

Gibby smiled. "Yes, I have nothing better to do than be looked after by you fools."

"Tell Mrs. Simple I'm convinced she doesn't have to worry about anyone stealing this idea from her. Balloons have been around for close to fifty years now. If it was a good and safe mode of mass travel, someone would have started a ballooning company years ago."

"Well, now, I'm not so sure about that. Mrs. Simple said a man came snooping around her barn a couple of days ago, asking her workers a lot of questions about the balloon."

That didn't worry Blake. He was sure it must have been someone sent there by Race or Morgan. "It was probably just someone interested in the novelty of ballooning."

The servant approached and set an open bottle of champagne and two crystal glasses on the table in front of them. He poured the bubbly liquid into each glass. After the server left, Blake and Gibby raised their glasses to each other.

"To the next successful mode of mass travel," Gibby said with a wide, confident smile.

Blake smiled and lifted his glass. "And may that be the locomotive engine that's showing great promise in Newcastle."

They laughed and sipped the champagne.

"Excuse me, Your Grace."

Blake looked up to see Lord Waldo Rockcliffe standing beside him, looking as if he might shake right out of his shiny, black knee boots.

Lord Waldo bowed. The man was so thin that Blake wondered if he would snap when he bent forward. Both Blake and Gibby rose from the table and greeted him.

"I'm sorry to disturb your evening, Your Grace, Sir Randolph, but I saw you over here and didn't want to pass on the opportunity presented to me."

Blake and Gibby remained silent. Blake wasn't sure what opportunity he was referring to.

Lord Waldo's light brown eyes twitched nervously, and his pale lips had a slight tremor. "I'd like you to consider me for the honor of marrying Miss Tweed."

That will be a cold day in hell.

"Would you allow me to come to your home, Your Grace, and formally ask for her hand?"

"Lord Waldo," Blake said as calmly as he could when all he wanted to do was grind his teeth together at the thought of this man with Henrietta. "Miss Tweed just made her debut last night. At this point, I'm not prepared to consider any proposal for her hand from anyone. She will need time to enjoy some of the Season and consider all the bachelors who hold her interest."

"I suspected that, Your Grace, but I wanted to be the first to make my intentions known to you. I intend to charm her, court her, and make her fall in love with me."

That will be another cold day in hell.

Blake thought of all the calling cards he'd received since word first leaked that he had a ward of marriageable age. Lord Waldo was shaking so badly that Blake decided not to tell him that more than two-dozen better men had already come asking about Henrietta. Waldo had a mighty long line to stand in.

"You, of course, are free to do all those things within the proper bounds of what is expected."

Lord Waldo bowed again. "Thank you, Your Grace. I'll be happy to be at your service whenever you wish. Again, I apologize for interrupting your evening." He looked at Gibby. "Sir Randolph, it's always good to see you."

Lord Waldo walked away. Blake and Gibby sat back down and picked up their champagne.

Blake took a long drink and then said, "Does that

fop really think he has a chance in hell of winning Henrietta's hand?"

"Sounds to me like he does."

"I'd sooner cut off my right foot than let that happen."

Gibby chuckled. "He has always seemed to be something of a weak-kneed ninny. In fact, I think this is the first time I've ever seen him without Rockcliffe."

"You're right. They are always together. I guess that means the Duke is somewhere here in the club."

"By the way, do you still detest the man?"

"Immensely."

"Hmmm. Too bad the popinjay doesn't know he doesn't have a chance in Hades with the lovely miss."

"Not a chance in hell."

"So tell me, how is the lovely Henrietta?"

Perfect.

"I'm sure she's fine. I haven't seen her today as Constance keeps her busy."

"There does seem to be quite a furor over the young lady. Have you checked on the wager at White's?"

"No."

"Did you read what the gossip sheets said about her today?"

Blake held his face as expressionless as if he was playing cards with Rockcliffe. "No."

"I guess you've been too busy with my life to worry about the life of your ward?"

Blake smiled. "You are such a bastard sometimes, Gib."

"It keeps me healthy."

"I've bet on my share of distasteful wagers at White's too many times to count, but the one concerning Henrietta is off limits to all of us. And you know I never read the scandal sheets."

"Not reading them was understandable when you were always in them, but with your ward in them, you need to give them close scrutiny."

"Why?"

"You know Lord Chesterfield said, 'There's always a grain of truth to every rumor.'"

"The hell he did."

"Well, somebody said it. You need to read the gossip pages because they will enlighten you."

"And I need that?"

"You can find out what other people are saying about her, and who she's really interested in, by reading the tittle-tattle in the newsprint."

"I consider it useless blather."

Blake poured more champagne into their glasses and, out of the corner of his eye, he saw two gentlemen in the far corner chatting and looking his way. No doubt, they wanted to come speak to him about Henrietta, too.

Blake sighed. "Maybe Henrietta's guardians *are* cursed. I've had little peace in my life since she arrived."

"What are you talking about?"

"I don't think I've ever told you, but Henrietta thinks her previous guardians were cursed, and that now I am. And with all the things in my life that have changed since I met her, I'm beginning to think there may be some truth to that curse. I haven't had a peaceful night's sleep since she got here."

"The sleepless nights I understand, but what the devil are you talking about a curse?" Gibby asked.

"I'm not sure I understand the whole story of how it came about, but Henrietta believes someone put a curse on her guardians and that's why all five of them have died in the past twelve years. Of course, she believes I'm part of that curse and next on the list to die. I've tried to tell her there is no such thing as a curse."

"Of course there is," Gibby said.

Blake gave him a look of disbelief. "Don't tell me you believe in all that hocus-pocus stuff?"

"Sure I do. I've known plenty of people in my time who were cursed in one way or another."

"How many do you know who have been given the curse of death?"

"There have been some. It all depends on what you believe. If someone believes a death curse has been put on him, he will die. On the other hand, you can't curse someone who doesn't believe in them."

"And how do you know this?"

"It was told to me by a woman who claimed she was a witch."

Blake smiled. "I've known plenty of witches, but not one who could conjure a spell and make it work."

Blake and Gibby laughed.

"I've been cursed, myself a time or two," Gibby said proudly.

"You don't think I'm going to fall for that story, do you?"

"It's true. I believe your grandmother must have

cursed me, because after I met her, I never wanted another woman the way I wanted her."

Gibby's words caused Henrietta's face to flash before his mind's eye. He saw her as she was last night with her head thrown back, eyes closed, the smile of wonder on her lips, while he kissed the slender column of her throat all the way down to the soft, shapely mound of her breast.

"Excuse us, Your Grace."

Slowly, Blake turned around and saw the two gentlemen he'd seen talking in the far corner of the taproom.

He held up his hand to stop them before they had opportunity to say more. "Don't tell me; you're sorry for interrupting me, but you want to make known your intentions to charm, court, and win the hand of my ward, Miss Henrietta Tweed."

The two men looked at each other in astonishment.

"It's the curse," Gibby said with a grin.

"You might be on to something, Gib," Blake said, and they both started laughing.

Sixteen

My Faithful Grandson Lucien,

Study on this from Lord Chesterfield: "In the course of the world, a man must very often put on an easy, frank countenance upon very disagreeable occasions; he must seem pleased when he is very much otherwise; he must be able to accost and receive with smiles those whom he would much rather meet with swords."

Your loving Grandmother,
Lady Elder

THE GREAT HALL GLIMMERED WITH LIGHTS FROM thousands of candles, or so it seemed to Henrietta as she stood at the entrance to the famed building with its twelve Corinthian columns lining the main ballroom. Blakewell and Constance were taking care of their wraps while she stood in awe of the chandeliers and wall sconces, radiating with extraordinary light and giving the room a breathtaking gleam.

The room was spectacularly decorated with flowers of every size, shape, and color, arranged in large pots, wound around the columns, and dripping from the ceiling. Henrietta had no idea where they found so many fresh flowers so early in the spring season. At one side of the room stood three long tables, each one filled with fancy silver trays loaded with such delicacies as chilled oysters, fowl baked in figs, lamb cooked in plum gravy, preserved apples, and pears simmered in a brandy sauce.

Her mouth watered at the sight of the delicious food spread before her, but she wouldn't sample the first taste. Constance had, once again, insisted she dine at home. That was a puzzle to Henrietta when the food was such a lavish production at both the parties she'd been to.

Sparkling champagne glasses were lined up ready to be filled and served. The violinist, cellist, and flutist played a lively tune, and the dance floor was overflowing with colorfully dressed ladies and finely dressed gentlemen swinging, twirling, and clapping as they moved about the room in time with the music.

Henrietta was still awed by the opulence of all the houses and buildings she had been in since arriving in London. The people in the quiet villages where she had grown up truly had no idea of the grandeur of the houses, the fancy details of the clothing, or the extravagance of the parties held by London's elite Society.

She noticed that Blakewell seemed to be in considerably less pain than during the previous evening. He had appeared more calm and relaxed on their short drive to the Great Hall. That pleased her. Though she had loved every moment of caring for him, she didn't relish seeing him in pain.

As they walked toward the champagne table, she glanced at the duke, and love for him swelled in her heart. She had realized she loved him last night and that she desired him tremendously.

She wanted to do things for him. She couldn't wait to see him. She wanted to be with him. It had to be love that she was feeling.

A stabbing pain pierced her chest as they stopped at the drink table. But he didn't love her. He wanted her to marry another man, not him. And she must marry soon. His life was in danger because of her. No matter what he thought, the curse on her guardians was real. He could only be saved by relinquishing her guardianship. And marriage to another man would do that.

Blake handed a glass of champagne to Henrietta and one to Constance before taking one for himself. He thought Henrietta looked sad; though she smiled at him, there was a hint of anguish to it.

"Now, Your Grace," Constance said, " tell me who would you most like to see Henrietta dance with first this evening, and I'll arrange it."

No one but me.

He took a sip of his drink and glanced from Constance to Henrietta. "I will leave it up to Henrietta as to whom she chooses to dance with."

"Thank you for that option, Your Grace."

"I'm certain she won't have to wait long for a request to dance." Constance turned to Henrietta. "Of all the gentlemen you met last evening, who caught your fancy?"

None had caught her fancy.

Henrietta hesitated, trying to figure out a way to sidestep Constance's direct question.

"The choice is an easy one. I shall dance with the first gentleman who asks me."

Constance gave her an approving smile. "That is always the best thing for a young lady to do at a ball. And you said it just in time," Constance added. "I see the first gentleman is on his way. I can tell by the way he's walking that he is headed straight for Henrietta. And I have no doubt that every bachelor here tonight will want her to save him a dance on her card."

"Good evening, Your Grace, Mrs. Pepperfield, Miss Tweed," Lord Snellingly said as he bowed low before kissing first Constance's and then Henrietta's hand. "Might I say that both you ladies look exceptionally lovely tonight."

"Thank you, Lord Snellingly," Constance said.

Henrietta remembered meeting Lord Snellingly the previous night. The man was tall, slim, and quite handsome in a classic way, but looking at him, she felt none of the butterfly sensations in her stomach, weak knees, or fluttering in her chest that she experienced when she looked at the duke.

Lord Snellingly stepped closer to her. "After meeting you last evening, Miss Tweed, I was inspired to write you a poem." He unfolded a piece of parchment and looked at Blakewell. "With His Grace's permission, of course, I'd like to read it to you."

The duke's brow furrowed deeply. "I don't think this is the place for poetry reading, Snellingly," he said.

"It's only three lines, Your Grace, and I'll say it quickly."

"Henrietta?" His Grace asked.

She stood very still. She wasn't sure she liked the idea that this man had written her a poem, and she was certain she didn't like the fact he wanted to read it to her in front of the duke and Constance. But she must look for a husband, so she had to consider every man a possibility.

If she couldn't have Blakewell, the man she loved and wanted, would it matter who she married?

"Very well," she finally said. "Since it's a short poem, please go ahead."

The man smiled gratefully at the duke and then turned his attention to Henrietta.

"The sun cannot outshine the light in my love's eyes.
"When she looks at me, darkness never falls.
"I am drawn to her the way a baby bird's chirp
draws his mother back to the nest."

Henrietta smiled at the man. "Thank you, Lord Snellingly, that was lovely."

Lord Snellingly beamed at her praise. "It is easy to write poetry for someone as beautiful as you, Miss Tweed." He turned to Blakewell and said, "With your permission, Your Grace, may I have this dance with Miss Tweed?"

"No way in hell" was Blake's first thought, but he saw Henrietta smiling at the man. He guessed she could consider the man handsome, but had she really fallen for that poetry blather?

Blake nodded to Snellingly and quietly watched as he walked away with Henrietta. A knot formed in Blake's chest, and he felt as if his stomach had flipped over. He had seldom experienced what he was feeling, but he knew what it was.

He was jealous. Damned jealous.

He found that unbelievable. He had never been

jealous over a woman in his life, but what else could it be? He didn't want any man touching Henrietta, not even to dance with her. What kind of hold did she have on him?

"She's handling herself very well," Constance said, breaking into Blake's thoughts.

"I knew she would," Blake answered, hoping his newly discovered feelings didn't show on his face.

"Is it me, or was that the worst poem you have ever heard?" Blake asked Constance.

"Lest you forget, Blake, I'm a woman. I've heard some very bad poetry through the years from beaux trying to impress me, but I admit that none of it comes close to being as bad as what we just heard. Now tell me, Blake, surely you have been thinking of someone who might be a good match for Henrietta. If you will let me know of your choice matrimonial candidates for her, I'll guide her in their direction."

He ignored her statement and said, "Tell me what is being said about her in the gossip sheets." Blake wouldn't give Gibby the satisfaction of asking him about it, but he wanted to know.

Constance sipped her champagne and then said, "Mostly good things."

"Mostly?"

"Yes, there is the usual nattering about her beauty, wit, and charm. Unfortunately, Lord Truefitt's "Daily Society Column" is reporting you are desperate to make a match for her so you can be rid of her as quickly as possible because she is a burden to your carefree life."

"Damnation," he whispered under his breath.

That might have been true when she first arrived, but it was no longer the case. She was growing on him. He actually liked knowing she was in his house and under his protection.

"My fear is that it will make inappropriate and unworthy men think they can pursue her hand."

Hence, the many calling cards from men he didn't know as well as advances from the likes of Lord Snellingly, Lord Waldo, and Count Vigone.

"How did something like that get started?"

"Who knows how anything gets started with the gossipmongers? But good will come from the bad, and it will all equal out," she smiled sweetly at him. "Between the scandal sheets, the wager at White's, and her being your ward, she has easily become the most popular young lady of the Season. Surely you've had inquiries about her."

"I have been inundated with men I know and men I don't know and don't care to know, all wanting to make their intentions known that they plan to ask for Henrietta's hand. Even if I wanted her to marry in haste, what would make the lot of them think I would not be very selective in whom I allow her to marry?"

"Come now, Blake, a chance is all they are looking for. What could be better for them? She has her pick of London's finest gentlemen. Surely there will be one who catches her attention and of whom you will approve. And the tittle-tattle is right, isn't it?"

"What's that?"

"The sooner the better, as far as you are concerned?"

Blake looked out over the dance floor and spotted

Henrietta dancing. His breath quickened just looking at her.

"Perhaps that was true when I first spoke to you, Constance, but not anymore. I'm in no hurry to find Henrietta a husband."

"I see," she said coolly, and then added, "However, it's no wonder every eligible man is prepared to try his luck at winning her hand. She is quite a catch, Blake. Beautiful, charming, and intelligent, and everyone knows you will bestow a wealthy dowry on her. She's definitely the diamond of the Season."

"I know."

Constance smiled at him, and Blake remembered why he was once attracted to her. She was enticing. He needed a woman to help him forget his craving for Henrietta, but his desire for Constance had long passed. She would be of no help to him in that way.

Blake returned Constance's smile, and then picked up another glass of champagne.

After more than two hours of watching Henrietta enjoy herself on the dance floor with so many men he'd lost count, Blake walked outside the front of the building for some fresh air. The flames from all of the candles and the crush of people had the Great Hall hot and confining, even though the night air had a chill to it.

The fog and mist were clearing, and he could see the light from the streetlamps in the distance. Maybe the downpours were finally leaving London. It had been wet for days. He stood just under the portico, breathing in deeply the cool, damp air. It felt good to be outside. It was making him crazy watching Henrietta dance, smile, and talk to all those fops gathered around her like yapping dogs. She was in demand, no doubt about that, but he hadn't thought one of the men pursuing her tonight was worthy of her hand. He blew out his breath in a huff. She had more than enough confidence to send most of those men scurrying away in a panic if they ever got into a verbal confrontation with her.

Earlier in the evening, Lady Houndslow had approached him, giving him a come-hither look meant to entice him straight into her bed, and at first he had given the idea considerable thought. But, after spending only a few minutes with her, Blake had no inclination to visit her, and he was more than happy he hadn't spent the afternoon with her before his trip to Valleydale with his cousins.

Blake had no doubt she would have agreed if he had asked to come to her bedchamber later tonight, but as soon as he could respectfully do so, he took his leave from her.

He wanted a rendezvous with a desirable woman to take his mind off Henrietta, but Lady Houndslow wasn't the woman to do it. An even bigger problem was that when he had looked at all the ladies in the ballroom, he didn't see a single one that he wanted to take to his bed.

Had Henrietta ruined him for all other women?

Blake needed to get away from the sound of the

music and revelry coming from inside the Great Hall, so he stepped off the portico into the darkness. At the bottom of the steps, something sharp scraped deep into the side of his head over his left temple, and he jerked back.

"Damnation," he muttered and looked up. He saw that a piece of iron had rusted and fallen down from the covered archway on the landing. In the darkness, he hadn't seen it. Grabbing hold of it, he yanked the bar down and threw it into the shrubs. It wouldn't catch any other unsuspecting person.

Blake grimaced and put his hand to the wound. It felt wet and sticky. He pulled his handkerchief from his pocket and dabbed at the bleeding injury.

"You're brooding, aren't you?"

Blake spun around at the sound of Morgan's voice. He slipped the soiled handkerchief into his pocket. "I'm in no mood for lectures, Cousin."

"I don't intend to give you any."

"Good."

"If you want, I'll leave you to sulk in private."

"Blast it," Blake exclaimed. "I'm not sulking or brooding, and you don't have to leave."

"All right, what are you doing standing outside all by yourself, staring into the mist like you've lost your best friend, or should I say your lover?"

"I'm getting some fresh air. It's damned hot in there."

"You wouldn't be so hot if you hadn't stood in there like a lost pup and steamed over every man that Henrietta danced with."

Damnation, Morgan saw too much. He always

had. Blake hoped he hadn't been that obvious to anyone else.

"I'm fine," is all Blake felt compelled to say.

"So nothing is bothering you?"

Morgan wasn't going to let it go, but Blake wasn't going to acknowledge Morgan's curiosity.

"Nothing," Blake lied. He hated doing it, but there were just some things he couldn't share with his cousin. What he was feeling for Henrietta was one of them. He was still trying to figure it out himself.

"Perhaps there is something to that curse she talked about when she first arrived. She's gotten to you, hasn't she? You haven't been able to take your eyes off Henrietta all night."

Blake swallowed his angry retort and, in a calm voice, said, "There is no curse, but since you're here, why don't you tell me what you've found out about Mrs. Simple and her balloons."

"That's a good, safe subject to change to," Morgan remarked.

Blake remained silent.

"All right, my man can't find one person in London who is interested in ballooning as a form of travel. Most of the men he talked to don't even care for it as recreation. Mrs. Simple seems to be the only person in London, other than Gibby, who appreciates ballooning."

"That is just as we suspected. What about Race—has he found out anything about Mrs. Simple's past?"

"I see him walking toward us. Let's ask him."

"Did I miss getting the signal, or are you two trying to have a secret meeting without me?" Race asked as he joined them. "It's a good thing I saw you coming out here. What's going on that I was going to be left out of?"

"I thought Blake was brooding, so I followed him out here to see what was bothering him."

"He was definitely brooding about Henrietta," Race said.

Blake swore under his breath. Damn his cousins and their meddling.

"Apparently not," Morgan answered. "The only thing he wants to talk about is Gibby, Mrs. Simple, and hot-air balloons."

"Figures. I'd probably say that, too, if I were in his dancing shoes. But, speaking of the old dandy, it just so happens that I heard back today from the man who was making inquiries for me about Mrs. Simple."

"What did he say?" Morgan asked.

"So far he hasn't found anything sinister in her past. Seems she was married to a tradesman who was always inventing things and trying to sell them. Everyone he talked to who knew Mr. Simple respected him and his wife, too. The fellow died a couple of years ago. He left Mrs. Simple a small amount of money and two balloons. This idea of using a hot-air balloon like a coach was his idea, and she has taken up the venture since he died."

"How noble," Morgan said dryly.

"And touching," Race added, "and all the more reason for Gib to want to help her. She has asked others to help finance this project. So far, my man hasn't found anyone who has agreed to give her money."

"So she really thinks she can make this business fly?" Blake asked.

Morgan and Race looked at each other and started laughing. Blake was puzzled for a moment until he realized what he had said, and then he laughed, too. Leave it to his cousins to make him laugh when it was the last thing he felt like doing.

"All right, enough making fun of me," Blake said after their laughter died down. "How do we keep Gib from putting money into this scheme since we can't prove Mrs. Simple has anything more sinister up her sleeve than just a dumb idea?"

"We'll leave that to you to handle however you see fit," Race said. "Sound good to you, Morgan?"

"Sounds very good to me."

"Cowards," Blake muttered good-naturedly.

"We just think you need something to think about other than Henrietta. You're becoming a bore."

Blake grinned. "And you two are becoming obnoxious fools."

Blake spent a few more minutes outside with his cousins before going back inside the Great Hall. He glanced around the perimeter of the dance floor, searching for Henrietta or Constance, but didn't see either of them. Walking farther into the room, he looked over to the dance floor and saw Henrietta.

His blood turned cold in his veins. She was dancing with Lord Waldo Rockcliffe. He was the last person Blake wanted her dancing with. They stood in a long line and held hands with their arms in the air, forming a canopy for other couples to dance under. All Blake could think was that he didn't want that bufflehead, hobbledehoy touching her. Blake had to restrain himself from rushing over and pulling her out of his grasp.

It gave Blake the shivers to see Lord Waldo dancing with Henrietta and touching her hands, even though she wore gloves. He would just as soon see her with Rockcliffe himself or the fake Count Vigone.

Blake was conflicted. It was so unlike him to care this much about someone. Never before had he minded sharing a woman's affections with another man.

As soon as Henrietta came off the dance floor, they were heading home. He had had all he could take for one night of her charming other men.

While Henrietta finished the dance that seemed to be going on forever, Blake picked up their wraps, called for his carriage, found Constance, and informed her they were leaving.

By the time Lord Waldo walked Henrietta over to him, Blake was calmer, but no less seething with jealousy.

Lord Waldo thanked her for the dance and then turned to Blake and said, "Your Grace, might I have permission to take Miss Tweed for a ride in Hyde Park tomorrow afternoon?"

Blake couldn't believe the man actually had enough courage to ask, and from the way the poor devil was shaking, it took every ounce he had. It was on the tip of Blake's tongue to say, 'No way in hell, you bloody bastard. Get your mucky hands off her and keep them off,' but instead, he stopped himself and studied the trembling sap with the pale brown eyes and pallid skin.

Henrietta was probably safer with Lord Waldo than Lord Snellingly, Count Vigone, or anyone else. Surely, she couldn't be interested in this man as a husband.

"Very well," Blake said. "A short ride, if Miss Tweed agrees."

And consider yourself one damned lucky man!

Henrietta looked at Lord Waldo and said, "That would be lovely." She turned to Constance and asked, "Will we be finished with all we have to do by half past three?"

Constance smiled at her and said, "We'll make sure that we are, my dear."

"Good, it's settled. I'll see you tomorrow," Henrietta said to Lord Waldo.

Lord Waldo said his good-byes and walked away with lightness in his step that set Blake's teeth on edge. Did that fool really think he had caught Henrietta's fancy? There was no way in hell Blake would believe that. She was too intelligent, too passionate, and much too strong to be attracted to him.

Henrietta had something up her sleeve. He was sure of it.

A few minutes later, they were in the carriage and on their way to take Constance home. Blake listened quietly as Constance and Henrietta talked about the different gentlemen she had danced with throughout the evening. His ears perked up when Constance asked specifically about Lord Waldo Rockcliffe.

"I accepted his invitation to ride in the park simply because he was the first person to ask me," Henrietta said, "just as Lord Snellingly was the first gentleman to ask me to dance this evening."

Blake smiled, feeling quite smug about her answer, until a terrifying thought entered his mind. What if Henrietta decided to marry the first man who asked her?

"Did you find him attractive?" Constance asked.

"Hmm. Yes."

Attractive? Lord Waldo? Really?

Blake cut his eyes around to Henrietta. She was in the darkest part of the carriage so he couldn't see her face very well.

"But not more so than all the other gentlemen I danced with. He has a nervous, boyish charm about him that's quite engaging."

Engaging? Lord Waldo? Would she marry him, if he was the first to ask her?

That thought caused Blake to sit up a little straighter.

"Since it's my job to guide you, Henrietta, I will say that, as the younger brother of a duke, Lord Waldo would be a splendid match for you. You and your children would always live well. But, truthfully, he seems much too immature for you. You are very, shall we say, confident, and he is lacking in that area. I feel that, over time, you might find him too weak for you."

Hear, hear, Constance. I know she will.

"There is something to be said for a husband who is malleable, is there not?" Henrietta asked.

Constance looked over at Blake. He had a feeling they were thinking the same thing. Was Lord Waldo exactly the kind of husband Henrietta was looking for—someone she could mold to her own wishes and ideas?

"You are right," Constance said. "Your answer proves my point. You are much too clever for a gentleman such as Lord Waldo, my dear. But look, we've arrived at my house. We will continue this discussion at a later time. I think you will see my point once you've had an afternoon ride in the park with him."

They said their good nights, and Blake helped Constance down from the carriage and walked her to her door. Before he climbed back inside the cab, he told his driver to take the long way home and not to stop at the town house until he was given the signal to do so.

Blake sat down beside Henrietta, rather than on the seat opposite her. He needed to be close to her. He had watched men hold her hand all evening. No doubt all of them squeezed her fingers affectionately, innocently let their fingers glide down her arms, or took other liberties when they danced with her. Blake knew all the tricks a man would try when he thought other eyes weren't watching.

Blake intended to touch her now and erase the memory of all the other men from her thoughts.

The light in the carriage was damn poor. He could see very little of her face, but he could smell the soft womanly scent of her, and he felt her feminine warmth. He stared at her in the darkness and all his built-up apprehension from the events of the evening washed out of him.

He was alone with Henrietta, and that is exactly what he had wanted all evening, to be totally alone with this beautiful, tempting woman.

Her hair was arranged beautifully on top of her head with a delicate pink ribbon woven through her golden curls. The diamonds and pearls that dripped from her ears sparkled and glimmered in the dim light from the lantern outside the carriage. He knew that a single strand of pearls graced her neck, though he couldn't see them for the fur around the collar of her cape.

The footman had kept the cab warm with a bucket of hot coals, and the gentle rocking of the carriage as it rolled along the streets was soothing. There was a dull ache in his shoulder and the side of his head where he'd scraped it earlier, but it wasn't enough pain to keep him from wanting to pull Henrietta into his arms and kiss her. He was hungry for the drugging taste of her again.

The only reason Blake could think that he wanted her so badly was because she should be off-limits to him. She was his ward. Forbidden fruit. But such tempting fruit.

"How many men did you dance with tonight?" he asked as casually as possible, considering how tightly he was strung.

"Perhaps eight or ten," she answered just as casually.

"How about twelve?"

She smiled up at him and his heart fluttered.

She laughed softly. "No, I'm sure it wasn't that many."

"Probably more. I don't think you missed a dance."

"I did try to accommodate all those who asked."

"And you adored the attention from all of them, didn't you?"

"Adored is not quite the right word. I accepted the attentions I received tonight."

"Did any of them squeeze your fingers or let their fingers glide down your arms?

"That's more than I want to answer, Your Grace."

"I know the answer."

And it drove me mad!

"Perhaps now I can show you attention."

"I would like that—Your Grace!" she exclaimed. "You're bleeding!"

Blake swore, and dug into his pocket for his handkerchief. "Sorry about that. It's just a little scratch."

"It's not bleeding like a simple scratch. What happened?"

He pressed the handkerchief to the wound. "It's nothing to be alarmed about. An iron bar was hanging down from an archway, and in the darkness I didn't see it. I scraped my head as I walked by."

"How many more mishaps will you have before you believe that your life is in danger as long as you are my guardian?"

Blake sighed. "Henrietta, I lead an active life. I agree it seems as though too many things have happened to me since you arrived, but that is only because you make us so aware of them. They are only little ordinary things that happen to everyone."

She took the handkerchief from him and softly wiped beside his ear. "Lean down and let me take a closer look at it. It might need to be stitched if it continues to bleed."

"There is no need to look at it. I am fine."

She pressed the handkerchief to the wound again.

"Your touch is gentle, Henrietta. I find that I like you more with every little mishap."

"The poisonous mushroom was not a little thing. The dislocated shoulder was not a little thing." Her eyes searched his with tenderness. "Don't you understand how I worry about you?"

"I'm beginning to." He took the handkerchief from her and put it back in his pocket.

He wanted to kiss her, nothing more. Just kisses, he swore to himself as he dipped his head low and covered her mouth with his.

Her lips were warm, soft, and inviting as they pressed against his in a slow lingering kiss that he was reluctant to break. She tasted of champagne and smelled of spring. He didn't want to rush this exploration of desire with Henrietta, but his body was hungry for her. He deepened the kiss, and he loved it when she responded by instinct and parted her lips for him. His tongue darted inside her mouth and explored its depths with slow sensual movements.

Desire grew inside him. He had to have a little more than kisses.

He tugged on the ribbon of her fur-lined cape and pushed it off her shoulders with eager hands, exposing her lovely pearl-draped neck, softly rounded shoulders, and the tempting swell of her breasts to his view.

Blake stared down at her loveliness. "Do you trust me not to hurt you?" His voice sounded far huskier than he intended.

She touched his cheek. "I know you will not hurt me. I would trust you with my life."

He reached over and kissed her slender, beautiful

neck and buried his nose in its softness. She reached up and wrapped her arms around his back, and he seemed to melt into the warmth of her exciting body.

His lips found hers and kissed their way down her cheek, over her jawline to her neck, sending little shivers of exhilaration popping out all over her skin. At the touch of his moist lips upon the fullness of her breasts, her breaths jumped erratically.

Blake grabbed hold of the bit of lace on her dress and her undergarment and pulled it down, exposing her breast. His mouth covered her nipple quickly, eagerly. He heard a contented groan but didn't know if it came from him or Henrietta. His tongue flicked and played with her nipple as she squirmed and moaned beneath his touch.

Blake could hardly keep himself in check. He had wanted to caress her breasts all day. He sucked and filled himself with the taste of her.

She arched her back and gave him ample access. He fed upon her as his body throbbed, begging him to take more of her for his own.

He only knew that being with her like this, wanting her for himself, felt right. It felt natural, and he didn't want that feeling to go away. He wanted to act on it.

A tremor of desire shook her body and Blake smiled. She was as affected by him as he was by her. That thrilled him immensely. And as much as he wanted, needed, to make her his, he couldn't.

Leaving her breast moist from his tongue, he brushed her lips with his, easing over them with the lightest contact. She opened her mouth and playfully caught his bottom lip with her teeth. His tongue thrust in deeply, sipping from her mouth. They teased each other with nips and kisses. With a loving hand, he raked his fingers down her rib cage and over her slim womanly hip and shapely thigh to press her tightly against his hardness.

He had to fight the temptation to continue and make her his.

Blake raised his head. His gaze swept down her face to her beautiful breast spread before him. Once again, he felt that unexpected longing for her. He felt something for her that went deeper than it ever had with any other woman, and he was troubled by it.

His voice sounded husky and raw as he said, "You are so tempting, my beautiful Henrietta."

"Thank you," she answered just as huskily as their eyes met and held.

He pulled himself away from her and straightened in the seat. Blake forced his rigid body to relax. Calmly, he said, "You are inquisitive and eager for my touch and all that I can teach you."

"Yes," she whispered.

"I like that." He pulled up the straps to her bodice, and then wrapped her cape around her shoulders as he said, "But I cannot teach you any more than I already have. That will be for your husband to do."

She sat up straight and said, "Yes, of course. I understand."

"Do you still want the attention of Lord Waldo?" Blake asked.

"No, I mean, yes. I mean, I can't answer that right now, Your Grace. I find that I am confused by my feelings."

So am I.

"Perhaps it's a good idea for you to reconsider and think a little longer before you decide you want to marry someone as malleable as Waldo."

She glanced at him. "Why?"

"I don't think there is any passion in him, while you are full of it."

Henrietta retied the ribbons of her cape into a bow. "I have very little knowledge of passion, Your Grace. I'm skeptical as to whether you are qualified to instruct me concerning it."

He chuckled. "Ah, but I have a lot of knowledge of passion. And believe me, passion is something you would not want to live without."

"Then perhaps I should consider Lord Snellingly as a suitable husband. He is handsome, he compliments me on my beauty, and he writes the most extraordinary poetry. He must be full of passion."

"Ha!" Blake muttered annoyingly. Sometimes Henrietta was just too intelligent for her own good. "Words on a piece of parchment or rhymes tumbled from the tongue are not passion."

"Perhaps I need to learn that for myself. I think I shall let Lord Snellingly know I would welcome a visit from him."

"You are a menace to my sanity, Henrietta."

She leaned against the cushion and stared straight ahead. "I was just thinking the same thing about you."

Blake reached up with his fist and knocked the roof of the cab twice, signaling the driver to take them home.

Seventeen

Lucien, My Dearest Grandson,

Read well these words of Lord Chesterfield and remember them: "The character which most young men first aim at is that of a man of pleasure, and pleasure is the rock which most young people split upon."

Your loving Grandmother,
Lady Elder

HENRIETTA SAT ON THE SETTEE IN THE DRAWING ROOM with Constance by her side and Lord Waldo in the melon-colored chair to her left. A huge bouquet of pink and white Persian lilies lay on the small table in front of her, a gift from Lord Waldo. She was surprised and disappointed that the duke wasn't present for her visit with Lord Waldo before the two of them left for their carriage ride in Hyde Park.

Constance had reminded Henrietta not to sit too close to Lord Waldo on the carriage seat and never to let his leg touch hers or even come in contact with her skirts while they were riding. If he should try to steal a kiss from her at any time during the afternoon, she was to avoid it if possible, but if she couldn't, she was to make sure the kiss landed on her cheek and not her lips.

Henrietta had already considered that possibility and decided that, should Lord Waldo try to kiss her, she would let him. She wanted to know if another man's kiss would bring her the exquisite pleasure and wonderful excitement she felt with Blakewell's kiss.

The night before, she had realized that she needed to get serious about deciding on a man to marry, and she had to do it quickly. The duke might not believe in the curse that had claimed the lives of her previous guardians, but Henrietta did. Too many things had happened to him since she had arrived. The next incident might take his life, and while the duke was willing to take that chance, she wasn't. She must free His Grace from the curse.

She had taken special care when arranging her hair and dressing for the day, not for Lord Waldo, but because she wanted to please His Grace. She wore a blush-colored dress trimmed with delicate white lace around the neckline and the capped sleeves. She would don a matching, long-sleeved pelisse that buttoned high up her throat before she went out for the carriage ride.

"And what is your age, Lord Waldo?" Constance asked.

"Twenty-eight last month," he said proudly.

"And your brother, the duke, has he bestowed lands or an allowance on you yet?"

He threw his shoulders back and beamed. "Yes, both. My brother has been quite generous to me and has promised to be even more so once I have an heir."

Henrietta couldn't help but smile. Perhaps it was a good thing the duke wasn't at home. Constance was questioning Lord Waldo as if Henrietta were her daughter. She didn't think the poor man could have withstood questions from both of them. One of his pale brown eyes constantly twitched, and he nervously kept wetting his lips in a most annoying way. Henrietta actually felt sorry for him. She would do her best to put him at ease once they were alone in his curricle.

When Henrietta had all she could take of the questions Constance was asking, she rose and said, "I think we should be going, don't you, Constance?"

Constance and Lord Waldo stood up, too.

"Yes, by all means," Constance said, looking at the clock on the mantel. "We certainly want you back well before dusk begins to settle." She turned to Lord Waldo. "A couple of hours should be plenty of time for you to see all the important people who might be in the park today, don't you think?"

"Yes, Mrs. Pepperfield. I'll not return Miss Tweed late, I assure you."

"Good. Since Blake is out of the house, Henrietta, I will be here when you return."

They walked to the vestibule, and Henrietta picked up her pelisse. Lord Waldo immediately tried to help her with it but dropped it before she could put her arm through the sleeve. After much fumbling, Henrietta managed to don her pelisse and button it. She placed a blush-colored bonnet on her head. Constance handed her her gloves, cape, and parasol, and she and Lord Waldo walked out the door.

"You are absolutely fetching, Miss Tweed, and I count myself the luckiest man in London to be with you today."

Henrietta smiled at him as they approached the carriage and said, "Thank you, Lord Waldo. I think the blue skies and beautiful sunshine might have something to do with that. We've had so much rain and so many gray clouds recently that the loveliness of the day spills over into our attitudes, don't you think?"

"Begging your pardon, Miss Tweed, but I don't think the day has anything to do with your beauty. You were just as beautiful last night, and you will be just as beautiful tomorrow."

"You are far too generous with your praise, Lord Waldo. However, I will simply accept it graciously."

As they reached the carriage, a small dog popped out of a crate and barked, startling her.

Lord Waldo reached down to the floor of the open carriage and lifted the dog out of the cushioned wooden box. The long-haired, white dog barked and happily licked Lord Waldo's face.

"This is Tulip," he said, "though I call her Tooley most of the time. My brother doesn't mind. She's a West Highland white terrier."

"She is a darling little dog," Henrietta said, backing up slightly.

"I know. My brother told me to bring her along with me. He said that all ladies love dogs, and caring for dogs shows that a man has compassion."

"That's wise counsel from your brother," she said, thinking that Lord Waldo mentioned his brother a lot. She remembered how close he had stayed to his brother at the two parties she had attended.

"I'll tell him you said that. He'll be pleased. Here, let me help you into the carriage and then you can hold her."

"Well, ah." Henrietta hesitated. "All right, perhaps I can hold her for a short time."

He held Tooley in one arm and held out the other hand for her to take.

"Thank you," she said and allowed him to help her up the steps and into the carriage.

Lord Waldo picked up a small blanket from the crate, plopped it over her new pelisse, and then placed the dog in her lap. Henrietta looked down at the terrier and realized she should have told Lord Waldo that she usually had bad reactions to most dogs and all cats. After being around them for only a short while, her eyes would run water, and she would start sneezing. She could only hope that, because Tulip was a small dog, she wouldn't have any problem.

Tulip, with her cute little face, stared at Henrietta and barked happily again.

Lord Waldo climbed up into the carriage beside her. He opened her parasol and handed it to her. He then took the leather ribbons from the floor and snapped the rumps of the two gray mares. With that, they took off at a breezy trot, with the dog barking.

"That bark means she wants you to rub her back. She likes to have her neck scratched, too, while she rides in the carriage."

Henrietta stared at the mound of barking fluff and hoped that, since she had her gloves on, maybe petting Tooley for a few minutes would not bother her.

"She certainly seems friendly enough," Henrietta said, stroking the dog's back with her free hand. The dog calmed, laid her head down, and snuggled into Henrietta's skirts, making herself comfortable.

"She loves people," Lord Waldo said, keeping the horses clipping along at a brisk pace. "See, she thinks you are the most beautiful woman in London, too."

Henrietta laughed. "I don't think she cares what either of us looks like, but she does seem to be enjoying the ride."

Lord Waldo glanced over at Henrietta and smiled. Some of his nervousness seemed to have passed, now that they were out of the house. His eye wasn't twitching, and he had stopped wetting his lips after every sentence.

"I'm glad His Grace wasn't home to visit with us before we left. Your chaperone made me nervous enough."

"You didn't seem nervous," she lied, knowing that she shouldn't, but how could she agree with him?

"Really, you didn't notice?" He threw his shoulders back and sat up a little taller in the seat. She could see his confidence grow.

"You did quite well holding your own with Constance. She could probably make most men quake in their boots. I found her quite intimidating the first time I met her, but now I don't feel that way. I think she is beautiful and confident, and she's knowledgeable about most things in life."

Henrietta's fingers sifted through the dog's long hair as the carriage bumped along. She couldn't help but remember how delicious it had felt when she combed through the duke's hair with her hands the night he was in so much pain.

"They are both quite intimidating, you know."

She threw him a questioning glance. "I'm not sure who you are referring to?"

"My brother and your guardian."

She had no idea about the Duke of Rockcliffe, but she certainly agreed that Blakewell could be that way—if allowed.

Henrietta felt the need to bolster Lord Waldo's confidence once again. "I see you as formidable as either of the two dukes. You have no need to feel inferior to them."

He turned to her, his eye twitching again. Her comment had been made to try to put him at ease, but it had only made him nervous again.

"You do?"

"Yes, of course," she answered, stretching the truth one more time.

"But dukes are the ones with all the power."

"Look, there's the first entrance into the park," she said, grateful for any reason to change the subject. "Spring is so beautiful here in Hyde Park, and the sky is such a pleasant shade of blue today. There's not a cloud to be seen. And see how many people have already arrived to enjoy the afternoon. My goodness, there must be hundreds of people here."

"My brother suggested we drive around the park twice to make sure we are seen by everyone, and then we should stop and find a place to sit and enjoy our refreshments."

"Once again, your brother seems to have offered the perfect idea. That sounds wonderful to me," she said, thinking that would be a good time to put some distance between her and Tooley, who seemed perfectly content curled on her lap.

Lord Waldo guided the horses through the east gate and onto the road that led to the Serpentine. The carriage traffic was thick as their curricle fell in behind a fancy closed carriage driven by a liveried driver and drawn by a pair of matching bays. The grassy areas of the park were packed with elegantly dressed people. Some of the couples strolled around the grounds of the spacious park with their children and pets, while others rode horseback or in two-seated carriages. Still others had found shaded areas to spread their blankets and enjoy the contents of their luncheon baskets.

Henrietta and Lord Waldo rode in silence for a few minutes, enjoying the activity in the park. Lord Waldo would occasionally wave to someone in the distance or yell a hello to someone in a passing carriage. All Henrietta could think was that she wished she were in the park with Blakewell, as she continued to rub Tooley and scratch her neck.

After two trips around the park, Lord Waldo stopped the carriage and handed off the horses to a groom. He helped Henrietta and Tulip down from the carriage, and carried the blanket and food basket while she carried her parasol and the dog. They found a shade tree and spread the blanket. As soon as she sat down, Henrietta's eyes began to water and her nose felt stuffy. She took a handkerchief from the black velvet reticule that swung from her wrist and dabbed at her eyes.

She tried to set Tooley aside, but the little dog did not want to be put down. "Go run and play," she said, but Tulip wasn't interested. The terrier was obviously too newly enamored of Henrietta to leave her lap.

Lord Waldo sat down a respectable distance from her and started emptying the contents of the basket onto the blanket. While he busied himself, Henrietta took time to really look at him. He wasn't an unattractive man at a distance, but in the cold light of day, she could see that as far as handsomeness, he paled compared to Blakewell. Lord Waldo's body was thin. He didn't fill out his shirt and coat. He appeared to be the same size from his shoulders to his hips, while Blakewell had broad, muscular shoulders and lean, narrow hips.

Lord Waldo must have spent little time outside as his face, neck, and hands were pale compared to Blakewell's sun-kissed, golden-colored skin. She looked at Lord Waldo's hands, pouring wine into a pewter cup. His fingers were long and bony, so unlike the strong, masculine hands of the duke.

"Here you are," Lord Waldo said, giving her a cup of wine.

She sniffled and said, "Thank you."

Suddenly Henrietta sneezed twice. "Bless you," Lord Waldo said.

Henrietta sneezed again.

"It must be the sunshine and fresh air making you sneeze. Here, eat a little of this kidney pie and cheese.

A little food will help you. My brother said wine, kidney pie, and apricot tarts were the best food for an outing in the park with a captivating young lady."

She smiled and took the plate from him. Tooley stared at the plate. Maybe if I feed the dog, Henrietta thought, she would get up and nose around the grounds. Henrietta couldn't believe Tooley didn't want to mark her territory.

While Lord Waldo ate and talked about his brother, Henrietta smiled, nodded, and answered in all the right places, but her symptoms worsened, and her sneezes became more frequent. She drank the wine but finally put the plate on the ground as far from her as she could reach and placed Tooley right in front of it.

Henrietta brushed the white dog hair from her pelisse and gloves while the little dog downed the food in a matter of seconds. Lord Waldo seemed not to notice or, if he did, he didn't care that she had fed the terrier her food.

Tulip sniffed around their picnic area for less than a minute and then perched herself right back on Henrietta's lap. She wagged her tail and barked happily. Henrietta couldn't deny little Tooley her affection when she looked so intently at her with those dark, bright eyes.

"I do say, I think the new blossoms are making you sneeze a lot. Do you always sneeze so much when you are outside?"

"No, never, I mean yes, sometimes, when everything is in bloom." She couldn't very well blame her sneezing and watery eyes on the dog now, since she didn't speak up and say anything right from the beginning.

"I think Tulip is as enchanted with you as I am. She hasn't left your lap all afternoon."

"I believe she likes to be held."

"My brother has spoiled her. When he is at home, Rockcliffe walks around holding Tooley all the time."

"Mmm," she said, growing very tired of hearing about Lord Waldo's brother.

Lord Waldo wiped the crumbs from his lips and put the remnants of food back into the basket. While doing so, he maneuvered himself so that he was suddenly sitting very close to her. Henrietta knew his intentions. He was going to kiss her. She didn't want him to, yet she did. She had to know if any other man could elicit the passion in her and make her feel the way Blakewell made her feel.

She watched as his face slowly descended toward hers. She had plenty of time to stop him or turn her cheek to him, but she remained still and allowed his lips to lightly brush against hers. Nothing happened. There was no feeling other than awkwardness. She smiled to herself, and without warning she sneezed, making Lord Waldo jump and the dog bark.

"I'm sorry, Lord Waldo, but perhaps we should cut our outing short and return to the house. I don't think my sneezing and watery eyes are going to get any better this afternoon."

A pink blush stained Lord Waldo's cheeks, and he blinked rapidly. "I think you're right. Perhaps we should try it another afternoon. I can see your eyes are starting to swell. Tooley will miss her walk in the park, but she'll understand. I think we should leave."

Henrietta's symptoms continued all the way home,

but she was actually growing quite fond of the little dog. When they arrived at the town house, she gave Tulip a last rub on her head and placed her in the cushioned crate. Lord Waldo helped Henrietta down from the carriage and walked her to the door.

She sniffed. "Thank you for a pleasant afternoon, Lord Waldo. I'm sorry we had to cut the day short."

"I think it was for the best," he said, opening the door for them to step inside. "You're not looking so well. I wish the day hadn't been quite so in bloom."

"Henrietta, you're home," Blakewell called to her from the top of the stairs.

She turned toward him and smiled. It thrilled her just to see him.

He hurried down the stairs and as he stepped off the last step, his eyes widened. "Bloody hell, what happened to you? You've been crying."

"No," she whispered.

Rage flashed across his face. He turned to Lord Waldo. "What have you done to her?"

Lord Waldo blinked rapidly as one eye twitched. "Done, I—I? Nothing!"

"Don't tell me 'nothing,' I can look at her and tell she's been crying."

"No, Your Grace," Henrietta tried to calm him, but he brushed right past her and advanced on Lord Waldo.

"Please, Your Grace, I haven't touched her." Lord Waldo backed against the doorframe, hitting his head.

The duke advanced on him. "You expect me to believe that when her eyes are swollen and her nose red?"

Lord Waldo trembled, his eyes twitched in fear as he nervously wet his lips with his tongue.

Henrietta tried again. "Stop this, Your Grace. You are being an ogre; listen to me. Lord Waldo was a perfect gentleman and did nothing to me."

The frightened man nodded.

"What is happening in here?" Constance said, rushing into the vestibule. "Why are your voices raised? Henrietta, have you been crying?"

"No, of course not. I've been rubbing my eyes."

"It must be the shrubs or flowers in bloom, Mrs. Pepperfield, Your Grace. She's been sneezing almost since we left the house. That's why we returned so early. We've hardly been gone an hour."

Blakewell backed away from Lord Waldo. He glanced from Henrietta to Constance to Lord Waldo again. In a much calmer voice, he said, "Perhaps it's time you said your good-byes."

"Yes, Your Grace; good-bye, Miss Tweed. Thank you for a lovely afternoon. Mrs. Pepperfield, it's always nice to see you." He bowed to Blakewell. "Your Grace."

When the door closed behind Lord Waldo, the duke turned to Constance and asked, "Has she ever shown this reaction when she was out with you in a carriage?"

"No."

He turned to Henrietta. "Now tell me the truth."

She sneezed into her handkerchief. "The truth is that I've had this kind of reaction to dogs and cats since I was a little girl. Lord Waldo brought his brother's West Highland terrier with him, and I'm afraid I let the dog get too close to me."

"I've heard of people having similar reactions to dogs and cats, though I've never personally known anyone," Constance said.

"Me either," Blakewell said.

"It's my fault. I should have told Lord Waldo I needed to keep my distance, but Tooley was so loving. I thought perhaps because she was small, I would be all right." Henrietta peeled off her gloves, unbuttoned her pelisse, and shrugged out of it. "I won't be able to wear these again until they are cleaned."

"I think the rubbish heap is the best place for those," Blakewell said, taking them from her. "Constance, I don't think she should go out tonight."

"Oh, I agree," Constance said with a horrified expression on her face. "Looking as she does? Absolutely not. It would be the kiss of death to go out in public." She turned to Henrietta. "Have your maid bring you cool, wet cloths to cover your eyes, Henrietta. Hopefully the swelling will be gone by tomorrow."

"I know it will all go away now that I'm not around Tooley. It was foolish of me not to speak up."

"We're all foolish from time to time, Henrietta," Blakewell said. "I'll discard these while you say good-bye to Constance."

The duke's eyes were still dark and stormy, but his expression of rage had relaxed.

"Wait for me in my book room, Henrietta, after you say good-bye to Constance."

Henrietta and Constance watched Blakewell walk down the corridor carrying her gloves and pelisse.

When he was out of sight, Constance turned to

Henrietta and said, "I've never seen a man so eaten with jealousy."

Shocked by the comment, Henrietta whipped around to face Constance. "His Grace? What do you mean by that?"

Constance took a deep breath. "I mean he's fallen for you, Henrietta, though I'm not sure he is ready to admit that to himself, or to you."

Henrietta's stomach did a flip.

Could that be true?

Eighteen

Dearest Lucien, my grandson who hasn't been to see me in weeks,

As I have told you many times, Lord Chesterfield was the wisest gentleman I ever had the pleasure of knowing. This is one of my favorite quotes from him about women: "Women are not so much taken by beauty as men are, but prefer those men who show them the most attention."
How does he know us so well?

Your loving Grandmother,
Lady Elder

BLAKE FOUND HENRIETTA IN THE VESTIBULE, CLOSING the door behind Constance, when he came back from throwing out her clothing. Her nose was still a little red from sneezing, but fortunately the swelling was leaving her eyes. He had wanted to strangle Lord Waldo when he thought he had accosted Henrietta and made her cry.

He took hold of Henrietta's hand and said, "Come with me."

Blake led her into the book room, closed the door, and leaned against it. Henrietta stopped in the center of the room and faced him.

As he stared at her, he realized Morgan and Race had been right. Blake had been brooding. For days. He might not be cursed because of Henrietta, but he was definitely bewitched by her. She consumed his thoughts and his dreams. Could what he was feeling for her be love?

Damnation. He certainly hadn't planned on that happening to him. Ever.

Not only had he not slept well last night for thinking about her upcoming outing with Lord Waldo, but he had left the house early that morning and gone riding to avoid seeing them together. Blake hadn't wanted to be around when Lord Waldo came for her. Now, he was glad he hadn't been. He never would have let her leave with that sap.

"Tell me that, after today, you are no longer seriously considering Lord Waldo for a husband."

She looked surprised for a few seconds, but her self-confidence quickly took hold. "I have not yet made that determination, Your Grace. Lord Waldo has many admirable qualities to recommend him."

Admirable qualities? Waldo?

"And what are they, Henrietta, for I have never seen an example of them, nor have I heard anyone express awareness of these admirable qualities you see in him. That is, other than your belief that he is malleable. I don't consider that a very high mark for a man."

She remained resolute. "He is considerate, kind, and easy to talk to, Your Grace."

"Ah, easy to talk to, I see. I guess that could be considered an admirable quality. During times when he is so easy to talk to, I don't suppose he ever mentions his brother, does he?"

Her shoulders and chin lifted ever so slightly, and Blake smiled. He loved watching her fight her way out when he backed her into a corner.

"He is very loyal to his brother, and to me loyalty is clearly another admirable quality."

Blake pushed away from the door and strode over to a washstand that stood in the far corner. He poured water from a pitcher into a basin, and then dipped a small cloth into it. After he had wrung most of the water out of the cloth, he walked over to Henrietta and said, "Close your eyes."

She acquiesced, and he tenderly pressed the wet cloth over her eyes.

"How does that feel?"

She breathed deeply. "Soothing."

"Good. The cool cloth should help the rest of the swelling in your eyes to go down and make you feel better."

She reached up and took hold of the cloth and said, "Thank you."

"All right, I'll give Lord Waldo one point. Loyalty is a good trait, and he has plenty of that for Rockcliffe."

Henrietta placed the cloth over one eye and stared at the duke with the other. "I don't know why you are taking me to task about him, Your Grace. We are both eager for me to marry, so you can be rid of the responsibility for me. If Lord Waldo should be interested in considering me for his wife, then I would mull over that opportunity carefully."

Blake's chest tightened. He watched her expression closely. She seemed serious, confident. But she was lacking emotion. He was convinced she didn't fancy the man, so why would she consider marrying him?

"I am not eager for you to marry the wrong man or the first man to ask you. Lord Waldo is a weakling, and you know that."

She placed the cloth over her other eye. "I know of no such thing. He is a man who will provide well for me and not demand much from me in return."

Lifting a skeptical brow, Blake moved closer to her. "Henrietta." He said her name huskily, seductively. "Now we are getting somewhere."

She stepped away from him and dipped the cloth in the cool water again. "Perhaps he's not as strong as you, as most men are not, but he's a capable man and, with the right direction, he can grow stronger."

Blake followed her. "Ah, I see. You think you can lead him as his brother does now, don't you?"

She squeezed the cloth and didn't answer him. She didn't have to. He knew the answer.

The room slowly darkened as late afternoon shadows covered the room. Soft lamplight danced on her rumpled hair and slithered across her lovely face. The wet cloth had made her eyes look much better, and the redness had faded from her nose. Everything about her was tempting him to pull her into his arms and make her his. Forever.

"You don't love him," Blake finally said.

Holding the cloth over one eye, she said, "I don't

know why we are talking about this, Your Grace. Lord Waldo has not asked me to marry him, but if he should, you didn't say I had to love the man I married."

He cocked his head and said, "I didn't know I had to. You must see him as a spineless ninny that you can control."

She dropped her hand to her side and huffed indignantly. "You go too far, Your Grace, to think that I believe such a cruel thing about him."

"But it's true, is it not?" He advanced on her yet again. She backed away. "You are interested in him only because you want a husband you can control. You have seen for yourself and heard talk about the way his brother leads him around, and you believe you will be able to do the same."

Her lips parted in shock. "When you put it like that, it makes me seem very shallow."

"If the shoe fits, wear it, as Lord Chesterfield was so fond of saying."

Henrietta's brows drew together in a frown. "I don't believe Lord Chesterfield ever said that, Your Grace."

Blake smiled mischievously. He was enjoying the battle with her. "Perhaps not, but he should have. You are not shallow, Henrietta. Far from it. But there are two things you are missing in your consideration of Lord Waldo." He took another step toward her. She took another step back and found herself against the wall.

Refusing to cower, she lifted her chin again and said, "I don't think I am missing anything."

"Oh, yes you are. One is that the Duke of Rockcliffe will continue to control his brother, no matter who he marries. Rockcliffe will not relinquish that authority, and Lord Waldo will not want him to. He worships his older brother. Neither of them wants their relationship to change, certainly not for a wife. Lord Waldo has been his brother's pup for too long to change." He leaned in closer to her and held his gaze steady on her clear, blue eyes. "You will not be able to wrest control of Lord Waldo from his much stronger brother."

"I disagree. I might be young and not very worldly, but I do know that a woman has certain charms that can persuade her husband to her will, her wishes, and her desires."

He took the wet cloth from her hands and threw it into the basin, splashing water over the sides of it. Her breaths were shallow and fast. Her chest heaved enticingly. "Ah, yes, your charms are many, Henrietta. Many. And you may be able to do that, for a time, but what of my other reason? I said there were two."

Her gaze locked onto his. "What is the other?"

He lowered his head, bringing his face very close to hers. He could no longer bear not touching her. He caressed her cheek with his fingertips, letting them slowly trace the outline of her lips. Just touching her face caused his lower stomach to tighten, and a surge of hardness caught between his legs. The pads of his fingers traveled over her chin and down the slender column of her throat to rest in the hollow at the base of her neck where he felt her pulse beating wildly beneath her warm skin.

Blake loved the excitement he felt building inside her.

"Passion," he said huskily. "I don't see a lot of passion for anything in Lord Waldo. He reminds me of cold, gray ashes that have not been kindled all summer."

She grunted. "I care not for passion," she whispered.

Blake smiled triumphantly. He placed one hand against the wall near her shoulder and leaned in so close that their noses almost touched. "You care not for passion?"

She nodded.

He put his other hand on the wall beside her, boxing her inside his arms.

Henrietta flattened against the wall. Her eyes seemed to spit fire at him, and he welcomed it.

"Henrietta, that is a statement that I cannot let go unchallenged."

He bent his head and kissed both corners of her mouth, each cheek, and first one damp eyelid and then the other. She remained still except for the rapid rise and fall of her chest.

"So," he whispered, "if Waldo never kisses you like this, you will never miss it?" His lips glided across her cheek, over her chin, and to the soft, sweet skin behind her ear. He breathed in deeply her womanly scent.

Hot throbbing desire for her seared him. Without letting his lips leave her skin, he moved back up to her lips and tempted her with short, sweet kisses that moved agonizingly slowly over her mouth.

"If he never kisses you like this, you will never dream of it again?"

She shook her head. "I will not miss it," she whispered past a soft, gulping breath.

He smiled to himself. Let her deny the truth. The way her body responded to him told him all he needed to know.

He kissed his way down to the softly rising mound of her beautiful breasts beneath her low-cut dress. His tongue came out and tasted her cool, damp skin. Her breaths were quick and shallow.

Blake loved what he was doing to her, and what she was doing to him.

Henrietta moaned softly and arched her back, giving him greater access to her throat and chest. He took full advantage of her offering. His hand slid up her midriff to cup her breast and push it up. His fingers searched for her nipple, hidden beneath the fabric of her dress and undergarments. Through her silky bodice and cotton chemise, he located the tight bud and gently tugged on it, making it tighten. He dipped his head and nipped it with his teeth, making it grow harder under his playful touch.

A tremor shook her body, and she gasped with pleasure, giving him immense satisfaction to know he made her feel so good.

Blake's loins thickened for her.

"Now tell me you will never long to be touched like this, Henrietta. Tell me and I will believe you," he whispered as his hand kneaded her breast and his lips found hers once more in a long drugging kiss.

"All right, yes, Your Grace, I will miss it," she admitted, dragging her lips away from his. "I will miss your touch. I will miss you all the days of my life."

Her arms went around his neck, and her lips found his in a deep, bruising kiss that took his breath. Blake pulled her into his arms and accepted her fierce attack with a deep hunger gnawing at him.

She pleased him, aroused him, and fulfilled him.

His tongue drove deep inside her mouth, and his body pressed hers hard against the wall. His strong arms slid around her back and pulled her up to him as his mouth ravished hers. Her soft breasts pressed against his chest. His lips left hers, and he brought his tongue down the long sweep of her neck, tasting her, devouring her.

She swallowed hard and moaned with pleasure. Her eyes were bright with wonder. "Kiss me, Your Grace. Kiss me, touch me, and fill me."

That was all the confirmation he needed.

"My sweet, Henrietta, you tempt me beyond my control to deny you."

Anticipation of her request ran wild inside him. He had no doubts, no fears. She wanted him as much as he wanted her. That gave him immense satisfaction. His desire to take her was frantic. He was desperate for her total surrender to him, and she was willing.

Heat from her eagerness seared him with such wanting. His tongue swept inside her mouth and plundered its depth. Their uneven breaths melted together. This time he had to completely possess and make her his.

With impatient hands, he took hold of her gown and chemise and lifted them up to her waist. His arms slid around to her back, and his fingers fumbled as he untied her drawers and slid them down her legs, helping her kick free of them. He didn't bother removing her garters or stockings. He would have loved to look at her shapely legs, but there was no time for that.

Quickly, he unbuttoned his breeches and shoved them down to his knees. He placed his hands on her waist and gently pressed her against the wall once again. He then fitted himself against her soft womanhood and pushed inside her with a deep, demanding thrust.

Her gasp was soft and her body went rigid. He quickly covered her lips with his and whispered, "Don't panic, it will be all right. I promise. Move with me."

He placed his hand between them, found the center of her passion, and softly manipulated the bud while he gave her body time to adjust to this new sensation. He continued to kiss her and caress her, and slowly she relaxed against the wall, surrendering her body to him. He wanted to completely fill her and satisfy her before he gave in to his own gratification.

Blake continued his tender assault on her senses, gently moving inside her until she cried out in unexpected wonder. Her body tightened, shuddered, and then relaxed on a contented sigh. Only then did he allow his own passion to explode inside her. He went still, gasping for breath as his heartbeat slowed, and his limbs stopped quivering.

They remained quiet for a moment, gazing into each other's eyes, and pressed against the wall. His body already ached to possess her again, but slower. He still wanted her. He hadn't yet sated himself, and he wouldn't withdraw from her until he had.

"Now tell me you would not miss passion," he whispered.

"I cannot tell you that," she answered softly.

"And I won't let you marry a man who cannot satisfy you, Henrietta. You are too passionate for Lord Waldo and too intelligent to fall for Lord Snellingly's blather."

"I fear you are right."

"Passion is a difficult thing to deny yourself, is it not?"

"Yes," she admitted freely, "Most difficult."

He slid her dress off her shoulders and freed her breasts. Bending his head, he took one erect nipple into his mouth again. She gasped with pleasure and arched her hips to meet his. He felt her entire body tremble with delight. He tore the other side of her clothing away from her yielding breast and covered it hard and fully with his palm.

"Your Grace," she whispered passionately.

He gazed into her eyes, as he moved inside her. "Call me Blake."

"I cannot."

"Yes, say it. I want to hear you call me by my name. I am no longer your guardian. I am now your lover." He pressed deeper, harder inside her. "I want you to talk to me the way a woman talks to the man she desires. Tell me what you want."

Henrietta reached up and untied his neckcloth. "Take off your shirt, Blake, for I have longed to see and touch your chest."

"That is the Henrietta I want."

Blake laughed and helped her unwind his neckcloth,

dispose of his collar, and lift his shirt over his head, without removing his body from hers.

When he stood bare-chested before her, she rubbed her palms with tantalizing slowness over his broad chest, lightly touching his tight nipples, making him moan with desire. Her light caress teased him and offered no mercy from the torment and pleasure she inflicted on him.

His breath trembled in his throat at her touch, but he managed to say, "You learn quickly what a man wants."

"I do this for myself, but if it pleases you, too, I'm delighted. I have longed to touch you like this," she whispered against his hot skin.

Henrietta leaned in close to him and kissed his chest, pulling his small nipple into her mouth. One arm went around her, and he cupped her head and helped guide her. His other arm snaked behind her and cupped her buttocks. He pulled her up tight against him and pressed all the way into her.

But he could only allow this sweet torture from her for a few moments. His endurance was near the end for a second time. He lifted her chin with his fingers, bent his head, and slanted his lips over hers in a slow tender kiss. The longing and the passion inside him were intense. When her lips parted and she leaned sensually into him, he deepened the kiss.

That sent a slow spreading of delicious warmth sizzling through him. He lifted his hips toward her. He raked her chemise down her arms to her waist, leaving it to bunch with the bodice and skirt around her middle.

Blake ran the palm of his hands and tips of his fingers over her naked shoulders and breasts, down to the slender curve of her waist and back up again. All the while, he gazed at her gorgeous body.

He took in her beauty, knowing that she could see his great need for her once again in his eyes. He ached deeply for her.

In seconds, her nipples swelled and hardened beneath his gentle tug. The soft, feminine sounds of delight she made elated him and added to his own enjoyment.

"Does that pleasure you, Henrietta?" he murmured against her lips, not wanting to stop kissing her long enough to speak clearly.

"You know how it pleases me, Blake."

He chuckled into her mouth. "I can hardly breathe myself," he whispered. "I love the taste of you."

He continued to massage her breasts, loving the feel of their soft, firm weight in his hands. Just touching her helped ease the intense hunger inside him and gave him such pleasure that he never wanted to stop. A burning heat surged through his loins, and a longing filled his heart. Her arms went around his back and she hugged him to her. Soon they were moving as one in a beautiful, glorious rhythm. Their tempo increased until Henrietta cried out in sweet passion. Blake felt her body relax against him, and he spilled his seed into her for the second time.

He had never felt so complete.

He bent his head and kissed that warm, soft spot behind her ear. He inhaled the scent of fresh washed hair. For a moment, he rested his face in the crook of her neck. He breathed deeply, drinking in her warm, womanly scent.

He kissed her silky feminine skin, feeling immense satisfaction in the way she responded to him. He savored the sensations that touching her gave him.

She was the woman he wanted forever in his life. He loved her with no doubts and no reservations. For the first time, he was certain he wanted no other woman but this one.

"We should arrange our clothing before someone knocks on the door," she whispered.

She was so warm and inviting that he hated the thought of moving away from her for any reason. But if Blake had learned anything about Henrietta, it was that she needed order in her life. She wanted her clothing straight and proper. He understood.

He withdrew from her and turned away to button his breeches and give her privacy to deal with her gown.

When his clothes were set aright and his neckcloth perfectly tied, he turned back to her and asked, "Do you need any help with your dress?"

She was calm, just as he expected. "No, thank you."

His fingers feathered the outline of her face as he looked down at her and whispered a deeper feeling than he thought possible, "You do realize that what just happened between us is irreversible."

"I understand. I am fully aware of the implications of what happened between us, Your Grace, and you needn't feel any guilt or responsibility."

His eyes searched her face. He saw her love for him in her eyes and he smiled. "My name is Blake, Henrietta. I want you to call me Blake."

She nodded.

"There is no need for guilt from either one of us." He smiled at her. "As for responsibility, that has not changed. I will take care of you, Henrietta. I know what needs to be done, but it's going to take some time to work out the details on how to go about it. I'm going to get started on that right away."

He turned and left the room.

Nineteen

Dearest Lucien,

What do you think about these wise words from Lord Chesterfield? "Good sense will make you be esteemed, good manners be loved, and wit give a lustre· to both. I have known many a man of common sense pass generally for a fool, because he affected a degree of wit that God had denied him."

Your loving Grandmother,
Lady Elder

HENRIETTA DIDN'T KNOW HOW LONG SHE STOOD IN the book room after Blake left. She simply couldn't move. In the aftermath of their heated passion, she had straightened her hair and her clothing, but her mind was in a state of disarray. She needed time to collect her thoughts and categorize them as to importance. She needed time to evaluate what had happened between them and draw some conclusions.

Blake had told her that she tempted him beyond

his control. She had no doubt about this. She felt the same way about him. Still, she would not deny herself his attentions. She encouraged him. She understood the ramifications and took responsibility for what happened. She must pay the price for her wanton disregard for his vulnerability concerning her.

She wasn't unhappy, nor was she distraught about their coming together in the heat of passion. How could she be dismayed over something she'd wanted so desperately from the man she loved with all her heart? She treasured every moment they were together. She loved experiencing all the wonderful things he'd shown her—how he could make her feel, and how she made him feel. She would never forget one touch or one kiss of their time together.

Blake's happiness, his well-being, and his life were of utmost importance to her. The only questions for her were: where did she go from here, and what would be best for Blake?

Henrietta knew he wouldn't want her to continue living in his house, tempting him. Few avenues were available to young ladies who were compromised, the convent being the most likely choice for her. She really couldn't imagine Blake marrying her off to an elderly baron who lived so far up north she would never see the lights of London again or allowing her to present herself as a pure young lady to a gentleman of Society, such as Lord Waldo Rockcliffe or Lord Snellingly. She supposed he could deem her qualified to be a governess or perhaps a paid companion to an elderly woman in need of a kind ear.

Henrietta took several deep breaths and smiled.

Yes, life as a paid companion or in the convent it would be. It wasn't that she wanted to do either one. She didn't. She didn't have the temperament for a life of servitude, and she knew it would be a struggle, but she would do her best to hold her tongue and be obedient.

Both, entering a convent or becoming a companion, had one major advantage. The duke would no longer be her guardian, thereby freeing him from the curse. That, and only that, was the reason she would agree.

Henrietta smiled again. Blake would be free to live out his normal life. Just not with her. Henrietta's smile faded. Her heart ached at the thought of never seeing him again. She would only have her memories of the wonderful times she spent with him in his book room.

"Oh, there you are, Miss Tweed," Mrs. Ellsworth said, walking into the book room with a tray. "His Grace told me you needed a cup of hot tea. I took it all the way up to your room thinking you were there."

"Thank you, Mrs. Ellsworth. A cup of hot tea would be nice."

"His Grace said you had a foul reaction to a dog. Dear, dear, and I can see that you did. Your lips are a mite red and your eyes a little swollen. Shall I pour it for you?"

Henrietta was not up to the chatty woman staying one moment longer than necessary. "No, thank you, Mrs. Ellsworth, you may return to your other duties. I'll take care of it."

Mrs. Ellsworth walked to the door and then turned back and said, "His Grace told me you wouldn't be going out to the parties tonight. What time should I have Cook prepare your supper?"

"The usual time will be fine."

The housekeeper smiled, nodded, and left.

Food was the last thing on Henrietta's mind. She couldn't feel any less like eating. Right now she wanted to plan how best to put order back in her life.

She poured herself a cup of tea and looked around the book room. A sudden sense of loneliness overwhelmed her. She would miss this room with all its wonderful memories. The duke's desk caught her eye. More mail had been delivered while she was in Hyde Park with Lord Waldo. It lay scattered on his desk.

Taking her cup, she walked over and sat down in his chair. She smiled. It would give her great pleasure to organize his correspondence for him one last time.

Blake waited impatiently in the drawing room of Gibby's town house. His butler had told him that Gibby was indisposed at the moment but would be below stairs momentarily. Blake assumed Gibby was getting dressed for the evening's parties. Blake couldn't sit still, so he paced in front of a camel-backed, gold-and red-striped settee.

He wasn't happy with the way he had treated Henrietta. She deserved better than a frolic in his book room, but… what could he say? He'd wanted her to such a great extent that he had simply lost the desire to control himself. He had failed to treat her like a lady, and that pained him greatly.

First, he should not have compromised her, and second, not in such a devilish way. He would make that up to her as soon as they married. He would make love to her in a soft bed with flowers and candles filling the room. But he had to do something right now that was even more important than matrimony.

"To what do I owe the honor of this pleasure?" Gibby said, walking into the room with all the dapper sophistication of an elderly statesman. He held up his hand. "Wait, don't tell me; I'll guess. You have come to your good senses."

"It's more like I have lost them."

A confused expression eased across Gibby's face. "Do you mean you've decided that Mrs. Simple's idea is a smashing one, and you not only approve, but you want to help us get her business, shall we say, off the ground?"

Blake harrumphed. He was in no mood for mindless banter with Gibby. "I'm not that insane yet, old man. I'm not even here to talk about Mrs. Simple."

"Well, that's discouraging. You've always done such a splendid job of maligning her character. Why should you stop now?"

"I've done no such thing, Gib," Blake argued. "I've only questioned you about her motives for your involvement in her ridiculous scheme."

"See, you even refer to it as a scheme instead of a business venture. You and your unexceptional cousins have had a variety of unsavory Bow Street Runners asking about her and her deceased husband all over London for more than a week now."

Blake sighed. That was true. He should have

known Gibby would figure that out. He might as well tell him the conclusion he'd come to about Mrs. Simple and her ballooning idea and get it over with. Clearly Gibby thought Blake had come to his house to discuss the woman's proposition.

After taking a deep breath, Blake said, "All right, we'll talk about Mrs. Simple first. Just so you know, I've spoken with Morgan and Race about this, and we're all in agreement that Mrs. Simple is not nefarious."

Gibby gave Blake an "I told you so" smile. "So it took all three of you putting your minds together to come to that conclusion, did it? Figures."

"But we do think she wants to take advantage of you," Blake added.

The old man lifted his eyebrows suggestively. "Mmm. Now, there's an idea that sounds promising. Usually the gentlemen take advantage of the ladies."

No one needed to tell Blake how true that statement was.

"I'm not meaning in that way, Gib."

"In what way?"

"I'm talking about her soliciting money from you—and you never getting anything for it in return."

Gibby walked over to a side table with a satinwood finish and poured claret into two glasses. He handed one to Blake and then motioned for him to take a seat in one of the fancy side chairs in front of the window. Blake obliged, and Gibby sat in the chair opposite him.

His aged eyes narrowed, and he cocked his head. "What makes you think I won't be getting anything in return for the money I give her?"

Blake sipped the wine and let it settle on his tongue
for a few moments before swallowing. "Balloons shuf-
fling passengers from one place to another won't make
enough money to pay back your investment or keep
Mrs. Simple out of debtors' prison, Gib, no matter
how much you give her."

A smile started slowly at the corners of Gibby's
mouth and widened into a big happy beam. He asked,
"So, all this time you have been thinking that I want
to be paid back with money?"

That gave Blake reason to pause. "Well, I didn't
think…"

"You didn't think. What an admission." Gibby
laughed heartily.

Blake studied Gibby with curiosity for a moment.
The old man was always full of surprises. He was still
a handsome devil. He looked at least ten, if not more,
years younger than he actually was. It never dawned
on Blake, and obviously not his two cousins, either,
that Gibby might be enjoying certain womanly favors
from Mrs. Simple.

"I have more money than I know what to do with,
Blake," Gibby said, before putting the wine glass to
his lips again.

"That doesn't mean you should squander it on
some woman's foolish notions."

"I don't intend to. I might be old, but I still like to
take pleasure in the attentions of a pretty woman from
time-to-time."

Blake relaxed against the back of the chair and took
a drink of his wine. "I hope you never get too old for
that pleasure, Gib."

"You, Morgan, and Race worry too much about me."

"We have to. We promised our grandmother that we would take care of you."

"Even in death, she torments me." Gibby chuckled again. "She only did that because she knew it would annoy the devil out of me. But I do miss her. It's too bad the old chit had to go before me. I would much rather have had it the other way around."

That reminded Blake of the reason he had come to see Gibby in the first place. He needed to get on with the mission at hand. He had a lot to do tonight.

"Unfortunately, we don't get to choose who goes first. But back to Mrs. Simple, I think you should give her enough money to make four balloons. That would give her a total of six. Suggest to her that she open a recreation business with the balloons rather than a travel business. Convince her that she will have more success with a venture like that, and I think you believe that, too. This way you won't be out too much blunt for whatever way she repays you."

Gibby looked out the window and said, "It's probably best I adhere to your wise counsel on this matter. Your judgment sounds reasonable, though I have found great enjoyment in the attention Mrs. Simple has lavished on me these past few weeks. I suppose it is time I brought it to an end."

Blake took in a silent breath of relief. "I'm sure her consideration is worth a few pounds to you," he said with a smile. "Perhaps the respect and interest she shows you now will continue even after you settle your debt of honor with her."

Gibby smiled and lifted his glass to Blake. "Perhaps she will, but I think it will stop once she gets the money. She'll be busy with her balloon venture."

With that settled, Blake drew his brows together in concern. "I need to ask you something, Gib."

The smile faded from the old man's face, as if he sensed a more serious topic was on the horizon.

"Go ahead."

"Do you remember that I told you Henrietta thinks she is cursed because all her guardians have died?"

"That's not the kind of thing I'm likely to forget. How many people think they are cursed?"

"Right." Blake paused, trying to think of the best way to say what he wanted to say. "I need to convince her that I'm not going to die—ah, that is, any time in the near future. Gibby, she really believes I'm in constant danger of dying soon."

"With good reason, considering what happened to all her previous guardians."

"I don't believe in curses, Gib. Those men died because it was their time. It was their fate to die when they did. But I can't convince Henrietta of that, and I don't want her living with the fear that I will die soon."

"You want to marry her, don't you?"

Blake shifted in his chair, surprised. "How did you know that?"

"Everyone in the Great Hall knew it except that whimpering sap Lord Waldo, that pompous Lord Snellingly, and a few other fools. You stood on the side of the room watching her with an eagle's eye the entire night. You marrying her will not come as a surprise to anyone, except maybe you."

"Damnation. Morgan told me no one else noticed."

"He lied."

"That bastard," Blake muttered. "And Race, too."

Gibby laughed again. "How can you be angry with them? They did it to spare you, and you would have done the same for either of them. Besides, they knew it was just a matter of time before you realized it yourself."

"Well, it doesn't matter, because first thing tomorrow morning, I'm going to apply for a special license for us to marry as soon as possible."

"The wait is usually about three days, but you being a duke, you might make it happen sooner."

"Do you mean that there might actually be an advantage to being a duke?"

Gibby chuckled. "Yes."

"My problem is that I don't want her living the rest of her life with this fear that I'm going to die tomorrow because the name 'the Duke of Blakewell' was on her father's list of guardians."

"I see what you mean. That would put a damper on her happiness, for sure."

"I know Henrietta. It would always be at the back of her mind, no matter how many years passed."

Gibby seemed to study over Blake's comment for a moment, and then he rose. "I know exactly what needs to be done. Give me your glass and let me refill it for you while I tell you about it."

Twenty

My Dearest Grandson Lucien,

On a few occasions, I have seen it my duty to disagree with Lord Chesterfield, and this statement is one of them that I choose not to accept: "I must freely tell you that, in matters of religion and matrimony, I never give any advice, because I will not have anybody's torments in this world or the next laid to my charge."

Your loving Grandmother,
Lady Elder

BLAKE STRODE THROUGH THE FRONT DOOR OF HIS TOWN house, taking off his gloves.

"Your Grace, I'm glad you're home."

"Not now, Ashby," Blake said, tossing his gloves, hat, and cloak into the butler's hands without breaking his stride. "I don't have time."

The hour was late. After Blake left Gibby, it had taken him longer at his solicitor's home than he had hoped.

"And don't put my cloak away. I'll be leaving again shortly."

"But Your Grace, I need to speak to you of an urgent matter that needs your prompt attention."

"Where is Miss Tweed—her room or the book room?"

"Her room, Your Grace, and she is the reason I need to speak with you."

"Then follow me up to her room, because that is where I am headed."

Blake took the stairs two at a time. He heard Ashby behind him, struggling to stay up with him. When he made it to Henrietta's door, he knocked and waited what seemed like forever for the door to open.

"Your Grace," Henrietta's maid said and curtseyed.

"Is Henrietta in here?"

"Yes."

"Then step aside; I need to speak to her."

The maid opened the door wider, and Blake entered. Henrietta sat at her dressing table with a quill and a sheet of foolscap in her hand. On the bed, trunks lay open, half-filled with clothing.

A knot of fear formed in his chest as Henrietta rose and faced him. He saw no aftereffects of her earlier reaction to Lord Waldo's dog. All he saw was the woman he loved and who was preparing to leave him.

"What are you doing?" Blake asked as calmly as he could, considering how fast his heart was beating.

"That is what I wanted to tell you, Your Grace," Ashby said in a breathless voice behind him. "Miss Tweed had asked for her trunks to be delivered to her room after her supper was served."

Blake ignored his butler and took a step toward Henrietta. Didn't she know he loved her? He thought she'd understood that before he left the book room. Didn't she love him and want to marry him?

Barely holding his anger in check, he asked again, "What are you doing?"

"I'm packing."

He took another hesitant step toward her. She seemed so composed, so confident that it irritated the devil out of him. "I can see that," he said from between closed teeth. "Why are you packing?"

Henrietta's gaze flew from her maid to Ashby.

"Leave us," Blake said coldly.

Ashby immediately turned and left the room, but the maid remained. "You, too," he said, throwing a quick glance toward her.

The woman looked at her employer, and Henrietta nodded for her to go.

"And close the door behind you," Blake said in a voice that was meant to tolerate no argument from Henrietta or the maid.

With the door firmly shut, Blake said, "Now explain yourself."

She gazed into his eyes and said, "I am taking responsibility for myself. For the first time in my life, I am taking charge of my life. I have decided that I will either go to a convent or hire myself out as a paid companion."

Blake felt as if icy water had been thrown in his face. "What did you say?"

Her eyes didn't waver from his, though there was a slight tremor to her bottom lip, the only sign that she wasn't as unmoved as he first thought.

"I have given the matter careful thought and decided it is what's best for both of us."

Anger burned inside him. He stalked closer to her. "And you made this decision on your own without consulting me?"

"You have no cause to use such an angry tone, Your Grace."

"I have every right. You were just going to write me a note and tell me you wanted to join a convent or become a paid companion without even talking to me about it?"

"No, of course not."

"Then what is in your hand?"

She glanced down at the paper. "The letter is for Constance, telling her of my decision to leave your house, and asking if she might know of a place I could stay while my plans are finalized."

"Your plans? And you don't think I should be angry that you want to leave me. Very angry, considering what happened between us just a couple of hours ago."

Henrietta laid the piece of paper and quill on her dressing table. "I could never leave you without saying good-bye and thanking you for—for all you have shown me and taught me."

This was incredulous. "Tell me, do you want to go to a convent? Do you want to be someone's paid companion?"

"It's not that I want to. I thought it the wisest choice to make under the circumstances. I cannot stay here with you any longer, and I can't rightfully marry any other man now that I've, that we, well you know."

Blake grabbed her by the shoulders and pulled her tightly against his chest. His body trembled as his gaze held steady on hers. He would like nothing better than to throw her down on the bed behind him and give her the loving she deserved. But, he had to settle that damned curse first.

"Listen to me, Henrietta; you are not going to move to a convent or anywhere else. Right now, you are coming with me."

Her eyes were wide with trepidation, and Blake felt a twinge of guilt for talking so roughly. He hadn't meant to alarm her, but he didn't want her to know where they were going for fear she would resist his plan.

He desperately wanted to kiss her, to reassure her that everything was going to be all right. Just holding her close, even for so brief a time, aroused him, but he had to deny those feelings for the time being.

"I don't understand. It's already so late; where are we going?"

He bent his face close to hers. "Henrietta, do you trust me?"

"With my life," she said without hesitating for even a second. "You know that."

"Then don't question me about where we are going or why. Just trust that I am doing the right thing for us, all right?"

She nodded.

He set her from him and took a deep, steadying breath. "Where are your bonnet and cape?"

He went to the open wardrobe and pulled out a black cape. From the bed, he grabbed a bonnet and a pair of gloves. "Let's go."

The carriage was cold, and Henrietta shivered when she climbed inside. Blake took the seat opposite her and stared out the window. She was confused by his brusque manner. He had been astonished when he walked in and saw she was preparing to leave. But what had he expected her to do? It was past time she took responsibility for herself and made decisions without having to account to her guardian.

He wanted her to go with him, yet he wanted to be secretive about where they were going. Why?

She had no fear of him. She knew he wouldn't do anything to hurt her, but where was he taking her? By going with him now, was she giving up her only chance to be in control and make her own decisions about the rest of her life?

Surely he knew she could not continue living with him after their tryst. Her heart constricted at that word. That made what had happened between them sound so distasteful, and it wasn't. She loved him more than her own life. Their coming together had been glorious, and it meant everything to her. She had to leave him to save him from the curse. She had to find a way to make him understand that.

The carriage was moving rapidly through the streets, yet it seemed to be taking a long time to get to wherever they were going. She wanted to ask him their destination, but she remained silent, too, proving to him that she gave him her complete trust.

From the carriage window, she could see that they were leaving the business district of the city. The streetlights grew farther and farther apart until only darkness could be seen out the window. Blake remained silent, staring out the opposite window from her.

She couldn't let her mind run away with possibilities of his intentions. He had asked for her trust, and this was one last thing she could give him. It didn't matter where they were going; she knew she had to leave him to protect him.

Finally the carriage rolled to a stop. She glanced over at Blake, hoping for a reassuring smile, but all she saw were his dark stormy eyes.

Blake opened the door and jumped down. Through the black night, she saw a house that had only a dim single light shining in the front window. There was something cold and forlorn about the place.

"Let's go," he said, reaching for her hand to help her down the steps of the carriage.

Henrietta felt his strong hand close around hers, and his warmth immediately soothed her.

He looked up at his driver and said, "I'm not familiar with this area of Town. Keep a close eye out for anyone who looks suspicious, and don't hesitate to sound the alarm if you need to."

"Never fear, Your Grace. I have a sharp eye and a loud whistle, if I be needing your help. I'll take care of your carriage for you, and be here when you're ready to leave."

Blake nodded to the driver and then took hold of her elbow. They started toward the front door of the lonely looking house. The warmth of his hand continued to comfort her. As they approached the house, a shiver ran up Henrietta's back. She kept telling herself that she trusted Blake, but she had to admit that her faith was wavering just a little.

Blake knocked on the door. A tall, buxom woman with a severe expression on her flat face opened the door. "I'm the Duke of Blakewell, and this is Miss Henrietta Tweed. We are here to see Mrs. Fortune."

"Do you have an appointment, Your Grace?"

"No. Please apologize to her for us that we are arriving so late, but we have a matter of great urgency, and we hope she will be able to help us tonight."

"I'll see if she's available. Please come in." She opened the door wider and stepped aside for them to enter.

Henrietta and Blake walked into the vestibule of the home, and the first thing Henrietta noticed was the strong smell of incense. The lone lamp she had seen from outside was placed in the middle of a table in front of the window. She thought it odd that the window was framed with black velvet draperies. In fact, she had never been in a house that felt so eerie.

The maid motioned to two chairs that stood in the corner in front of a large gold cherub that rested on a fluted column.

"Wait here until I return," she said.

They took their seats in the dimly lit room, and the woman disappeared through a doorway that was closed off from the vestibule with two black velvet drapery panels.

Henrietta could hold her tongue no longer.

"Where are we, Blake? Who is Mrs. Fortune, and why are we here?" The questions tumbled past her lips. Her eyes questioned his.

He leaned toward her, a concerned expression on his face. "I didn't want to tell you for fear you would refuse to come with me. I have brought you here because I'm hoping she can help you."

Her breaths quickened. "Help me? How? Blake, if you fear that I might be with child after our encounter this afternoon, I will not agree to have anything done about it. I will have the child and care for it myself."

Blake jerked back as if she'd struck him. "Damnation, Henrietta, where did you ever get a notion like that? No such thing ever entered my mind. I would never ask anything so vile of you under any circumstances. Do you think me a monster?"

"No, but I don't know what to think," she whispered earnestly. "What am I to think? There is something eerie about this house, this place."

"We are here because of that blasted curse you always talk about. I'm not quite sure if she casts spells on people, reads their minds, or sees into their future. She might even do all three. I don't know that I'm willing to believe she can do any of it, but if by some chance she can cast spells, I'm hoping she can remove them and free you from that bloody curse you dread."

Henrietta's breath stalled in her lungs. She was amazed at how quickly she could go from feeling despair to feeling exhilarated. "Don't tease me, Blake. Are you certain of this?"

Blake laughed derisively and rubbed his forehead above his nose. "I cannot say anything for certain, Henrietta; I haven't met the woman. I don't believe in this curse, but you do. I'm doing this for you, so you won't go through our married life thinking I'm going to die any time soon."

She gasped. Surely he didn't say what she thought she heard. Dare she ask him to repeat it? Her eyes searched his face for humor. There was none.

"What did you say? Did you say our married life?"

"Yes," he said softly and reached over to take her gloved hand in his. "I want to marry you and spend the rest of my life showing you how much I love you."

"You love me?"

His looked deeply into her eyes and smiled. "I love you, Henrietta. It took you going to the park with that greenhorn and his dog for me to admit it to myself, and now I'm admitting it to you."

Joy filled her. "Blake, I think I fell in love with you the first time I saw you stride by the doorway of your drawing room as if you didn't have a care in the world. I love you with all my heart."

He shook his head and laughed. "Imagine my surprise when I came home to find you writing a note and packing to leave me."

She laughed with happiness, too. "This afternoon, after we—we…" Henrietta felt heat rise in her cheeks. "Anyway, when you told me you had to sort out the details of what needed to be done, I thought you wanted to figure out how to get me out of your house, out of your life."

"I'm sorry that's what you thought. All I could think was that I had to find a way to release you from this curse so you could marry me with no fear."

"Blake, I don't know what to say."

"How about saying, 'I'll marry you.'"

"Yes, I'll marry you, my love."

"I would never allow you to enter a convent. You are much too passionate for that kind of life. Besides, what would I do without you to challenge me at every turn?"

Henrietta's heart was racing so fast she felt light-headed. "Blake, do not fool me about this. Tell me truthfully about Mrs. Fortune. Is this just an elaborate plan to trick me into believing that you have had the curse removed?"

Blake slid out of his chair and fell on one knee in front of her. He took both her hands in his.

His gaze settled solidly on hers. "Hear me well. This is no ruse. I would not do that to you, nor would Gibby be a part of any such deception. He said this woman is sought for séances, readings, and other things which I have no desire to know about."

"And Gibby told you about her?"

"Yes, and he suggested we seek her for answers. I told him that I intended to marry you, but I worried about you and that hellish curse. If you are unnerved by being here, we will leave right now before we even meet Mrs. Fortune."

"Blake, I'm overwhelmed that you would do this for me. I'm thankful you want to do it for us."

"Henrietta, I love you. I would do anything for you. I am going to marry you, curse or no curse, but if you are uncomfortable, just say the word and we will leave."

Henrietta threw her arms around his neck, and he caught her up in a tight hug.

"Oh, no, Blake, I don't want to go. I want her help."

The black velvet draperies parted, and Henrietta and Blake separated.

The buxom woman stepped out and said, "Mrs. Fortune will see you now. Follow me."

Blake rose to his feet, and Henrietta stood up. They followed the woman through the heavy fabric opening and down a long, dimly lit corridor before stepping through another doorway. The room was lit by a single candle that eerily looked as if it was suspended in air. Henrietta had thought the front of the house mysterious, but this room was downright creepy. She inched closer to Blake and slipped her hand into his. He squeezed her fingers affectionately.

As they drew closer, Henrietta could see that the candlestick had been placed in the center of a small round table that had been draped in black velvet. The windows were also covered in black velvet draperies and shades, blocking out any hint of light from the outside. She wondered why everything in the room had to be so dark.

A tall, thin woman appeared before them. She seemed to walk out of the blackness of the wall and into the room, but Henrietta knew that was impossible. The woman was dressed in mourning clothes, including gloves and a tulle veil that covered her face. Her carriage was straight, and her head had a proud tilt. She stopped on the other side of the small table.

"You asked to see me?" she said in a voice that sounded as polished as any member of Polite Society.

"Yes," Blake said, guiding Henrietta farther into the room. "We've been told that you may be able to help us."

"Tell me what you desire."

"Miss Tweed believes there is a curse that follows her. We want to know if you can determine if that is true, and if it is, can you remove it?"

The woman laughed softly, and Henrietta thought she sounded much younger than her widow's weeds indicated. "I don't know what you have been told about me, Your Grace, but you must think very highly of my abilities if you think I can remove a curse someone else cast."

"Then you can't help me?" Henrietta said wistfully.

"That I don't know. Come sit here at the table, and let me look into your eyes and read you."

Read me?

Blake pulled out a black fabric-covered chair for Henrietta. When she sat down, he remained behind her and placed his hands on her shoulders. She was comforted by his touch.

Mrs. Fortune took the chair opposite her. The single candle was at the level of the woman's face. Henrietta tried to make out her features but the tulle veil was too opaque to distinguish any facial appearance.

Mrs. Fortune tilted her head toward Blake and said, "I understand why you don't want to leave her side, but you cannot touch her. You must go with my helper to the front of the house. Do not try to come back to us or interrupt us for any reason. If you do, I will have to discontinue my reading, and I will not be able to help her."

"I understand," Blake said.

Henrietta's heart slammed against her chest. She

reached up and covered Blake's hands with her own, trying to hold him to her.

He reached down and whispered into her ear. "I won't be far away. Just remember I love you, and that no matter what happens, everything is going to be all right for us."

She nodded, and then he slipped his hands from beneath hers. She listened for his footsteps until she could no longer hear them. She swallowed hard and lifted her shoulders.

"Give me your hands, palms up," the woman said, reaching out to Henrietta so that the candlestick was between her wrists.

Tentative at first, Henrietta didn't move. She took a deep breath. And another. Why was she hesitating? This woman might be able to help her. She could possibly break the curse and put order back into Henrietta's life, but there was the fear of the unknown. What would this woman find out?

With renewed courage, Henrietta swallowed her remaining fear and confidently reached out her open palms to Mrs. Fortune. The woman slipped her hands beneath Henrietta's and lifted them off the table, closer to the light. Her grasp on Henrietta was warm, sure, and firm.

"You must answer truthfully everything I ask you."

Henrietta nodded.

"Your hands are cold. Are you frightened of me?"

"No. I'm frightened of what you might tell me."

"But you want to know regardless."

"Yes."

The woman held Henrietta's hands closer to the candle. She felt the heat from the flame.

"Who cast the curse on you?"

"I don't know who cast it. An old woman by the name of Mrs. Goolsby told me I was cursed when I was seven years old."

"That is very young to be cursed. What did she say about the curse?"

"She said that anyone who had charge over me would die. My parents and five guardians have died in the past twelve years."

"Who is your guardian now?"

Henrietta's heartbeat hammered in her chest. Her hands grew colder, even though they were so near the flame that she felt its heat.

"The Duke of Blakewell," Henrietta said and leaned in closer to the flame. "You must do something about this curse. I don't want him to die."

"You love him?"

"Very much. More than my own life."

The woman laughed softly once again. "Die he will, Miss Tweed. All of us must die at some time, but let me see if he will live to be an old man. Stop trying to see my face. Stare into the candle flame."

Henrietta had no idea how the woman could tell she desperately wanted to look into her eyes and know if she spoke the truth. But Henrietta obeyed and transfixed her gaze on the lighted candle.

"The colors are soothing, are they not, amber and yellow mixing together? That's right, look at it, and let its heat comfort you. You are cold. It can give you warmth. It can calm you. Continue staring into the flame and relax your hands."

Henrietta felt her grip on the woman's hands go

slack. "That is good. Keep staring at the flame. Do your eyes feel heavy?"

Henrietta nodded.

"Close them and rest. I will read your life. Do not think about me. Just relax. Feel the warmth on your face. Let it comfort you."

Henrietta relaxed into the chair. Her eyes became heavy. She felt at peace, and darkness closed around her like a fine wool blanket.

"Miss Tweed, open your eyes."

Henrietta opened her eyes, blinking several times. The candle had burned low. She could see all of Mrs. Fortune's veiled face.

"Did I fall asleep?"

"Not exactly. You communicated with me during the reading. I asked you many questions, and you answered me."

"I did. Does that mean you can help me?"

"Come, let's go join His Grace, and I will tell you all I know."

Henrietta followed Mrs. Fortune through the velvet drapery panels, down the corridor, and back into the dimly lit vestibule. Blake turned from the window where he stood and rushed to Henrietta's side, sliding his arm around her waist.

"What happened?"

"From what I read of Henrietta's life, there has never been a curse on her."

Henrietta gasped in relief. Blake squeezed her close to his side.

"Then how do you explain what the old woman told me about the deaths of my guardians and it coming true?" Henrietta asked.

"The woman, Mrs. Goolsby, must have been a soothsayer. I cannot know for sure, but I believe she simply looked into your eyes and read your future. She knew these deaths would occur in your life, and she feared you because of it, but not because of anything having to do with a curse."

"She read my future?" Henrietta glanced from Mrs. Fortune to Blake. "But I don't understand. She told me I was cursed."

"Of course, I cannot say for sure, but my belief is that she probably didn't understand her powers to see into someone's future. Many people who have the gift deny it, and some even run from it, though they can never really give up or escape the gift. Some never embrace it or try to strengthen it. They refuse to make use of their talents to help others and become confused about what they are actually capable of doing. Sometimes it is wise to do so, especially if it frightens them. Perhaps this woman was like that."

"And Blake, my current guardian?" she grabbed hold of his arm and held tight.

"Have no fear. I see him with you in your future when you are both too old to climb the stairs in his home. And you will spend many more wonderful hours together in his book room."

Henrietta glanced up at Blake before setting her gaze on Mrs. Fortune. "You know about the book room?"

"How could I not? It is your favorite room in the house."

Henrietta's cheeks burned as her breath quickened. "Are you sure we will have a long life together?"

"I am. You are not cursed. You will have many

more cherished memories together. I saw into His Grace's future, too. He opened his mind to me the minute he saw me."

"I did?" Blake asked, disbelief showing on his face.

"Don't sound so skeptical." Mrs. Fortune laughed lightly again. "You were easy to read. You came in wanting my help, believing I could help you." She turned her face toward Henrietta. "You were not so easy to read. You doubted more than His Grace, but I finally calmed you enough to see into your life."

"You really read my future, too?" Blake questioned.

"Of course. As I said, you were easy because you were so willing to help Miss Tweed. I cannot change the past, nor can I alter the future. I can tell you only what I see. Neither of you has cause to worry. I don't see death in your futures for many years to come."

Henrietta gave her a grateful smile. "Thank you, Mrs. Fortune. Thank you."

"Once you sought my help, it was my duty, and my honor, to be of service to you."

"You said you think Mrs. Goolsby must have been a soothsayer, but what about you? Are you a soothsayer?"

"I am your servant, Miss Tweed. Call on me any time I can be of service to either you or His Grace."

"I will always remember what you have done for me," Henrietta said.

The woman nodded once.

Blake pulled a small drawstring bag out of his pocket and laid it on the table beside the lamp. "If I can ever be of service to you, Mrs. Fortune, please let me know."

"Likewise, Your Grace."

Blake opened the door, and they rushed out into the night.

Twenty-One

Dearest Lucien, My Grandson,

While reading last evening, I found this fine quote from Lord Chesterfield. It seems even he couldn't hold to his own vow not to offer advice on matrimony. I find it comforting to find the man had a few flaws after all.

"Do not be in haste to marry, but look about you first, for the affair is important; let her be of an unblemished and unsuspected character and of rank not indecently below your own."

Your loving Grandmother,
Lady Elder

HENRIETTA AND BLAKE QUICKLY CLIMBED BACK INTO the carriage, and the driver took off at a fast, rumbling pace. Blake immediately pulled her into his arms and kissed her passionately.

With his lips not far from hers, he said, "I want you to tell me that all this dark talk of curses is over."

She smiled and said, "Completely over, my darling."

He looked deeply into her eyes as he embraced her. "I want you to mean it, Henrietta. No more fear or dread."

"Or worry. I mean it," she said with all the love she was feeling for him. "I believed her when she said we will grow old together. I believe she saw our future and our past. How else would she have known about the book room?"

"How else?" he said with a grin.

"I only regret one thing."

"Tell me."

She gave him a teasing smile. "That we did not take the time to ask her how many children we will have. Maybe we should go back."

"No. I think she told us quite enough. I want to look forward to those surprises with you."

She cupped his cheek with her gloved hand. "And I look forward to many years of loving you."

"And now for what I didn't do properly in Mrs. Fortune's house or earlier in the book room. Henrietta, I love you. Will you marry me?"

Her smile widened. "Oh, yes, my love, I will marry you," she whispered as his lips covered hers in a deep passionate kiss.

His hand slipped under her cape, and he found her breast and softly caressed her as his lips moved over hers.

"Mmm, you feel so good. I might have to see what I can do about speeding up that three-day waiting period for the special license so that we can marry sooner."

"That would be wonderful, my love." Henrietta sighed contentedly, feeling happier than she thought possible.

"I have something for you. A wedding present."
Blake pulled a piece of parchment out of his coat
pocket and handed it to her.

"A wedding gift? When did you have time to get
it? I don't have anything for you!"

"You have given yourself to me. That is all that I
need or want. This is yours, and no one can take it
from you."

Her curiosity brimmed as she unfolded the sheet
of paper, filled with writing. At the bottom of it, she
recognized the seal for his dukedom.

She glanced up at him. "It is much too dark in here.
I can't read what it says."

"I will tell you. When I left you this afternoon, I
not only went to see Gibby; I went to see my solicitor
as well. I had him draw up a document for me to sign
that says you are to have complete and total control
over the inheritance you bring into our marriage from
your father. You are to be its administrator and look
after it however you see fit. It is all yours to do with
as you so please."

Henrietta felt her heart leap in her chest. "Blake, you
didn't have to do that. It will be my dowry to you."

"No, my love. It is yours to keep. I've already
signed it. Not even our son, should we be fortunate
enough to have one, will ever have control of your
inheritance, unless you sign it over to him. I want you
to know that you are free to live on your own, as you
wish, or you can marry me and be my love forever."

"I will marry you, and be your love the rest of
my life, Blake. I'm stunned. I'm grateful. I'm happy.
Thank you."

Henrietta kissed him softly on the lips and then handed the paper back to him.

His eyes questioned her. "You don't want it?"

"Of course I do." She smiled. "But, would you mind carrying it for me in your pocket, as I don't have one and I don't want to lose it."

He laughed and put the paper back in his coat.

"I am looking forward to having you by my side, Henrietta. There is never a dull moment when you are with me. You complete me."

Excitement grew inside her. "And you have made me feel content for the first time in my life. Thank you for giving me a home I'll never have to leave."

"Never," he whispered as his lips closed over hers again.

Their kiss deepened, and Henrietta parted her lips for him. A breathless fluttering settled in her stomach. His mouth and tongue ravaged hers in a slow savoring kiss that thrilled her. His kisses filled her with sweet torturous longing to be completely his once again. She loved this man who was strong and demanding, yet filled with tenderness, too.

He drew away from her once again. "The carriage is stopping. Let's go inside and finish this."

They stepped outside, and both noticed that two carriages were standing in front of theirs.

"Bloody hell," Blake cursed. "Those are Morgan's and Race's carriages. What the devil are they doing here, this time of night? Have they nothing better to do than plague me?"

"Do you suppose something is wrong?"

"Probably not. I'm sure they just want to find

out why neither of us appeared at any of the parties tonight. I'll get rid of them quickly."

Ashby opened the door for them as they approached and said, "Your Grace, Lord Morgandale and Lord Raceworth are here to see you. They are waiting in your book room."

"They're no doubt in there drinking my good brandy, but why?" Blake said as he took off his cloak and then helped Henrietta with hers.

"I'll say good-night to you so you can find out why they are here," Henrietta said while removing her bonnet.

Blake grabbed her hand and pulled her close. "You will do no such thing. You are coming with me. My cousins are annoying, but they mean no harm. They should be the first to know that we are getting married as soon as legally possible." He reached down and kissed her on the tip of her nose. "Or maybe they already know that."

"How could they?"

"Gibby."

They walked into the book room holding hands. Race and Morgan sat in the two wing chairs, each drinking a glass of brandy.

"I see you two made yourselves at home, as usual," Blake said.

The gentlemen rose. "Why stand on ceremony with family?" Lord Raceworth said. "Henrietta, how good to see you. You're looking lovely tonight."

"Thank you, my lord," she replied.

"And there are no lasting bad effects from your outing in Hyde Park with Lord Waldo?" Lord Morgandale said.

"None, but how did you know about that?"

"Lord Waldo was telling everyone tonight how you couldn't stop sneezing when you went for a ride in the park with him."

Blake made a growling sound. "Henrietta will never have to endure that man's attention, or the dog's, again."

"Dog?" Lord Raceworth asked.

Blake didn't let go of her hand as he said, "It's a long story, and the night is already short. What the devil are you two doing here this time of evening? It had better be damned important."

"Well, of course, it is," Morgan said. "We talked to Gibby earlier, and he told us everything."

"Everything?"

They both put their glasses down and reached into their coat pockets. Each cousin pulled out a folded piece of paper and extended it to Henrietta.

Hesitantly, she took them and said, "I don't understand."

"We've known from the beginning about the deaths of your previous guardians," Lord Raceworth said.

"And we know all about the curse and your fear for Blake's life," Lord Morgandale added. "Because of that, we have each drawn up a document that says that if anything happens to Blake, although we feel certain nothing will, but just in case an accident, illness, or whatever happens, we will be your guardians. You are part of our family now."

"And we will take care of you," Lord Raceworth finished for him.

Tears clouded Henrietta's eyes as she hugged Race and then Morgan. "I don't know what to say. I never dreamt anything like this would happen to me. Blake, you didn't know about this?"

"How could I? I'm as surprised by my cousins' actions as you are."

"Welcome to the family," Lord Morgandale said, giving her a kiss on the cheek.

Henrietta wiped the wetness from her eyes and rushed back to Blake's embrace. "Blake, I'm overwhelmed."

"Quite frankly, so am I." He glanced first at Race and then Morgan. "You won't ever have to be her guardians, but I do appreciate the offer and, for it, I'm indebted to you, Cousins."

"We were hoping you would be," Race said with a gleam in his eyes.

"Pardon me, Your Grace."

Blake turned toward the doorway. "Yes, Ashby?"

"Sir Randolph is here and wants to know if he may be allowed to join you."

Blake looked at Henrietta and gave her a knowing smile. "Of course, send him in."

A moment later Sir Randolph sauntered in, smiling from ear to ear. Without bothering with a greeting, he said, "I knew you wouldn't mind if I came over, Blake. I couldn't wait to find out what happened with Mrs. Fortune. Did it go well?"

"Ah, yes, we were wondering about that, too," Lord Raceworth said.

"It was exactly what we needed to do, Gib. Henrietta was never cursed. The old woman had just looked into her future and knew what was going to happen in her life." Blake tightened his hold around Henrietta's waist. "Everything is going to be fine."

"I'm completely at ease about the curse and have put it out of my mind," Henrietta said.

"Splendid," the old man added gleefully. He reached into his pocket and pulled out a piece of paper and handed it to Henrietta. "But since you can never be too careful, I've just come from my solicitor, and here is a document saying I will be your guardian if anything ever happens to Blake. I'm asking him to sign this and make it legal. It won't matter if I die; I'm an old man anyway."

Everyone laughed except Sir Randolph.

"I'm missing the humor in this. I'm trying to do the right thing here."

Henrietta took the paper from him and gave him a kiss on the cheek. "We are laughing because Blake's cousins just gave me similar documents." She held up the papers for him to see. "I'm simply overwhelmed by your generosity and compassion for me. I truly feel that I'm a part of your family now."

"I'm honored all of you are rushing to take care of Henrietta, but nothing is going to happen to me. Now, I would appreciate it if all of you would leave, so that I can have a few minutes of privacy with my beautiful fiancée before I have to say good-night to her."

After the door shut behind the three men, Henrietta turned and threw her arms around Blake and held him tight. "I am so happy I could cry."

"Please, don't, my love," he whispered into her ear. "I don't want to see you cry, even if they are tears of joy."

"Blake, I love you with all my heart, and I will do my very best always to make you happy."

"I could not be happier."

Heated with the sweet rush of desire, Henrietta lifted her lips to him again. Blake kissed her deeply, madly, and she matched his fierce hunger as they gloried in their new-found love for each other.

His lips left hers and burned a hot trail of moisture all the way down the column of her neck to the hollow of her throat. There, he stopped and tasted her skin with his tongue.

Henrietta trembled beneath his loving caresses.

"Once I apply for the special license tomorrow, it will be three days before we can marry."

"I don't want to waste three days of our lives by not being together."

"I was just thinking the same thing. I want you in my bed tonight," he whispered against her lips. "I don't want to spend another night without you."

"I am yours, my love—tonight, tomorrow, and always."

Blake reached down and, hooking one arm under her knees, he swept her into his arms and started up the stairs, kissing her as he went.

She laughed and mumbled against his lips, "I can walk, you know."

"Yes, I know, but I should do this before I get too old to walk up the stairs, as Mrs. Fortune predicted I will be one day."

As he walked down the corridor, they passed by Henrietta's bedroom door. They looked inside and saw Peggy still busy packing her clothing.

"Perhaps I should go speak to my maid," Henrietta said.

Blake kept walking. "You can tell her our good news tomorrow. I'm not letting anyone else interrupt us tonight."

He opened the door to his bedchamber, stepped inside, and kicked the door shut behind them. Blake laid her down on his bed and snuggled down beside her.

Gazing lovingly into her eyes, he whispered, "This time I am not going to be such a rake as I was in the book room."

Henrietta touched his cheek and smiled at him. "You were not a rake, my love."

"Lord Chesterfield said that 'few men can be men of pleasure, but every man may be a rake.' At the very least, I was hasty in my pursuit of our pleasure this afternoon, but only because my desire for you was so great, and I was eager to wipe any thought of Lord Waldo from your mind."

"Who?"

Blake laughed. "This time, my sweet Henrietta, I'm going to make love to you properly, slowly, and all night long."

"That sounds intriguing. I think I will love it."

Blake smiled at her. "I'll make sure you do."

He bent his head and captured her lips with his own as his hand caressed her cheek.

Henrietta thrilled to his touch.

The End

Dear Readers,

I hope you have enjoyed reading Blake and Henrietta's story in *A Duke to Die For* as much as I enjoyed writing it. Blake's cousins, Lord Raceworth and Lord Morgandale, have their own stories to tell.

It is also my hope that you found pleasure in reading the numerous quotes from Lord Chesterfield. While doing research, I stumbled onto this man who wrote hundreds of letters to his son over the course of several years late in the eighteenth century, and I was intrigued by him.

In *The Rogues' Dynasty Trilogy*, you'll find many of Lord Chesterfield's words sprinkled throughout the pages. All quotes at the beginning of each chapter are taken word for word from his letters to his son. I took creative liberty in attributing quotes to him that I know he didn't say, but in each case, I have a character in the book question the authenticity of the quote. I do this merely for fun and entertainment, not to give credit where it isn't due.

Please mark your calendars now to look for Lord Raceworth's story in *A Marquis to Marry*, which will be published in October 2009, and Lord Morgandale's story in *An Earl to Enchant*, which will be in book-stores in April 2010.

In the meantime, you can e-mail me with questions or comments at ameliagrey@comcast.net or through my website at ameliagrey.com.

Happy Reading,
Amelia Grey

Read on for a preview of

A Marquis to Marry

Book Two in The Rogues' Dynasty series
by Amelia Grey

Coming from Sourcebooks Casablanca
in October 2009

One

My Dearest Grandson Alexander,

I am confident you will agree with these wise words from Lord Chesterfield: "At all events, a man had better talk too much to women, than too little."

Your loving Grandmother,
Lady Elder

ALEXANDER MITCHELL RACEWORTH, THE FOURTH Marquis of Raceworth, stared at the cards in his hands, but his mind was on the surprisingly bold, albeit beautiful, Miss Maryann Mayflower. She sat beside him at the card table, slowly rubbing her foot up and down his leg. It was her second Season, and the talk around the clubs was that she would do anything to make a match before it ended.

That rumor gave Race pause, even though the invitation she issued under the table was tempting. He wouldn't mind a tryst in the shrubbery with a willing miss, but he wasn't interested in getting caught in a parson's mousetrap.

For the past three years, Race had held a popular afternoon card party in his garden during the Season. Only this year, the coveted outdoor event had to be moved inside because of a hellish rainstorm. The social gathering was so well attended that he had to move the furniture out of his drawing room and the dining room and place it in other areas of the house so that he could accommodate more than three-dozen guests who had come to play whist, cribbage, and speculation.

"Excuse me, Your Lordship."

Race looked up at his stocky housekeeper. "Yes, Mrs. Frost."

"Could I have a word with you in private?"

The woman was well trained. She wouldn't interrupt him unless it was something important. "Of course, I'll be right with you."

He looked at the players at his table. There was the comely blonde next to him who wasn't letting a little thing like a housekeeper standing so close keep her from seducing him with her foot. The other lady at the table was the quite charming and unattached widow, Mrs. Constance Pepperfield, and the other gentleman of the foursome was his cousin Morgan, the ninth Earl of Morgandale.

Race laid his cards face down on the white-linen-covered table. "Excuse me, ladies, Morgan. I have to bow out of this hand. As you know, this is the problem with being the host of a party."

"Must you?" Miss Mayflower asked, pouting.

"I'm afraid so," Race assured her pleasantly and moved his leg away from hers. "It seems duty is calling me. Morgan, can I depend on you to charm the ladies while I'm away?"

"More than happy to."

Race rose and went in search of Mrs. Frost. He found her in the vestibule, closing the front door.

"You needed to see me?"

"Yes, Your Lordship," she said with a grimace on her plump face. "I'm sorry to disturb you, but I knew you would want to know that the Dowager Duchess of Blooming is here to see you."

Race's brows drew together. He didn't like surprises. "A dowager duchess to see me? I wonder whatever for."

"I have no idea, My Lord."

Unlike his cousin Blake, the fifth Duke of Blakewell, who was notorious for forgetting appointments, Race knew every entry on his social calendar. He certainly would have remembered if a dowager duchess had requested to call on him. But what was he going to do? He couldn't see her this afternoon. His house was filled with people chatting nosily around card tables.

"Where is Her Grace now?" Race asked Mrs. Frost.

"In her carriage. I didn't speak to her. The duchess sent her companion to the door to say she would like a few minutes of your time, if you would be so kind. I told her you had a party going on. The companion apologized for the interruption and said Her Grace was content to wait in her coach until you are available to speak to her."

"That's odd," Race mumbled more to himself than to his housekeeper.

"It was a quick win for me after you left," Morgan

said, walking up to Race. "Those two ladies don't know much about cards. I got them both a cup of punch and told them I'd check with you to see if you wanted us to wait for you or continue. What's going on?"

Race stepped away from Mrs. Frost and in a low voice said, "I don't really know. The Dowager Duchess of Blooming is here to see me."

His cousin's blue eyes narrowed. "Good Lord, who is she?"

"The devil if I know." Race brushed his light brown hair away from his forehead and studied over her name, drawing a blank. "There are at least a dozen dukes, if not more. I'm not acquainted with all of them. And I certainly don't know how many dowagers there are."

"The area of Blooming is up near the Northern Coast," Morgan offered. "That is probably the reason we're not familiar with the name."

"I haven't a clue why the dowager would be here to see me."

"Maybe she was a friend of our grandmother's and would like to converse with you about her."

"Damnation, Morgan, I can't do that now with a house full of lively guests to help entertain. She's come without an appointment and wants to wait until I'm available to see her."

Morgan grinned. "And I can see you are on the verge of telling her just where she can wait."

Race smiled mischievously. "Tempted? Yes."

"Our grandmother would roll over in her grave that you would even think of treating an older woman—titled or not—any way but as if she were a queen."

"Don't remind me." All humor vanished from his face. "Why wouldn't Her Grace do the proper thing and leave, and then later make an appointment to see me?"

"It tells me she wants to do more than just converse about our grandmother. Is there any chance she's here because you slept with one of her maids, or worse, one of her granddaughters?"

Race glared at his cousin.

"Blast it, Race, whoever it is you've slept with, I suggest you turn on that famous charm. Better to win her over up-front. She'll go easier on you when you have to ask her forgiveness later."

"Bloody hell, Morgan. I don't even know who she is, so how can I know if I've slept with someone she's related to?"

"Are you in any other kind of trouble that I don't know about?"

"No," Race stated, cocksure.

"Hmm," Morgan said, and then added, "It's too bad Blake and Henrietta missed the party. With him being a duke, they would know exactly what is and isn't acceptable in a situation like this."

"Why the devil isn't our cousin here? What's he doing today, anyway?" Race asked in an annoyed tone.

"He married Henrietta two weeks ago." Morgan grinned. "You figure out what he's doing on a rainy Sunday afternoon."

Race uttered a curse under his breath. "Oh, right."

"Where is Gibby? He's been around long enough he should know what to do."

"I don't know what he's up to. I received a short note from him earlier today saying he couldn't make it."

"So what are you going to do about the duchess? You can't leave her in her carriage in front of your house. That's an outrage."

As much as Race didn't want to concede to Morgan or the dowager, his grandmother had raised him and his cousins to respect women. As inconvenient as it was now, he couldn't change his nature. And, he had to admit that the woman had piqued his interest. While he'd had his share of unannounced females showing up at his door, none of them had been old or titled.

"You know I'll do the proper thing," Race finally admitted.

He called to Mrs. Frost, who had remained silently by the front door. "Go out to the carriage and inform Her Grace that I insist she come in and join the party. If she refuses, which I expect she will, have some of the servants move enough furniture out of the music room to make a comfortable place for her to sit down. See that she is served a cup of tea and some of Cook's plum tarts, and tell her I'll make time to see her."

Race turned to Morgan and grinned. "Satisfied?"

"I am, but she'll probably think you've treated her atrociously." Morgan chuckled lightly. "You will be the talk of the ton after this little escapade."

"Probably," Race agreed. "No doubt it will give the scandal sheets a week's worth of articles."

"Or more, and they'll love you for it. Gossip makes them money. And look on the bright side. It could encourage other ladies to show up at your door unannounced."

"I don't see any harm in that."

Morgan clapped Race on the back, laughing as they rejoined the party.

Several games of cards and at least two glasses of wine later, Race was enjoying another good hand at a table with two delightful young ladies and their father when Morgan tapped him on the shoulder.

Race looked up at his cousin and frowned.

Morgan leaned down and whispered, "Have you met with the mysterious duchess?"

"Not yet," Race said, glancing down at the two aces in his hand. "I was giving her time to have a cup of tea."

Morgan cleared his throat. "She's been in the music room over an hour. I think her cup might be empty by now."

That got his attention. Race sighed. "Do you mind taking over this hand for me? Some problems just won't go away without a little push."

Race downed the remaining wine in his glass and, with a grimace, excused himself from the game once again and headed for his music room. Upon entering, he saw a gray-haired woman sitting in a side chair with mountains of furniture piled up behind her. He stopped in front of her, bowed, and kissed her hand. "Your Grace, you should have joined us. I take it you aren't fond of cards, but I trust my servants made every effort to keep you comfortable."

"Please, My Lord, I am Mrs. Princeton." She rose and curtseyed. "May I present the Dowager Duchess of Blooming."

The woman pointed to a much younger lady standing by the window and staring at him with an amused expression on her face. Race's heart skipped a beat. The duchess was not an old, unattractive lady. She was a stunning beauty.

She walked toward him with a slow, confident stride, stopping a respectable distance away. "You know, I've heard that about you," she said.

His stomach did a slow roll. "What's that?"

"That you can charm a leopard out of its spots and a nun out of her virtue."

Race raised one brow. "I wouldn't believe everything you read in the gossip pages."

"In your case, I think they may be right."

Race cocked his head and slowly perused her. She had the prettiest eyes he'd ever seen. They were a light shade of green, large and expressive. She wore a deep forest-green traveling dress, accented by a matching pelisse. Her glossy, dark brown hair was swooped up to the top of her head, with soft wispy curls framing her face.

"Then tell me, Your Grace, are you a leopard or a nun?"

Mrs. Princeton gasped.

Race cleared his throat. For a moment he'd forgotten the other woman was in the room.

The dowager hid her smile behind her hand, not answering his question, but saying, "My Lord, thank you for agreeing to see me. I realize that you are unacquainted with me or my circumstances. This is my companion, Mrs. Princeton. My husband died shortly after we married. His son from his first wife is now the Duke of Blooming, and he and his duchess reside at Chapel Glade in Blooming."

Her words brought to mind the vague memory

of gossip about a young lady who was married to an older, reclusive duke because of an indiscretion. Could she be that lady?

"I see," he said. "I have to admit that you have caught me at a busy time, Your Grace, and I feel at a complete disadvantage."

"I'm sure that's not a place you often find yourself."

"To say the least."

That amused smile played at her beautifully shaped lips again, and it irritated the hell out of him. So much for thinking she'd be horrified at being left alone to sip tea for the better part of an hour.

"Do you mind if we speak alone?" she asked.

"No, of course not, if you are comfortable with that."

"I am. The rain has stopped. Perhaps your housekeeper could take Mrs. Princeton on a tour of your garden."

She smiled again and Race's heart fluttered so fast he felt thunderstruck. What the devil was that feeling all about? And why was he so sensitive to every move she made?

She was the most intriguing woman he'd ever met—and it had nothing to do with her being a duchess. Because of Blake, Race had been around dukes and duchesses all his life, and he wasn't awed by them, as were most of the people in Polite Society. Her Grace's beauty was very appealing, but that's not what unnerved him, either. He had the pleasure of beautiful women around him all the time.

She unsettled him because of her poise, her self-confidence, and her regal manner. She was simply alluring and, when he looked at her, he was completely captivated. His fingers itched to touch her. He had never met anyone like her. Everything about her told him that, in her, he had met his match.

After Mrs. Princeton had left with his housekeeper, the duchess said, "I believe I owe you an apology for showing up at your door unannounced."

"Why do I get the feeling that you don't apologize often?

He saw a brief look of appreciation flash in her eyes.

"I'm sorry that, in my eagerness to speak to you, I rushed right past my good sense. I should have written and asked for an appointment to see you," she admitted.

"That's difficult to dispute. I confess to being a little surprised that you didn't."

A soft smile lifted just one corner of her lips. "Only a little?"

She was teasing him. *All right, a damned lot!* She was controlling their conversation, and he seldom let that happen with anyone other than his cousins.

His gaze focused fully on hers. "Tell me what I can do for you, Your Grace."

"I'm here because you possess something that belongs to my family, and I would like it back now."

Race went still. That proclamation raised Race's eyebrows and the hair on the back of his neck, too. He couldn't have been more taken aback if she had suddenly slapped him. *What kind of accusation was that? You have something that belongs to my family and I'd like it back.*

Race grinned, and then he laughed. She was truly

a strong-willed lady who didn't mind speaking her mind. He liked the courage he sensed in her, but he couldn't let her get away with being so brash.

His laughter caused the first crack in her over-confident demeanor. She bristled noticeably. It made him feel damned good to see her rattled.

"I'm sorry for laughing, Your Grace."

"No, you aren't."

Her voice was taut and steady. He could tell she strained hard to keep her face stoic.

"All right, I'm not. You have amused me greatly."

Her chin and shoulders lifted a fraction. She didn't like what he had said any more than he had liked her accusation.

"I wasn't aware I had the capacity to be so humorous," she said.

"Then let me enlighten you."

A couple of steps took him close enough that he could have touched her if he'd lifted his hands. He caught the scent of freshly washed hair and lightly perfumed skin. His body reacted strongly to her feminine draw.

He had expected her to back away from him, but she stood her ground without flinching. He heard her labored breathing and, for a moment, he watched the rise and fall of her chest. She was so fascinating he found it difficult to concentrate.

Yet, he couldn't let her accusation go unchallenged.

His gaze swept up and down her face before settling on her gorgeous green eyes. "First, I'm amused that you were so blunt. If you truly thought I had something that belonged to you, there are nicer ways

to say it than 'It's mine and I want it back.' Second,
I'm amused because I don't have anything that belongs
to your family, and third, if I had anything you
thought belonged to your family, I wouldn't turn it
over to you simply because you demanded it."

He bent his head closer so that his nose almost
touched hers. The fragrant scent of mint tea lingered
in the air. With great effort, he resisted the impulse to
rest his lips against hers and feel their softness.

In a husky voice, he said, "And finally, Your Grace,
just who the hell do you think you are to imply that I
have stolen anything from your family?"

A light blush tinted her cheeks, but she didn't
shrink from his nearness. Rather than his forward
advancement intimidating her, she relaxed. Only a
little, just enough to hint that he might have caused
her a moment of compunction before she summoned
an inner strength to carry her forward.

Her face remained dangerously close to his. Her
courage didn't waver. "Your points are well taken,
and I must apologize once again. I didn't intend for
you to feel I was accusing you of stealing anything
from my family. I assure you that is not the case. I
merely said you have it in your possession."

He heard sincerity in her voice, and that gave him
some measure of assurance that she wasn't just trying
to trick him.

"What is it that you think I have?"

Her eyes sparkled. "Oh, I know you have them.
The Talbot pearls."

Race's mouth tightened. His grandmother, Lady
Elder, had left him the priceless antique necklace in

her will. Five thirty-two-inch strands of perfectly matched pearls.

His gaze scanned her face once again, looking for deception. "My grandmother's necklace?"

"My grandmother's pearls," she insisted.

Her courage was impressive and her beauty undeniable, but her assertions were troubling. Her gaze stayed locked on his. He liked the fact she looked him in the eyes and didn't cower under his nearness. She obviously wasn't lying—she actually believed what she was saying.

"Your audacity is almost as priceless as the pearls, but stand in line, Your Grace. You are the fourth person this month to approach me about the pearls. Though, I admit, none have come forward with as creative a story as yours."

Concern flashed in her glinting eyes. "What do you mean?" She reached down, picked up some papers from the table beside her, and extended them to him. "I have documents proving the necklace belongs to my family."

Race didn't offer to take the folded sheets of aged parchment from her. "Interestingly enough, the gentlemen who have come before you are not as clever as you. They are not claiming ownership of the pearls. They all want to buy them."

Her fan-shaped brows furrowed, and alarm etched her face. "Who are these men?"

For the first time, Race felt anger rise inside her, and it was seductive. Desire for her filled him. He wanted to pull her into his arms, crush her against his chest, and feel her soft, pliant lips beneath his in an eager kiss.

Instead, he kept control of his thoughts and said, "The first person to approach me was Mr. Albert Smith, a one-armed antiquities dealer who wants them for an unnamed buyer. Does that unnamed person happen to be you?"

"Absolutely not. I'd never pay for what already rightfully belongs to my family."

"Then perhaps you are acquainted with Sir Harold Winston. He is employed by the Prince Regent himself. It seems Prinny has long had his eyes on the Talbot pearls. He wants to add the collar to His Majesty's Crown Jewels."

"That's absurd. The Crown already has more pearls, diamonds, and gems than all other countries put together, including Rome and the Catholic Church."

"Ah, then that only leaves the mysterious buccaneer, Captain Spyglass." He tilted his head in consideration. "Perhaps you have formed an alliance with him?"

"I have heard of the man, but know this, My Lord, I have formed no alliance with anyone. Moreover, Captain Spyglass is nothing but a pirate."

"So some say," Race admitted.

"What does he want with the pearls?"

"No doubt to add to his collection. He's been buying up pearls from all over the world and garnering quite the collection, from what I understand."

"Why is he buying pearls?"

Race bent his head closer to hers once again. "Are you sure you don't know, Duchess?"

"I can only tell you the truth. I have never met nor have I ever had dealings with Captain Spyglass or any of these men you speak of. These documents prove the Talbot pearls belong to my mother. They were stolen from my grandmother fifty years ago."

He refused the papers yet again. He didn't know if he should believe her about any of the men. Though in truth, it hardly mattered. He didn't know what kind of madcap scheme she had mulling around that pretty head of hers, or why she had brought it to his door, but he wasn't interested.

"Documents are easily forged to look old and authentic, Your Grace. There is no way I'm selling the pearls to a one-armed man, a pirate, or the Crown. And I'm sure as hell not going to be bluffed out of them by a beautiful duchess."

About the Author

Amelia Grey grew up in a small town in the Florida Panhandle. She has been happily married to her high school sweetheart for more than twenty-five years.

Amelia has won the Booksellers Best Award and Aspen Gold Award for writing as Amelia Grey. Writing as Gloria Dale Skinner, she has won the Romantic Times Award for Love and Laughter, the Maggie Award, and the Affaire de Coeur Award. Her books have been sold in many countries in Europe, in Russia, and in China, and they have also been featured in Doubleday and Rhapsody Book Clubs.

Amelia loves flowers, candlelight, sweet smiles, gentle laughter, and sunshine.

Lady Anne
AND THE
HOWL
IN THE
DARK

by Donna Lea Simpson

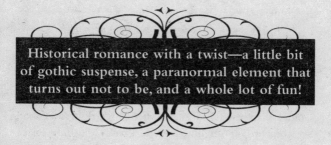

Historical romance with a twist—a little bit of gothic suspense, a paranormal element that turns out not to be, and a whole lot of fun!

LADY ANNE ADDISON IS A RATIONAL AND COURAGEOUS woman. So when she's summoned by a frightened friend to Yorkshire to prove or disprove the presence in their woods of a menacing wolf—or werewolf—she takes up the challenge.

Lady Anne finds the Marquess of Darkefell to be an infuriatingly unyielding man. Rumors swirl and suspects abound. The Marquess is indeed at the middle of it all, but not in the way that Lady Anne had suspected... and now he's firmly determined to win her in spite of everything.

978-1-4022-1791-3 • $6.99 U.S. / $7.99 CAN

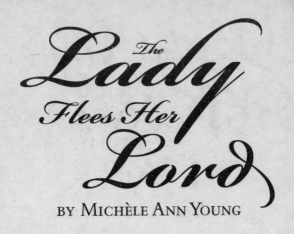

The Lady Flees Her Lord

BY MICHÈLE ANN YOUNG

DESPERATE FOR PEACE AND SAFETY…

Lucinda, Lady Denbigh, is running from a husband who physically and emotionally abused her. Posing as a widow, she seeks refuge in the quiet countryside, where she meets Lord Hugo Wanstead. Returning from the wars with a wound that won't heal, he finds his estate impoverished, his sleep torn by nightmares, and brandy the only solace. When he meets Lucinda, he thinks she just might give him something to live for…

Praise for Michèle Ann Young's *No Regrets*

"Dark heroes, courageous heroines, intrigue, heartbreak, and heaps of sexual tension. Do not miss this fabulous new author." —Molly O'Keefe, *Harlequin Superromance*

"Readers will never want to put her book down!" —Bronwyn Scott, author of *Pickpocket Countess*

978-1-4022-1399-1 • $6.99 U.S. / $7.99 CAN

No Regrets

BY MICHÈLE ANN YOUNG

"A remarkable talent that taps your emotions with each and every page." —Gerry Russel, award winning author of *The Warrior Trainer*

A MOST UNUSUAL HEROINE

Voluptuous and bespectacled, Caroline Torrington feels dowdy and unattractive beside the slim beauties of her day. Little does she know that Lord Lucas Foxhaven thinks her curves are breathtaking, and can barely keep his hands off her.

"The suspense and sexual tension accelerate throughout." —*Romance Reviews Today*

978-1-4022-1016-7 • $6.99 U.S./$8.99 CAN

THE
PRINCE
OF
MIDNIGHT

BY LAURA KINSALE

New York Times bestselling author

"Readers should be enchanted."
—*Publishers Weekly*

INTENT ON REVENGE, ALL SHE WANTS FROM
HIM IS TO LEARN HOW TO KILL

Lady Leigh Strachan has crossed all of France in search
of S.T. Maitland, nobleman, highwayman, and legendary
swordsman, once known as the Prince of Midnight. Now
he's hiding out in a crumbling castle with a tame wolf as his
only companion, trying to conceal his deafness and despera-
tion. Leigh is terribly disappointed to find the man behind
the legend doesn't meet her expectations. But when they're
forced on a quest together, she discovers the dangerous and
vital man behind the mask, and he finds a way to touch her
ice cold heart.

"No one—repeat, no one—writes historical
romance better." —Mary Jo Putney

978-1-4022-1397-7 • $7.99 U.S./$8.99 CAN

MIDSUMMER MOON

BY LAURA KINSALE

New York Times bestselling author

"The acknowledged master."
—*Albany Times-Union*

IF HE REALLY LOVED HER,
WOULDN'T HE HELP HER REALIZE HER DREAM?

When inventor Merlin Lambourne is endangered by Napoleon's advancing forces, Lord Ransom Falconer, in service of his government, comes to her rescue and falls under the spell of her beauty and absent-minded brilliance. But he is horrified by her dream of building a flying machine—and not only because he is determined to keep her safe.

"Laura Kinsale writes the kind of works that live in your heart." —Elizabeth Grayson

"A true storyteller, Laura Kinsale has managed to break all the rules of standard romance writing and come away shining."
—*San Diego Union-Tribune*

978-1-4022-1398-4 • $7.99 U.S./$8.99 CAN

SEIZE THE FIRE

BY LAURA KINSALE
New York Times bestselling author

AN UNLIKELY PRINCESS SHIPWRECKED
WITH A WAR HERO WHO'S GOT HELL TO PAY

Her Serene Highness Olympia of Oriens—plump, demure, and idealistic—longs to return to her tiny, embattled land and lead her people to justice and freedom. Famous hero Captain Sheridan Drake, destitute and tormented by nightmares of the carnage he's seen, means only to rob and abandon her. What is Olympia to do with the tortured man behind the hero's façade? And how will they cope when their very survival depends on each other?

978-1-4022-1396-0 • $7.99 U.S./$8.99 CAN

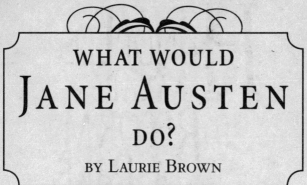

WHAT WOULD JANE AUSTEN DO?

BY LAURIE BROWN

Eleanor goes back in time to save a man's life, but could it be she's got the wrong villain?

Lord Shermont, renowned rake, feels an inexplicable bond to the mysterious woman with radical ideas who seems to know so much... but could she be a Napoleonic spy?

Thankfully, Jane Austen's sage advice prevents a fatal mistake...

At a country house party, Eleanor makes the acquaintance of Jane Austen, whose sharp wit can untangle the most complicated problem. With an international intrigue going on before her eyes, Eleanor must figure out which of two dueling gentlemen is the spy, and which is the man of her dreams.

978-1-4022-1831-6 • $6.99 U.S. / $7.99 CAN

Hundreds of Years to Reform a Rake

by Laurie Brown

His touch pulled her irresistibly across the mists of time

Deverell Thornton, the ninth Earl of Waite, needs Josie Drummond to come back to his time and foil the plot that would destroy him. Josie is a modern career woman, thrust back in time to the sparkling Regency period, where she must contend with the complex manners and mores of the day, unmask a dangerous charlatan, and in the end, choose between the ghost who captivated her or the man himself—but can she give her heart to a notorious rake?

978-1-4022-1013-6 • $6.99 U.S./$8.99 CAN

Wicked by Any Other Name

BY LINDA WISDOM

"Do not miss this wickedly
entertaining treat."

—Annette Blair,
Sex and the Psychic Witch

STASI ROMANOV USES A LITTLE WITCH MAGIC IN HER LINGERIE shop, running a brisk side business in love charms. A disgruntled customer threatening to sue over a failed spell brings wizard attorney Trevor Barnes to town—and witches and wizards make a volatile combination. The sparks fly, almost everyone's getting singed, and the whole town seems on the verge of a witch hunt.

Can the feisty witch and the gorgeous wizard overcome their objections and settle out of court—and in the bedroom?

978-1-4022-1773-9 • $6.99 U.S. / $7.99 CAN

The WILD SIGHT

BY LOUCINDA MCGARY

"A magical tale of romance and intrigue. I couldn't put it down!" —Pamela Palmer, author of *Dark Deceiver* and *The Dark Gate*

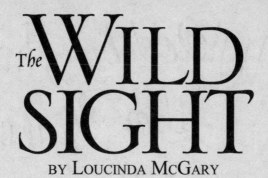

HE WAS CURSED WITH A "GIFT"

Born with the clairvoyance known to the Irish as "The Sight," Donovan O'Shea fled to America to escape his visions. On a return trip to Ireland to see his ailing father, staggering family secrets threaten to turn his world upside down. And then beautiful, sensual Rylie Powell shows up, claiming to be his half-sister...

SHE'S LOOKING FOR THE FAMILY SHE NEVER KNEW...

After her mother's death, Rylie journeys to Ireland to find her mysterious father. She needs the truth—but how can she and Donovan be brother and sister when the chemistry between them is nearly irresistible?

UNCOVERING THE PAST LEADS THEM DANGEROUSLY CLOSE TO MADNESS...

"A richly drawn love story and riveting romantic suspense!" —Karin Tabke, author of *What You Can't See*

978-1-4022-1394-6 • $6.99 U.S. / $8.99 CAN

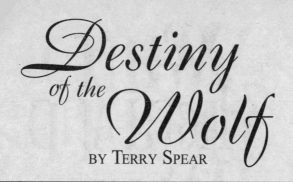

Destiny of the Wolf

BY TERRY SPEAR

Praise for Terry Spear's *Heart of the Wolf*:

"The chemistry crackles off the page."
—*Publisher's Weekly*

"The characters are well drawn and believable, which makes the contemporary plotline of love and life among the lupus garou seem, well, realistic." —*Romantic Times*

"Full of action, adventure, suspense, and romance... one of the best werewolf stories I've read!" —*Fallen Angel Reviews*

ALL SHE WANTS IS THE TRUTH

Lelandi is determined to discover the truth about her beloved sister's mysterious death. But everyone thinks she's making a bid for her sister's widowed mate...

HE'S A PACK LEADER TORMENTED BY MEMORIES

Darien finds himself bewitched by Lelandi, and when someone attempts to silence her, he realizes that protecting the beautiful stranger may be the only way to protect his pack... and himself...

978-1-4022-1668-8 • $6.99 U.S. / $7.99 CAN

Wild
Highland
Magic

BY KENDRA LEIGH CASTLE

She's a Scottish Highlands werewolf

Growing up in America, Catrionna MacInnes always tried desperately to control her powers and pretend to be normal…

He's a wizard prince with a devastating secret

The minute Cat lays eyes on Bastian, she knows she's met her destiny. In their first encounter, she unwittingly binds him to her for life, and now they're both targets for the evil enemies out to destroy their very souls.

Praise for Kendra Leigh Castle:

"Fans of straight up romance looking for a little extra something will be bitten." —*Publishers Weekly*

978-1-4022-1856-9 • $7.99 U.S. / $8.99 CAN

ROGUE

BY CHERYL BROOKS

Tychar crawled toward me on his hands and knees like a tiger stalking his prey. "I, for one, am glad you came," he purred. "And I promise you, Kyra, you will never want to leave Darconia."

~~~~~~

"Cheryl Brooks knows how to keep the heat on and the reader turning pages!"

—Sydney Croft, author of *Seduced by the Storm*

~~~~~~

PRAISE FOR THE CAT STAR CHRONICLES:

"Wow. Just… wow. The romantic chemistry is as close to perfect as you'll find." —*BookFetish.org*

"Will make you purr with delight. Cheryl Brooks has a great talent as a storyteller." —*Cheryl's Book Nook*

978-1-4022-1762-3 •$6.99 U.S. / $7.99 CAN

SEALed
with a
Promise

BY MARY MARGRET DAUGHTRIDGE

NAVY SEAL CALEB DELAUDE IS AS DEADLY AS HE IS CHARMING.

Professor Emmie Caddington's quiet intelligence and quirky personality intrigue him. When he discovers that her personal connections can get him close to the man he's vowed to kill, will their budding relationship be nothing more than a means to revenge...or is she the key to his salvation?

Praise for *SEALed with a Kiss*:

"This story delivers in a huge way." —Romantic Times

"A wonderful story that will have readers experiencing a whirlwind of emotions and culminating with an awesome scene that will have your pulse pounding." —Romance Junkies

"What an incredibly powerful book! I laughed and sniffled, was turned on and turned inside out." —Queue My Review

978-1-4022-1763-0 • $6.99 U.S. / $7.99 CAN

Romeo, Romeo

~ BY ROBIN KAYE ~

Rosalie Ronaldi doesn't have a domestic bone in her body...

All she cares about is her career, so she survives on take-out and dirty martinis, keeps her shoes under the dining room table, her bras on the shower curtain rod, and her clothes on the couch.

Nick Romeo is every woman's fantasy— tall, dark, handsome, rich, really good in bed, AND he loves to cook and clean...

He says he wants an independent woman, but when he meets Rosalie, all he wants to do is take care of her. Before long, he's cleaned up her apartment, stocked her refrigerator, and adopted her dog.

So what's the problem? Just a little matter of mistaken identity, corporate theft, a hidden past in juvenile detention, and one big nosy Italian family too close for comfort...

"Kaye's debut is a delightfully fun, witty romance, making her a writer to watch." —*Booklist*

978-1-4022-1339-7 • $6.99 U.S. / $8.99 CAN

Line of
SCRIMMAGE

BY MARIE FORCE

SHE'S GIVEN UP ON HIM AND MOVED ON...

Susannah finally has peace, calm, a sedate life, and a no-surprises man. Marriage to football superstar Ryan Sanderson was a whirlwind, but Susanna got sick of playing second fiddle to his team. With their divorce just a few weeks away, she's already planning her wedding with her new fiancé.

HE'S FINALLY FIGURED OUT WHAT'S REALLY IMPORTANT TO HIM. IF ONLY IT'S NOT TOO LATE...

Ryan has just ten days to convince his soon-to-be-ex-wife to give him a second chance. His career is at its pinnacle, but in the year of their separation, Ryan's come to realize it doesn't mean anything without Susannah...

978-1-4022-1424-0 • $6.99 U.S. / $8.99 CAN